The Tyranny of the Word

FROM THE SAME AUTHOR

The Tyranny of the Word

by

Brian Stableford

A Black Coat Press Book

ISBN 978-1-61227-881-0. First Printing. September 2019. Published by Black Coat Press, an imprint of Hollywood Comics.com, LLC, P.O. Box 17270, Encino, CA 91416. All rights reserved. Except for review purposes, no part of this book may be reproduced or transmitted in any form or by any means, electronic or mechanical, including photocopying, recording, or by any information storage and retrieval system, without permission in writing from the publisher. The stories and characters depicted in this novel are entirely fictional. Printed in the United States of America.

I

Behind the funeral cart, Brother Primael walked with a stride as steady as he could contrive, a solitary mourner, incongruous in his isolation. His isolation was not unobserved, however. The cottages that the cart passed remained stubbornly closed; no one came out to watch the vehicle pass by, but in the gloom behind the raggedly-draped windows, there was occasional movement, and the Benedictine, whose sight was still keen in spite of his almost-seventy years, glimpsed brief gleams that must have been the reflection of eyes.

On the hillside, higher up than the burial ground, two black-clad figures were standing in the open, ostentatiously, as if posing. Whereas the inhabitants of the cottages did not want to be seen at any price, they intended their presence to be known, as the threat that it was—naked, albeit premature. One was tall, the other short, but their cowls were raised, and Primael could not make out the detail of their faces. The taller man was holding a wooden cross, which he held up as if he were delivering an anathema, with the shorter one made the sign of the cross with his hand.

Under other circumstances, Primael would have been offended by that, but not alarmed, believing that he had the entire community of the Abbey to shield him against any oppression on the part of the rival order, but his companions were now exceedingly conspicuous by their absence. The Abbot had not forbidden them to attend the funeral, but his decision that Ollivier had to be interred in the public burial-ground of the village and not in the Abbey grounds had spoken volumes. No one but Primael had wanted to accompany the dead man to his final earthly abode, even though, like Primael, he had been a tutor and mentor to most of them.

Primael told himself, sternly, that he had nothing to fear from the two Dominicans, who were probably as frightened as he was, given the context is which they were operating, in

5

what had to be reckoned enemy territory in more ways than one. He did not tell himself that he probably had precious little life left to lose, because *precious* was the operative word; however little time might remain to him, he did not want to lose it, and above all, he did not want to waste it in prison, while the Inquisition prepared charges against him and its secular minions prepared their instruments of torture in order to facilitate his confession to sins he had not committed.

Since the foundation of their Order long ago, in the Midi, the Dominican predators had had little or no purchase in Bretagne, in spite of the aftermath of the scandal at the Château de Tiffauges and the trial of Gilles de Rais, which continued to fester and to fuel rumors of diabolism after more twenty years, even as far afield as Paimpol—but times were changing. It was common knowledge among the peasants and townsmen of the region, let alone in the Abbey, that as soon as Louis the Prudent, the Universal Spider, was dead and buried, and Burgundy no longer a distraction, new political alliances had been redrawn by the Regent and her husband. The Kingdom of France was now in the process of annexing the whole of Bretagne by means of armed might; the Regent had not licensed the black friars to launch a massive heresy-hunt, backed by her invading troops, but it was a card that she would not hesitate to play if she thought it politic.

Anne and Charles had as much Breton blood in their veins as any other kind, but that was not inhibiting them from launching mayhem and murder within the realm, and it would not stop them from attacking the churches and abbeys of the region if any orators elected to preach against the invaders. Heresy charges had long been an important instrument of political propaganda and manipulation, in the deployment of which the Dominicans—who were fighting their own long war for power and influence within the Church while France and Bretagne fought theirs—were expert, making full use of the special privileges granted to the order by Rome.

Ever since returning from his missionary service in Spain and the brief sojourn at Tiffauges thereafter, when he had not yet turned twenty, Primael had led a sheltered life in the Abbey, supposedly isolated from worldly turmoil, but his pastoral duties often took him outside the walls, especially since the Abbey had acquired medical texts from which he and Ollivier, their primary custodians, had learned healing arts. He was aware of all the news that reached the scattered communities within a league of Paimpol, and all the rumors too. He had more than adequate grounds for his anxiety.

Until the last few days, Primael had never had any reason to fear that he might become a scapegoat in the deadly game of heresy-hunting, but Ollivier's illness and death had changed his situation drastically. He had no protection but the Abbey—what remained of his family, the Quemerles, was of no political consequence whatever, even in Quimper—but he had always thought the Abbey a more than adequate shield, especially since the passage of time had left him in a position of seniority there, effectively equal to Ollivier's even though the latter was two and a half year older, and had been the principal tutor to numerous sons of the aristocracy, sent to complete a veneer of education there from as far away as Rennes. He and Ollivier had been on excellent terms with superior of the Abbey, who had been Herik Berthou before entering Holy Orders and taking the conspicuously un-Bretagnian name of Brother Michael. Primael's position and reputation for scholarship had made him a person of considerable consequence within the monastery—until Ollivier had returned from Tardivel and fallen ill, triggering the rumor that his illness, his disfigurement and his eventual death were a divine punishment visited upon him for a horrible sin: that of practicing necromancy.

The wise thing to have done, in the present circumstances, Primael knew full well, would have been to imitate his brethren, stay in his cell, and not to follow Ollivier's coffin: to hide, as everyone else was doing; but Ollivier had been his friend for forty years—and Ollivier, he felt quite certain in his heart, had been innocent of any sin, unless scholarship were to be reckoned a sin in itself. Ollivier had always taken more interest in the texts of occult science that they had both read than Primael had, but surely only as a scholar, with not the slightest shadow of evil intent. The delirium of his final fevers had been mere delirium, and the obsessive repetition therein of various arcane formulae had been an unconscious trick of the mind, such as the mind often played in delirium, and even in ordinary bad dreams. He had not been remembering or attempting to work magic spells. Primael was sure of that, sure of Ollivier's innocence.

But then, Primael still felt sure in his heart that Gilles de Rais had been innocent as well, and that innocence had not helped Gilles when the conspiratorial web had trapped him. Unlike Jeanne d'Arc, poor Gilles had not been redeemed by a belated intervention by Rome and given the status of a martyr; his demonization continued apace, having only increased its magnitude since his death. There was no justice in politics, within the Church as well as without.

The funeral cart continued to make its slow and painful way up the hill towards the burial ground. The weather was gray and overcast, and a cold wind was blowing from the east. The stout peasant who was guiding the cart and the thickset companion who was sitting beside him wore sullen scowls upon their faces. Even the two old bay mares that were pulling the vehicle were holding their heads very low, as if they had no enthusiasm at all for the work, although they could not have had any notion of why the burden they were carrying was dangerous, and the crude coffin was certainly a good deal lighter than the cargoes of hay, oats and turnips that were their more usual haulage.

The Benedictine could almost feel the pressure of the gazes watching from the cottages physically. While he went about his normal business he had always commanded respect, and had been treated with due deference, but he had a dire sensation of that respect having slipped away mysteriously, replaced by suspicion and hostility. Ollivier—whose surname had once been Abalain, and who had had noteworthy relatives—had been even more respected for the greater part of his life, and thus granted a proportionately greater due deference, but almost overnight, since falling ill, he had become a telling illustration of the fragility of such respect, and the damage that malevolent rumor could do in a time of war, when fear was abroad and hunting for objects on which to seize.

How had the rumors of Ollivier's dabbling with the Devil started? Primael had no idea. Who could possibly have anything to gain by spreading the slander? Rumors of sorcery and necromancy were by no means uncommon in Bretagne, especially in the vicinity of the Forest of Ploermel—greatly reputed as the principal residuum of Broceliande, the legendary lair of all kinds of enchantments—but for most of Primael's life, the Abbey had been regarded as a powerful bastion of defense against sorcerers and phantoms, the Dames Blanches, the Marie-Mortes and all the Devil's imaginary instruments. How had that changed so swiftly?

No one within the Abbey, so far as he knew—although the Abbey was not without its ration of secrets, of the various sorts to which the Church was, by nature, always hospitable—had anything to gain by invention and disseminating such slanders, and no one in the parish of Paimpol either…but the question of where and how the rumor had taken wing was irrelevant now; the fact was that it had, and that it had attracted the attention of the Dominicans, who must have immediately begun to wonder whether it might be useful in their insidious progress to power within the bosom of the Church.

Primael raised his hand to his forehead and brushed the skin mechanically, although he was not sweating. His throat was dry, and his legs ached, even though the September sun was not unduly hot nor the hill excessively steep. He felt guilty for having hoped briefly that Ollivier's death might put an end to the matter, because it smacked of wanting to obtain some personal advantage from his friend's death. He felt guilty, too, for walking awkwardly and a painfully, when he would have liked to hold his head up high and maintain a stern stride, to illustrate his rectitude; but there was nothing he could do about the fact that he was old, and his joints were stiff. He put his hands carefully within the folds of his cloak, because the cold wind was making his gnarled fingers ache, and fingered the tattered pages of the missal nestling in its pocket—a gesture that automatically brought prayers to the tip of his tongue, although he did not pronounce them, even silently. The missal was a copy that he had made himself, long ago, before he had ever seen a printed book.

Courage, he said to himself, instead. *You are doing God's work. He will not fail you.*

But he was not reassured.

When the cart finally reached the gates of the burial ground, a small company of small boys who had been hiding behind the low wall suddenly popped their heads above the parapet, and hurled a few handfuls of mud and stones in the direction of the approaching cart, crying: "Necromancer! Filthy necromancer!" before running away as fast as their feet could carry them. The missiles did not hit anything; the boys had acted too precipitately, hastened by fear.

Was it just a childish display of bravado, Primael wondered, or had someone put them up to it? Not the Dominicans surely—but if not them, who?

Just a display of bravado, he concluded, uneasily. He contemplated shouting after them, angrily, but they were already out of earshot, and in any case, the cart-driver was already sending a volley of oaths in their direction, not because he wanted to defend Ollivier against the charge, but because he knew that he had been in more danger of being hit by the stones and mud than the dead man, who would not have suffered anyway.

Did the boys even know what the word *necromancer* signified? Primael wondered. Probably not; to them it was just a term of vulgar abuse Had they known, they would probably have calculated that hurling the insult, even at a dead man—perhaps especially at a dead man—was a little too daring. The Abbey had been in existence for five hundred years, although it had been burned in its early days by the Normans and completely rebuilt for a second time a little more than a hundred years ago, but its presence and influence had never contrived to stamp out local superstition completely; it had certainly contrived to apply Satanic labels where once there had been mere pagan grotesquerie, but sometimes Primael wondered whether the fact that the churches in the region were full on Sundays really signified that the peasantry were less ungodly now than their ancestors had been before their conversion, or whether it merely testified to their awareness of the importance of apparent conformity.

He was a Breton-born commoner himself, but in the eyes of many of his own kind, that only meant that he was now a defector of sorts, currying favor with the authority of the Church. As soon he had he had learned to read and write, having crossed the threshold of the seminary, he had ceased in the eyes of the local peasants to be a *true* Breton, and had become a "Norman," in the special meaning that Bretons intended by that term. But Primael still felt Breton, in his blood and bones. He was still Primael Quemerle, and had even retained his given name within the bosom of the Order, just as Ollivier Abalain had become Brother Ollivier. The Church was tolerant of such local usages—but even that, he now suspected, might become something that the Dominicans might seek to use against him, if he were unfortunate enough to fall under their jurisdiction.

There was no one standing by the freshly-dug grave. The cart-driver and his thickset companion had been ordered by the Abbot to lay the coffin in the ditch and cover it over. Primael waited patiently for them to unload the coffin, to manipulate the ropes, and to lower it into the hole. They worked slowly, and awkwardly, as if making a show of the fact that it was not work to which they were accustomed, and not a kind of labor to which they ever wanted to become accustomed. They did not speak to Primael, but when they had finished they assumed a respectful stance, caps in hand, and did not even glance in the direction of the watching Dominicans. They were playing their part carefully.

Primael had no need to consult the missal in order to recite the necessary formula, which he knew by heart, but he did it anyway. He too was putting on a show—but he knew that there was no reason to be ashamed of that, given that the recitation in question was all show itself, a symbolic defiance of death and an affirmation of faith in the Resurrection. This was still holy ground; Ollivier's posthumous banishment from the Abbey had been deliberately incomplete, and it seemed to Primael that the diplomatic compromise in question made the present show of faith all the more necessary. The formula was recited properly, in good Latin. Everything else was in order; Ollivier had been confessed by Brother Michael, and absolved of his sins. He was sure and certain of the Resurrection, if...

If? Primael grimaced slightly. How could there be an *if?* How had that syllable arrived in his train of thought, unbidden?

"I was his friend," said Primael, aloud, although he did not look at the cart-driver and his accomplice while they were filling in the grave, with much greater efficiency and rapidity than they had maneuvered the coffin into it. "I have known him since childhood. He was a good man."

Perhaps surprisingly, the driver looked up from his labor and said: "Aye," in a tone very different from the one he had used to curse the children. He said no more, because no more was necessary, and because he was shifting soil, with the hasty regularity of a man concluding a task with which he was anxious to be done.

Primael had never had occasion to preach a sermon against necromancy, but he had heard such sermons preached, and not only in his youth. Old as he was, his memory still retained some of those preached on the subject of Gilles de Rais.

"A man forsakes all claims of friendship and amity when he delves into forbidden lore," one stern priest had said. "A man who seeks to deal unnaturally with the dead must be shunned absolutely by the living. A man who forsakes the Scriptures in order to delve in proscribed books is delivering his soul to the Devil."

And what of the pythorem *of Endor who summoned the spirit of Samuel at the request of King Saul?* Primael had thought at the time. *Do the prophets really do the bidding of the Devil's henchmen? Something is amiss in the legend.* Nowadays, he no longer found any reason for surprise in the suspicion that something might be amiss with Biblical legend. He had read too much, even without delving overmuch into forbidden lore, not to know that legend was a labyrinth, in which there were many wrong turns.

"Ollivier has joined the ranks of the dead himself now," said Primael, still speaking aloud, in the Breton vernacular that he still thought of his own, because he was talking to himself rather than to the cart-driver. "He is now a memory to the living, and the memories which I have of him are memories of goodness, piety and altruism. I am here in order to bid farewell to a man I have known all my life, and to attest that he is fully deserving of divine resurrection. I will not permit the fact that he has lately been abused by foolish and malicious men to prevent me from doing so, or make me feel the slightest shame."

Perhaps because he was using the language of the local peasantry, the cart-driver must have assumed that the words were addressed to him. "Aye, Father," he said, again, like a weak echo of his former remark. Then he wiped his forehead; he really was sweating, in spite of the brisk wind, which carried a suggestion of autumnal chill.

The grave was now filled in.

"You may go," Primael said, to both the waiting men. "I shall stay a little longer, to complete my farewell."

Both men seemed surprised. Although he had been behind the coffin, they had observed the difficulty he had in negotiating the hill. They had expected him to ride back to the Abbey on the cart.

"It's all right, lads," he said, with the faintest of smiles. "It's all downhill."

The driver's eyes flicked in the direction of the black-clad figures on the hillside. Primael's smile widened slightly.

"Have no fear for me, my son," he said, a trifle presumptuously. "Crows of that species don't pluck out the eyes of their victims in broad daylight."

The driver's eyes were raised, not piously toward heaven, but to indicate that the daylight was murky, and that even noon, when it came, would not bring a more conspicuous brightness.

"Thank you, lads," said Primael, sincerely. "I'll remember you in my prayers."

The driver and his companion turned away, and took half a stride in the direction on the gate of the burial-ground—but they both stopped with the stride incomplete, with a comical simultaneity. There was a sudden clatter of hooves in the gateway, a huge bay horse, liberally flecked with sweat, was abruptly reined in some twenty paces from the grave. A man leapt down, patting the trembling horse upon the neck to offer thanks for its unusual effort—it was obvious that the mount had been ridden a long way, and urgently.

The newcomer was a young man in his twenties, plainly dressed, without livery or ornament—but he strode toward the graveside with the pride and grace of an aristocrat. He barely glanced at the two men whose departure he had interrupted momentarily, and who had already resumed their hurried retreat. For a split second it seemed that he might dismiss Primael with the same casually scant attention, but then his gaze was arrested and he looked at the Benedictine with respect—and recognition. His own stride was cut short momentarily, and he bowed. Primael recognized him, too: Corentin de Tardivel, at whose manse Ollivier had stayed for three months before falling ill on his return

I am not entirely alone, then, he thought. *There still another man in this benighted land willing to mourn Ollivier Abalain, and to be seen to do so, other than as a matter of compulsory duty.* He was so grateful no longer to be alone that his gratitude overrode the awareness that, of all the company he might have had at present, under the eyes of the Dominican spies, this was undoubtedly the most dangerous.

Having bowed, the young man moved on, to stand before the grave. As he looked down at the freshly-moved earth, there were tears in his eyes.

"Be welcome, Corentin," Primael said. "I did not know that the Abbot had sent a messenger to Tardivel."

The other looked up, and smiled—but thinly, as if he did not have the heart for a proper greeting. "You do well to remember me, Brother Primael, even though it's no more than five years since I was your pupil. I fear that I must have changed a great deal since then."

"Hardly at all," said Primael, slightly surprised. "If I seemed to hesitate before greeting you, it's because old age is eroding my alacrity."

"No apology is necessary, Master," Tardivel assured him. "Pupils always remember their teachers far better than teachers remember pupils, who are transient and numerous. It's a matter of simple arithmetic."

Primael's memory was working hard, recovering and collating the information it had regarding the young man. Where was Tardivel, exactly? Some way to the north, not far from Trehonteuc, in Herbriant. Wooded country, not the interminable Breton heathland: another fragment of what had once been Broceliande.

"Ollivier was in your manse for nearly three months," Primael remarked. "He must have fallen ill during the return journey. He was seventy years old, and the trek was doubtless arduous on his donkey."

"He had a mule," Tardivel corrected. "Yes, he was my guest for nearly three months, on the most recent occasion. It was kind of Brother Michael to release him for so long: a favor for which I'm still in his debt, and for which I hoped that he does not consider me ingrate, for I was coming to ask him for another. I only learned this morning that he will not be able to grant it, when I paused at the inn in Brehonnec to water my poor horse, and was told that Ollivier had died."

That was obviously not all that the vicomte had been told at the gossip-well, for his eyes shifted in the direction of the two Dominicans, who had altered their stance and were now exchanging remarks, presumably discussing the unexpected arrival of a second person at Ollivier's graveside. Primael knew that it would not take the black friars long to learn the identity of the man in question, given that he was known in the vicinity and that he had paused to ask questions at a wayside inn. They were far enough away not to have been able to see the tears in his eyes, but the young man's attitude had testified clearly enough to the fact that he was no enemy of the man they suspected of having made a pact with the Devil.

"It might not have been entirely wise for you to come here, Sire," said Primael, mildly, "once you had heard what is being said about Ollivier in the vicinity."

The young man's lip curled. "Ollivier was my mentor," he said, "and lately the best friend I have ever had. And this is holy ground, is it not? That sheaf of paper in your hand is a missal, I assume, so I know that he has been buried in accordance which the rites of the Church. And if I can trust my eyes and my heart, you are not here under duress, or even out of duty. He spoke about you a great deal, Brother Primael, as a loyal friend and a true man of God."

"I was proud to be his friend," Primael said, "and I still am. He was a fine scholar, and I never knew a kinder man. I could not desert him, even dead, and even with carrion crows gathering over a reputation slain by delirium."

"Delirium?" Tardivel echoed, the tone of his voice becoming uneasy. "What did he say?"

"Mostly gibberish—but I fear that one of the younger monks who took a turn at sitting by his bedside got it into his head that he was reciting spells—spells intended to raise the dead. That absurdity spread through the convent like wildfire and soon breached the walls."

Tardivel's face was pensive, as his mind doubtless made the connection between what Primael had just told him and the gossip that he had picked up in Brehonnec.

"He was a true man of God," Primael repeated, feeling the need to emphasize the conviction. He was the best man I knew. The others knew that too, but his illness had a terrible effect on his face, and the younger monks were alarmed by his disfiguration. They are men of God too, but not entirely free from superstition. You completed your education in Paimpol, and you doubtless know as well as I do what convictions persist, not merely in the town but even within sacred walls."

Tardivel nodded his head, his expression increasingly anxious. "I fear that I might not be doing you a kindness by being here, Brother Primael," he said. "If the black friars were chattering about you before I arrived, they might chatter more excitedly when they discover that I have come from Tardivel, as they surely will. Had I realized that they would be here, I would have been more discreet, but in my naivety, I thought the Abbey far above foul suspicion."

Primael hesitated, not knowing which of the threads implicit in that speech to take up. In the end, he contented himself with saying, a trifle warily: "We are living in troubled times, and suspicion is sometimes direly indiscriminate." After a slight pause, he added: "We have had no news of Tardivel recently." He left it at that, discreetly.

The scion of Tardivel grimaced, wryly. "The Order of Preachers has a sacred mission, it seems," he said, "to root our heresy everywhere. It has taken them a long time to extirpate it in the Midi, but the task is complete there now—or so they think. If they are to maintain the impetus of their organization, they require new objectives. There is little chance of the present Pope declaring a crusade against Bretagne as his predecessor did against the Cathars centuries ago, but if the Dominicans can only launch a covert war against us, it will be no less ferocious for that. The Bishops in these parts have always opposed them in the past, but an alliance is being forged, with the encouragement of the French crown. If the Dominicans are scouting targets even in Paimpol, they must at least have arrogance, if not confidence. Herbriant is an easier target, and the Château de Tardivel is its heart."

"I have never visited Herbriant," Primael remarked, "and know nothing of its manse. Is it a true castle?"

"Hardly," said Corentin de Tardivel, dryly. "But citadels are no longer safe refuges, since Tristan L'Hermite's artillerists became expert at blasting through their walls with the aid of long cannons. Tardivel has the advantage of being of no strategic value in France's war, but if the Church cared to make it a symbol of heretical opposition, and it became desirable to raze it, the task would not be unduly difficult, I fear, for a company equipped with good arbalests, let alone cannons."

"I'm sorry to hear that your peace is in danger of being disturbed, Sire," Paimpol said, and added: "Since you have come here to visit the Abbey, would you care to walk down the hill with me? Or would you prefer to ride ahead?"

The young man sketched a slight smile, evidently understanding the full implication of those questions.

"My horse is worn out," he said. "He will not be able to walk quickly, but if we will not slow you down too much, Brother Primael, I would be glad to accompany you. First, however..."

He knelt down beside the grave, bowed his head, placed the fingers of his right hand on his forehead, closed his eyes, and remained in that position for a full two minutes. If he was reciting a prayer, his lips did not move. Nor, when he finished, did he make the customary sign of the cross.

In the meantime, Primael said his own prayer, made the sign, and said: "Amen."

Then Corentin de Tardivel picked up the reins of his horse, which was waiting patiently nearby, and the two of them left the burial ground together, united in grief, and in defiance of the spies intent on thinking evil, whether any existed or not.

II

"Can you tell me more about the substance of the rumors that have caused Ollivier to be sent to the public burial-ground rather than interred in the Abbey grounds, with only a single mourner?" Corentin de Tardivel asked Brother Primael, as they made their way slowly down the hill. "The innkeeper's account was a trifle confused."

"Such lies often are," remarked Primael. "Given that they have no substance, I doubt that I can tell you anything that your informant did not, for nothing has reached my ears but the same scabrous rumors, probably filtered by diplomacy. Since his illness disfigured his face, it is said—within the Abbey, alas, as well as without—that Ollivier must have been stigmatized for the crime of secretly practicing necromancy, consulting the souls of the dead in search of enlightenment. If rumors originating in distant places can be trusted, such accusations are commonly leveled at dedicated scholars all over Europe, especially after they are dead. I dare say that Ollivier's reputation will only be further exaggerated now that he has been laid to rest. He was a great reader, it is true, a scholar of alchemy and astrology as well as Aristotle and the Cabala. He and I visited Granada in the early days of our priesthood, dispatched as junior members of a mission to the Moors and the Jews—this was long before the Spanish launched their more violent crusade—but rumor among novices not even born then now seems intent on interpreting his part in that mission, retrospectively, as having brought him into contact with Moorish magic and diabolism.

"We brought back manuscripts from that mission, as we had been ordered to do by our superiors, and some of those manuscripts ended up, in the custody of Gilles de Rais, before being ceremonially burned. Gilles was reputed when we met him to be a great scholar, albeit a secular one. Since then, alas, his reputation had been direly tarnished. The fact that Ollivier visited him at Tiffauges is now being remembered, and the allegation made that he brought manuscripts away with him before Gilles was arrested and tried. Thus far, the rumors have only cited his name, but now that he is dead, and I have been seen standing by his graveside, while Brother Michael and the rest of the community remained in the Abbey, attention might focus on me...but I swear to you, Sire, that I have never dabbled in necromancy, and if I have sometimes read in forbidden books, it has been purely in the interests of enlightenment, never in rebellion against God's law."

"I know," said Tardivel.

"You *know?*" Primael echoed, surprised. "How can you possibly know?"

"Ollivier told me. He considered you a great friend, and made many a laudatory description of you."

"He was very kind," Primael repeated, in a soft voice.

"Exceptionally," Tardivel agreed. "It would have upset him greatly, I know, to think that rumors circulating in his regard might cast a shadow over you. It troubles me, too, to think that my coming here might add a further measure to your difficulties. When I set forth, I did not anticipate..."

"Of course not," said Primael. "You have nothing for which to apologize, Sire. You are not to blame for the malevolence of the ignorant, and if it is has taken aim at you as well as Ollivier, then I am glad to be able to stand beside you, as I was to stand beside his coffin, even though I am a very feeble buckler. Virtue ought not to hide; it must be courageous."

"Even at the cost of martyrdom," muttered Tardivel. "Yes, Brother Primael, the Church certainly teaches us that." He fell silent, pensively.

"The favor that you came to ask of the Abbot," said Primael, tentatively, "was to request that Ollivier come to Tardivel again?"

"Indeed," the young man agreed. "I wish I had come sooner, for more reasons than one. If Ollivier had been able to leave Paimpont before these evil rumors gathered pace..."

"He could not have done so," Primael interjected, dully. "As I said, he fell direly ill as soon as he had returned from Herbriant."

"And people doubtless see a causal connection there?" the young vicomte said, warily.

"I do not, Primael was content to respond, "except in the sense that the journey must have wearied him." As he spoke, he was looking at the road ahead, tacitly measuring the distance that still separated them from the Abbey, and the effort still required in order to reach it, now that they were no longer walking downhill, the road having leveled out. The distraction was minimal, but it still prevented him momentarily from noticing that Corentin de Tardivel had fallen silent. When that awareness caught up with him, he looked at the young man quizzically, and frowned as he saw that Corentin was studying him obliquely, evidently making some kind of calculation.

Tardivel apparently realized that his attention might appear rude. "I apologize, Brother Primael," he said, "but I have several matters on my mind, and am only beginning to consider them as carefully as they will require. Ollivier told me that your medical knowledge was at least equal to his, and that some aspects of your scholarship are even more extensive. Since I was coming here to ask Brother Michael to release him again, I wonder whether you might be willing to substitute for him.

"Someone at Tardivel is ill?" Primael queried.

"My mother and my sister have been ill for a long time. Ollivier was a great comfort to them while he stayed in the manse, and they have regretted his absence deeply since he had to leave, as I have. Given the circumstances"—he glanced behind him at the hillside where the Dominicans had been standing—"it might be the case that Brother Michael would not be sorry for an opportunity to send you away from the Abbey for a while. I'm sure that he is aware by now that the black friars were watching you just now, and that I arrived while you were completing the rite. Perhaps, after all, it might be best..."

Primael did not know what to say, although he could see the logic of the young man's thinking.

"I will pay my respects to Brother Michael," said Corentin de Tardivel, with the air of a man making a decision. "I will confer with him regarding the interests of the Abbey and the interests of Tardivel. With your permission, I will suggest to him that, since Brother Ollivier cannot do so, you might accompany me to Herbriant instead. He will have a better idea than I have of the possible consequences of that measure. I ought to warn you, though, in fairness, that Tardivel is not a fortunate abode at present. My sister's condition had worsened before I left, and my mother has…not been herself for a long time. She has summoned other assistance, but I fear…well, if you consent, and Brother Michael is prepared to grant permission, I will have plenty of time to prepare you further on the journey. Can you ride?"

"Of course," said Brother Primael, but he turned to glance at the huge bay, and added: "But I fear that I have not ridden anything taller or faster than a donkey for quite some time."

"I think I can hire you a mule," the vicomte replied, "or purchase one, if necessary. In anticipation of success, it might not be premature for you to make up your pack while I consult the Abbot."

They had reached the Abbey now, and Primael rang for the doorkeeper. "That will not be difficult," he said, dryly. He had always taken his vow of poverty more seriously than some of his brethren—even Ollivier. His pack would not weigh down even the paltriest mule too heavily.

"Good," said Tardivel. He offered the monk his hand. "I'm truly sorry, Brother Primael, that we are not meeting again under happier circumstances. I always had the greatest respect for you as a teacher and as a man of God. Thanks to you, Ollivier and Michael, I am sure that I received a better education here than I could have obtained at the new university in Nantes—not that my father would ever have dreamed of sending me there, considering it almost to be part of France already."

"The world has changed since I was young," Primael observed, sadly. "There was no university then nearer than Paris. Now there is even one in England, so I'm told. In fifty years' time, literacy will be commonplace, and not merely in the aristocracy; the new printing presses are already making books easily available to the laity. Monastic scribes like me, who have kept literacy and learning alive in Europe for a thousand years, might soon become superfluous."

All that Tardivel said to that doleful remark was: "Indeed." A novice came to fetch him then, in order to take him to the Abbot.

Primael headed for his cell. Half a dozen of his brethren gathered around him before he reached it.

"Ollivier has been laid peacefully to rest, then?" said Brother Medard, a trifle shamefacedly.

"He has," Primael confirmed. "Under the eyes of God and two silent witnesses—crows, or perhaps only jackdaws. Personally, I think the reputation of the Dominicans overrated."

"It used to be," murmured Brother Thaddeus, in a tone the saved him the trouble of adding: *but times are changing.*

"But you were not alone at the burial," Brother Leon put in. "You came back with the new Vicomte de Tardivel."

"He was Ollivier's pupil, and mine, some years ago," said Primael, although he really did not feel that he had to explain himself. He was unable to identify the owner of a voice that muttered something that included the phrase "birds of a feather." He felt compelled to add: "He did not know about Ollivier's death; he was on his way to see the Abbot when he heard the news."

"Why?" said Brother Medard bluntly.

"I'm not sure," Primael retorted, in the knowledge that it was a diminution of the truth, if not actually a lie.

The evasion was pointless; the younger men were perfectly capable of jumping to conclusions of that kind. "If he asks for you to go to Herbriant instead of Ollivier, Brother," said Thaddeus, seemingly with earnest solicitude, "you might be well advised to decline the invitation. The Abbot surely won't order you to go against your will." Primael got the impression that his fellow monk would not have been in the least sorry if the Abbot were to do exactly that.

It was Primael's turn to ask: "Why would I do that?" although he hated the necessity of feigning ingenuousness. He was at least twenty years older than the brethren who were surrounding him; in essence, they were still his pupils, and he was still their mentor, in practice if not nominally. Normally, he kept his distance from them, having become increasingly reclusive over the years.

"Doubtless he was a dutiful pupil while he was in your care," said Medard, "but rumors have spread since then. It didn't do Ollivier's reputation any good to spend much of this year holed up with him."

"Are you saying that malicious gossip accuses Corentin de Tardivel of diabolism, as well as Ollivier?" Primael snapped, impatiently.

"That too," said Thaddeus, "but Herbriant has had a dark reputation for centuries; it's said that the Druids used to make human sacrifices at secret altars among the oaks, and the Dames Blanches are known to haunt the place."

Primael sighed. "Not one of you is Breton-born," he observed, casting a glance around, "and you don't really understand our folkways. Herbriant is said to be a relic of Broceliande, like Ploermel, so it's saturated by all the ancient superstitions of the Dames Blanches, and such quasi-Christian modifications as the Marie-Mortes, as well as dark tales of what Druids did—but you know full well that all of that is frank nonsense."

"Do we?" countered Brother Luhan. "Dealings with the Dames Blanches and the Marie-Mortes are diabolism, even though local superstition presents the Dams Blanches as benign and even the Marie-Mortes as not supposed to be malevolent."

"Local superstition is right to consider such ideas as harmless," Primael said. "So should we."

"And Brother Ollivier's necromantic ravings?" queried Thaddeus. "Should be consider those harmless too?"

"Yes," said Primael, positively. "Perfectly harmless. Delirium lends itself readily to meaningless repetition, and even if Ollivier had been unconsciously reciting formulae that he had read in Albertus Magnus or any similar source, they could not possibly have had any effect."

"That's true," put in Brother Thomas, supportively. "Let's remember who and where we are."

"We know very well where we are," Medard countered. "The Bible tells us that the dead really can be raised by incantation, and if such things can happen, there's no likelier location than Herbriant, where diabolism is still rife in the forest, if not the manse. What was Ollivier doing there for three months, with Corentin de Tardivel? He didn't breathe a word to us before the fever robbed him of his reason. Why would he keep silent, unless it were something dubious?"

"Because it was one of your business," Primael riposted. "And your scholarship is faulty. The mythology of the Dames Blanches has nothing to do with diabolism. Such beliefs are vestiges of the old pagan religion that was here long before the Franks, let alone the Normans, and might even predate the Gauls. They are false, but quite harmless. We should have no truck with any of that because of its irrelevance, not because it's Satanic. We are men of God, who know the truth. If he remembers my teaching, so does Corentin de Tardivel."

"He might prefer to remember Ollivier's teaching," said Medard, darkly.

"What's that supposed to mean?" retorted Primael, and swiftly added: "Well, whatever it was supposed to mean, it's the simple truth: he might. Ollivier was a man of God, as I am, whose teaching was orthodox, as mine is. I've known Ollivier since the day we first entered these walls as novices. I've taught novices like you and laymen like Corentin alongside him for forty years."

"And you were missionaries in Moorish Spain together," Thaddeus added, in a carefully neutral tone.

"And in Tiffauges," Leon put in.

"We were indeed together in Granada and in Tiffauges," agreed Primael, defiantly, "where neither he nor I committed any sin ourselves, nor saw any evidence of any."

He felt guilty as he said it, though, because it was not quite true. He had never seen Ollivier or Gilles de Rais commit any mortal sin, but he was not entirely stainless himself, despite having never dabbled in necromancy. Nor did he dare to go so far as to allege publicly that Gilles de Rais had been innocent of practical research in occult science. It was not impossible, or even improbable, that the Dominicans had ears within the Abbey, and that anything he said was in danger of being reported, remembered and used against him.

"We can believe that of you, Brother," said Thaddeus, in a soothing tone that might not have been entirely hypocritical.

"But not of Ollivier, do you mean?" said Primael, exasperated.

"I didn't say that," Thaddeus was quick to reply, his gaze darting sideways briefly, like that of a man who was only too well aware that sensitive ears of more than one inclination might be attentive.

"Brother Michael is a man of God too," Brother Joel interjected, addressing the company. "We can trust him to guide us through this time of troubles."

"He's prudent," agree Medard, "and not responsible for his brethren—but it anyone here runs into trouble, he won't be able to avoid being caught up in it, and we'll all feel the consequences."

"It's the uncertainty I don't like," said Leon, doubtless thinking that he was citing a common thought. "There's no recent news out of Nantes—no reliable news, at any rate."

"What might be happening in Nantes isn't our concern, any more than what is happening in Paris," said Primael, sternly, trying to play the orthodox mentor. "Our responsibility is to the Rule, Rome and God."

"Easy to say," said Medard, "but Paimpol is in Bretagne, and Bretagne is now a vast battleground. If it were just the Duke's heirs and the French, things would be bad enough, but with two contending English parties and the Holy Roman Emperor involved as well, it's a mess. As if the dirty Bretons were worth fighting over—meaning no offense, Brother Primael."

Primael did not tell him that none had been taken. "It's not our concern," he said again. "Our responsibility is to serve God, nor princes."

"You're right, Brother, of course," said Thaddeus, "but in order for us to attend exclusively to our own concerns, the outside world needs to let us alone. The Dominicans have established houses in Rennes and Quimper, and they seem to have their eyes on Paimpol too. They have no men-at-arms at their beck and call at present, but it's only a matter of time. If they can't get them from the Bishops, they'll get them from the French, the English or the Austrians. And once they begin to discover heresy, they won't stop. You know how the Inquisitorial process works: every extorted confession produces further accusations. What starts in Ploermel or Herbriant won't take long to spread to Paimpol—and to the Abbey. I'm making no accusation against Ollivier, and certainly not against you, Primael, but you must see that what has happened in the last few weeks, and today in particular, is storing up in danger, for you, the Abbot, and the whole community. I dare say that nothing will happen tomorrow, or next week—but next year might be a very different matter. As Medard says, the Abbot is a prudent man, and a good one—and so, no doubt, are you—but we need to be prudent too."

"So prudent," said Primael, acidically, "that not one of you came to lay your brother and mentor decently to rest."

"It wasn't us who made the decision that he wasn't to be buried in the Abbey grounds, Brother," said Thaddeus, still trying to maintain a soothing tone, as if he were playing to an invisible gallery. "We simply got the message. But no one blames you for administering the rite, and we admire you for it, as well as being grateful to you. You were a good friend to Ollivier, and I sincerely hope that he deserved your friendship as fully as you believe."

Primael had had enough, and thought that there was no point in any further argument. He pushed through the small crowd, went into his cell, and closed the door. Then he made up his pack, just in case.

As he had forecast, it did not take him long. He barely had time to kneel down by his bed and say a prayer before the novice knocked on his door and told him that the Abbot wanted to see him right away.

No one attempted to intercept him on the way, and one or two of the brethren who had questioned him earlier looked away when they saw him. Primael inferred that word was already spreading that he might suddenly have become a dangerous man to know.

Corentin Tardivel was not in the Superior's chamber. Brother Michael invited Primael to sit down in a armchair by the fireplace, although no fire was set there, and he took a similar chair himself.

"You do not approve of my sending Ollivier's body to the village burial-ground," he said, without preamble. "I don't blame you for that, Primael. In your position, I would disapprove as well. I won't bother to offer you the excuse that I have to think of the good of the community, in the longer term; you're an intelligent man, perhaps more intelligent than I am, or even Ollivier. That's partly why you're in danger. If you were a fool, you'd be safer."

Primael said nothing, but simply waited, a trifle resentfully.

Brother Michael sighed. "Your family and mine have known one another a long time, Primael Quemerle," the Abbot said, "and we have been in this place together for many years. In a way, though, we don't know one another at all. The Rule is conducive to that; it's one of its great strengths. It regulates action to the extent that we can all live together in harmony, side by side, year after year, without ever knowing anything about one another. As long as everyone follows the script, the organization functions smoothly and well. None of us, I suppose, finds it entirely easy, but we all know what the benefits are.

"Unfortunately, circumstances outside our control sometimes intervene. You know, and I know, that the illness that disfigured poor Ollivier's face was some kind of canker, an accident of happenstance—but popular superstition tends to react badly to such misfortunes, and there are people within these walls, sensitized to the notion of God's wrath, who find it difficult not to see divine punishment in such tragedies. A single rolling stone can sometimes start a landslide, alas.

"I have to send you away, Primael, just as I had to send Ollivier to the burial ground. I don't ask you to approve of that decision, because in your situation, I wouldn't approve of it either. I can't even ask you to understand, because I know that once you do understand more fully—and the time isn't far off when you will—you'll doubtless disapprove of me even more. But I will ask you to believe that I'm acting with the best of intentions, not only with regard to the community but in your own regard. None of this is your fault—you're the best man I know, and surely better than I am—but you're in danger now, and you can't protect yourself, so I feel compelled to try. I might not succeed, but I need to try. I want you to leave the Abbey, Primael. I want you to go with Corentin de Tardivel to his château, and I want you to lie low there, until the war is ended by some kind of treaty, and I can assess the situation as it might go forward from there. That might take some time, I fear—perhaps longer than either of us has to live—but that's in the Lord's hands, not ours, and all we can do is trust in his mercy."

The Abbot did not sound like a man who had confidence in that mercy. Primael realized, somewhat to his dismay, that he had none himself. He could not remember exactly when he had lost it, but it was certainly gone. Nor would it have made any difference if Brother Michael had referred to justice or wisdom rather than mercy.

Dear Lord, Primael thought. *Can that be true? Have I lost my ability to believe in your every aspect?*

Aloud, he said: "Obedience is the Rule, Master. You do not owe me an explanation." He could not help wondering, though, what might have happened if he had decided to test the suggestion that had been made to him a little while ago, that Brother Michael would not expel him without his agreement to be expelled.

"I will pray for you, Brother Primael," the Abbot said, "and I will ask the Lord to forgive me."

"You are not in need of forgiveness, Master," said Primael, softly. "You have not done anything wrong."

"The fact that you think so, Brother," said the Abbot, "says more about you than about me, alas. Corentin is having a mule saddled for you—the same one on which Ollivier returned from Tardivel. Are you sure that you will be able to ride it? It's a long way to Herbriant."

"I can ride," said Primael, confidently. It has been a long time, I know, since I sat on anything but a donkey, but in my youth, as you will doubtless remember, I rode much further afield than Tardivel, on mounts that did not lack strength and spirit. The exercise will doubtless revive me, for I fear that my recent sedentary habits have made me a trifle lazy, and Ollivier's illness and death have left me somewhat dejected. Herbriant is mostly forest, I believe, and the pure air there will be a tonic. The excursion will, as you say, be beneficial to me. But may I ask you one question, Master?"

"Yes, my son," said the Abbot, although his eyes narrowed slightly, perhaps in anticipation of being required to find a difficult answer, or perhaps trying to weight up exactly what Primael might know, suspect or think.

Primael took a deep breath, and said: "Do you believe, Master, that Brother Ollivier was guilty of practicing necromancy?"

Brother Michael let four or five seconds go by—quite unnecessarily, in Primael's view, before saying: "I know that he tried, my son, but not with the Devil's aid, or on the Devil's behalf. He consulted my advice on the matter long ago, and I granted him permission to do so, although I instructed him sternly to keep his research secret from the brethren, including you. He was a good man, through and through, exactly as you believed him to be—and it was his goodness that led him to keep the secret from you, his best friend, not his shame."

"But he did not keep it from you," said Primael, colorlessly.

"I was his Superior," said Brother Michael.

"And his confessor," Primael observed.

"I was his confessor too," the Abbot agreed, "but I knew what he was doing independently of his confessions, for many years, and I am not breaking the seal by revealing the fact of his experiments, or even the fact that his formulae did not work, or worked so imperfectly that he could not be sure that they had achieved anything except to stir up his imagination. As his confessor, however, I absolved him of all his sins before he died. If I was wrong to do so, that secondary sin is mine, not his. He has no quarrel with Heaven. Nor have you, I believe—but still, it is politic for you to go, and I am sending you away. I'm truly sorry—but the world has changed since the Order sent you to Spain in search of unknown documents and consented to your brief liaison with Gilles de Rais, and what was innocent then would not seem innocent now, even if Gilles had not been so foully slandered and discredited."

"He was a scholar," said Primael, dully.

"Like Albertus Magnus," Michael agreed, "who was the greatest scholar of his era—and who is now, for that very reason, being posthumously smeared with a reputation for having dabbled in black magic. Scholarship itself, regarded as a virtuous vocation when you were young and elected to dedicate your life to it, is now looked upon with suspicion even within the Order, let alone among more fanatical sectors of the Church. The Church once thought that it had complete control of learning, because it had complete control over the use and dissemination of the written word, but that was not really true even before the Germans began making printing presses and they began sprouting like mushrooms in all the capitals of Europe. The Church is now direly alarmed about what people might be able to read in future, and what they might want to read.

"You and I know, because we have actually read grimoires, that they are mostly nonsense, and that if there is any power at all in any of their formulae, then the duty of men of God is to study it, to understand it and to employ it in the service of God and virtue. That is why I sanctioned Ollivier's research, while recommending that he kept it secret. He was a good man, and I knew that he would only employ anything that he discovered in a virtuous fashion. I cannot tell you what he confided to me in the confessional, but I can tell you that his research bore very modest fruit before he went to Herbriant—modest, but not entirely negligible, in his opinion. Necromancy, he told me, does not work in the fashion that popular superstition sometimes supposes; it cannot reanimate cadavers, and such specters as it raises are elusive to sight, but Ollivier became convinced that the dead could be raised and consulted, under the right circumstances—as, indeed, the Old Testament assures us.

"He would have told you what he had done and what he had found, I feel sure, once he was certain in his own mind, and if he had not fallen ill. I heard his delirious ramblings, as you did—as several of your more scatterbrained brethren, I fear—and I heard him repeating formulae that he had read in texts that, mercifully, are no longer in the Abbey. I shall do whatever I can to preserve the texts that are still here, but if orders come from above to destroy some of them, I will do it, with a heavy heart. I hope, sincerely, that the ones Ollivier took secretly to Tardivel will be safe there just as I hope that you will be safe there, but more wars than one are raging around all the havens of peace that still exist in Bretagne, and the future is unknowable.

"Corentin de Tardivel can tell you far more, and is not bound by the secrecy of the confessional. I trust you to make up your own mind about the reliability of what he tells you, and to make your own judgment as to where virtue lies in this matter. I hope, in time, that you will judge my decisions more kindly that perhaps you can at present. I hope that it might be possible one day for you to return here, because, in my opinion, the Abbey needs you, the town needs you and the Order needs you—but Tardivel needs you too, and for the moment, it might be best for you the Abbey, the town and the Order if you were there rather than here. That is why I am sending you away. God be with you."

"And with you," Primael replied, automatically, unable, for the moment, to make any further comment, or even to make up his own mind about what he thought and felt.

III

At least thirty of the brethren had gathered in the court-yard to watch Primael depart with Corentin de Tardivel. He did not make attempt to shake anyone's hand, but contented himself with a general salute, which almost all of them returned, with varying degrees of conviction, as he rode through the gate. Many, he thought, would be glad to see him gone, and in view of what the Abbot had told him, elliptically, he could not hold it against them.

Tardivel's horse had a much larger stride than Primael's mule, but it had little difficulty adapting its gait to the leisurely walk that the mule adopted. Tardivel did not ask his companion to urge the lesser mount to a trot. Although his own horse had been rested and watered, it could not be reckoned fully recovered from the morning's exertions.

Primael did not see the two Dominicans as he and Corentin skirted the hill where the black friars had taken up their position earlier in the day, but he had no doubt that his departure would not go unseen, and would certainly not be unreported to the Dominicans' superiors. After all, the two were in the vicinity to search for evidence of heresy, and they would not be doing their duty if they did not report something, however trivial or unreliable.

Seek and ye shall find, he thought, *and if ye do not find, ye shall invent.*

It was easy enough for riders to converse while they were going at such a slow pace, even though Primael was obliged to look up at his traveling companion at a slightly uncomfortable angle, but their conversation was wary and somewhat desultory at first, neither being certain how to broach the matters that were on both their minds. To begin with, he and Corentin did not talk about anything but practical matters: the length of the journey, the stages in which they would undertake it, and whether it would be strictly necessary to seek lodgings for the night, or whether Primael would be able to sleep in the open, given that the weather was still relatively benign. He assured his companion that sleeping on the ground would not be any harder than sleeping on the mattress in his cell.

In the first stage of their itinerary they followed a road alongside one of the streams that fed the lake, in a north-easterly direction, through farmland, but it did not take them long to reach heathland, and roads that were little more than trails, negotiable for men on foot and for horses, but not for carts. Streams and stands of trees were sparse, and human habitations even sparser; their inhabitants lived primarily on meager hunting and fishing, and sickly vegetable plots, but the land was, in general, too poor to support an abundant population.

Primael did not believe, however, that it had always been so unyielding, for he found it difficult, in that case, to explain the enigmatic presence, in places, of menhirs, either singly or in geometrical arrays. It was not impossible that the huge stones had been transported into the wilderness deliberately, distanced from settlements, but it was also possible that the terrain had been very different once, and that what seemed eternal now was, in reality, only temporary, the bleak aftermath of a more fruitful era, of which only strange stones and fanciful tales remained to stand as witnesses to forgotten purposes and ambitions.

It was a landscape conducive to meditations, but also to a certain peculiar unease, which encouraged conversation as a kind of spiritual antidote. They had not been traveling for long when Tardivel evidently thought that the time had come to begin preparing his guest for the prospect that confronted him, as an alternative to the quiet and exceedingly orderly life that he had been leading for thirty years and more.

"I can promise you a good bed, efficient fireplaces and good carpets when we reach Tardivel," the vicomte said. "The house is perched on a rock with steep slopes, and looks forbidding from beneath, but its architecture is safe and it is comfortable within. There will be more meat in the diet than you are accustomed to, and the bread often leaves something to be desired by those used to fine wheat, but I have a good cook, who works wonders with whatever materials she has. On the whole, life is good there, and I think you will find it comfortable."

"More comfortable than the Abbey, I dare say," said Primael. "I shall adapt to it as best I can. The Abbot might require me to stay for some time, if your hospitality will allow it."

"Have no fear on that score, Brother," said the vicomte. "My fear is rather that you might be reluctant to accept it when you discover how…certain other things are there. If you can soothe my mother's occasional distress, though, as Ollivier seemed capable of doing, I'll be eternally grateful to you. And if you could do something for my sister…although I fear that might be a hopeless case…"

"I have not very much medical skill, in spite of my reading," Primael said, dolefully. "With regard to your mother…much depends on what you mean by her distress."

"She has fits sometimes—convulsions. Some people call it madness. I prefer the term epilepsy. But we have books at Tardivel, and I know that Hippocrates is said to have suggested opening the skull surgically in order to drain off the phlegma causing the seizures. Ollivier did not think such treatment appropriate, and I was glad."

The young man looked at Primael uneasily, as if wondering whether he might be an enthusiast of craniotomy. "My father treated her cruelly, and had her confined to her apartment," he added, "but she is certainly not mad. Between her fits, she is perfectly reasonable…more so than my father, at any rate. According to Ollivier, the word madness has no definite meaning, and people are sometimes accused of it who are as reasonable as you or I, sometimes because of temporary physical afflictions and sometimes because they have ideas contrary to common belief. If the latter is truly evidence of madness, you will find a great deal of it at Tardivel—but I dare say that you would find it everywhere, if you were able to look into people's thoughts, instead of merely hearing their guarded confessions."

Primael had often suspected so, and knew what a privilege it was to live in the Abbey, where ideas were so carefully policed. But perhaps the policing of routine and ritual only made it easier to keep secrets, given that the two men he had thought he knew more intimately than anyone else seemed to have been doing for years—from him, but not from one another. Aloud, he said: "People are sometimes very free with assertions of others' madness."

"Indeed they are," Corentin de Tardivel agreed, wholeheartedly. "And people say so many other things that are not true that I am loath to trust their judgment on a matter of such personal importance as my mother's reason."

Primael could sympathize with that. His own mother had died while he was barely adolescent. He could not help feeling, though, that his companion was beating around the bush somewhat in his elaborate sketch of what he would find at the Château de Tardivel, even though neither of them was aware of the real issue at stake. He cast about for a way of broaching the subject, but found that he, too, was urged by instinct and habit toward indirection.

"Incidentally," he said, glimpsing a path that might take the conversation were they were both a little reluctant to go, "I seem to have told you an accidental untruth when I said that we had had no news from Tardivel for some time. It appears that I am out of touch with the gossip that circulates among the younger monks. I have been a little too successful in isolating myself in my scholarly pride, it seems."

"But whatever you were told while I was talking to the Abbot did not deter you from accepting my invitation?"

"No. Initially, I dismissed it all as nonsense. I'm no longer so certain of that, but I would not have declined your invitation on account of the allegation, even if my superior had not instructed me to accept it."

"I'm glad to hear it," said Tardivel. "Might I know what it is that is being alleged against me within the Abbey walls?" Evidently, he wanted Primael to make the first move, the first fatal pronunciation.

Primael broke through the barrier of reluctance. "That you practiced necromancy with Brother Ollivier," he said, "and that the people of Herbriant have commerce of some kind with the Dames Blanches." Once said, it seemed to have been easy enough, but he was aware that his heart was beating faster, and had the curious sensation of having crossed a threshold: that although his mule was plodding along a tedious track between shallow hills clad in purple heather and yellow gorse, he was in a world whose meanings had shifted. There was no menhir in sight, for the moment, but he suspected that if there had been, it might have taken on a ominous significance in his imagination.

"Is that all?" said the young man, lightly. "And which part of it might not be nonsense, in your estimation?"

"I'm Breton-born," Primael replied, carefully. "I have a clearer idea of the harmlessness of the legends of the Dames Blanches than the fools who come to the Abbey from France, Flanders or England, who cannot detach such ideas from notions of demonic tempters."

"They are certainly not tempters," Tardivel agreed. "If I did have commerce with Dames Blanches, then it would not worry you?"

"It would not," said Primael. "Even if they were really demons, I would not be afraid of them, but they are said to be generally benign. Nor am I afraid of tales of follets and farfadets…or necromancy. When I hear such suggestions, I do not automatically reach for my cross in order to launch an anathema, as that tall Dominican did whom we saw on the hill"

"Ollivier said that you are a wise man as well as a good one," Tardivel said, with a hint of relief in his voice—but only a hint, as if he considered the hurdle just crossed was only the first of many, and by no means the highest.

"And then again," Primael went on, "even before you arrived at the burial-ground, while local boys were testing their daring by hurtling insults at my friend's coffin, I had been led to wonder whether the practice of necromancy is necessarily evil. Specifically, I was thinking of the woman who summoned the prophet Samuel at the behest of King Saul, whom the Vulgate calls a *pythorem*, which I take to mean a seeress. The English, I know, call her a witch, but that was a concept that did not exist at the time when the Holy Book was written, and the English used the same term as a justification for foully murdering Jeanne d'Arc, who has now been proclaimed a martyr and might one day be recognized as a saint. I can find no evidence in the scriptural text that the seeress Saul consisted was evil, and what Samuel prophesied at her request was accurate, so I wonder—speaking purely as a scholar, you understand—whether someone following in her footsteps ought to be condemned as evil merely for the fact of invoking the dead."

"That's very diplomatic of you, Brother Primael," said Tardivel, with a brief and rather contrived laugh. "You will not be surprised, I think, to hear that I agree with you wholeheartedly—but you might not be so ready to absolve me of sin when you know the whole truth about my necromancy. What did Brother Michael tell you about what Ollivier and I attempted?"

"Absolutely nothing," said Primael, carefully. "Whatever you or Ollivier might have confessed to him, he held the secret to be sacred."

"But silence can sometimes be as eloquent as speech. And whatever Ollivier might have confessed to you of his own sins, you would similarly regard as sacred. Very delicate—and reassuring, as you doubtless intended it to be. You need not worry, though. You shall know everything, in time, perhaps far more than you want or need to know, and I have already made an irrevocable commitment to trust your discretion. Please give me a little time to organize the thoughts in my own mind, though. Believe me when I tell you that you might

39

find the truth more challenging that you presently imagine. If you were a lesser man, I would say with confidence that you might find it stranger than you can imagine, but I remember you well enough from the days when you tried to educate me in Latin, and Ollivier has told me enough about you for me to believe that you will at least be able to understand, even if it horrifies you."

"It does not seen to horrify you," Primael observed, a trifle uneasily.

"I have certainly grown accustomed to it," the vicomte said, "but I'd be a liar if I said that my invocations do not make me anxious, in certain of their aspects...and certain manifestations."

"Manifestations?" Primael queried.

"Indeed."

"Of the dead?"

"Among other things." Tardivel uttered that phrase simply and flatly, but Primael was able to see the range of its implications. Tardivel was not simply a necromancer, then...or what was held to be necromancy was not simply a matter of divination by consultation with the spirits of the dead. That was not surprising. He had read a manuscript of the *Liber Juratus Honorii*, and Johannes Hartlieb's commentary on it, in which the summoning of the spirits of the dead was represented as merely one aspect of the summoning of spirits, called demons or daemons—and what a difference of interpretation those different orthographies signified! What a world of difference there was between the Christian definition of demons as agents of Satan, and the sense in which ancient philosophers had employed the term daimon, or daemon, to mean a benign guiding spirit!

On the other hand, Primael remembered what had actually been said to him at the Abbey in the brief interval when he was endeavoring to reach his cell and prepare his pack. It was not spirits of either of those kinds to which reference had been made—and he and Tardivel were both Breton-born.

"Do those other things include Marie-Mortes?" he asked, curiously

"Yes, they do," said the vicomte, bluntly. "And stranger things. I would not care to put a limit myself on how many kinds there might be, or how strange they might be. Mother has warned me against trying to summon them, although I have not told her much about my discoveries or my dreams, for fear of fueling her own visions. I cannot be sure what she sees when the physical disturbances disrupt her ideas—secrets are kept within families as well as within Abbeys. She is surely not mad, but she places too much faith in her intuitions. My particular necromancy is…far more focused. I consider myself to be prudent, although others might not agree, and none of us can choose the circumstances in which we operate. I am aware that occasions might arise in which prudence is an insufficient protection."

Primael considered that statement for a moment, and felt need of an intellectual anchorage before proceeding. "Forgive me for being simplistic, he said, but I am trying to orientate my thoughts. Let us be clear: you have practiced necromancy successfully with Brother Ollivier, and your mother sees the spirits of the dead, along with other entities, when she has convulsions?"

"I have certainly practiced necromancy successfully with Ollivier. My mother's case is different, although she is a seeress of sorts. She does not use formulae, attempting to exercise thereby what Ollivier called the tyranny of the word—indeed, when I quoted that phrase to her, she said that I had an entirely mistaken conception of the tyranny in question. She is not convinced that spirits can be commanded and compelled, as the *Liber Juratus Honorii* and the *Clavicula Salomonis* allege, but she certainly accepts that they can come of their own accord, with their own reasons, and not merely in dreams, although that is where they are most commonly manifest.

"These are deep waters, though, and you will have the opportunity to consult my mother yourself. The matter I want to emphasize regarding what Ollivier and I have done is that in

41

saying that I have practiced necromancy, successfully, I am not confessing to having had any truck with the Christian Satan, the ruler of Hell and ultimate enemy of humankind. I have made no pact with the Devil, any more than Ollivier had—or my mother. I will not tell you that my research has been carried out for purely scholarly motives, as his was, but I do consider my motives, and my success, to be entirely virtuous."

"But you have conjured spirits of the dead, both with and without Ollivier's aid?"

"Yes, I have. Ollivier was my teacher in that instance, to begin with, but what he taught me would not have had any great effect if I had not been able to add something myself. We drew upon different resources of knowledge, combined what we knew, and obtained an initial success. Ollivier had to return to the Abbey when the term of his leave ended, but he was supposed to return soon, bringing more books with him. While he was gone, I suspended new research for a while, and concentrated on refining what I had already achieved, but when time went by and Ollivier did not return or send any message, I began to try new conjurations again, modestly. Then I decided that it might be wise not to continue without him, and that I should come to Paimpol in order to ask the Abbot to release him again. We had only begun to understand, you see, and in terms of understanding, I was far inferior to him. Whether this will help, I don't know, not having had a chance as yet to decipher it."

Corentin de Tardivel put his hand over his breast to indicate that he had something wedged inside his jerkin—sheets of parchment, Primael guessed, given to him by Brother Michael, on Ollivier's behalf, perhaps a record that Ollivier had tried to make of his discoveries, in spite of his crippling illness.

"And did Ollivier's initial contribution to your endeavor," Primael asked, "consist of manuscripts that that he had brought back from Granada, or manuscripts that he obtained from Gilles de Rais?"

"Both. You have seen some of them yourself, but not all. The important thing, however is that the manuscripts would not have been adequate in themselves to enable Ollivier to do what he did for me. There are indications that have never been written down, and necessarily so. Even those that are in writing are difficult to decipher, unless one possesses keys that are not easy to obtain. By the same token, however, the knowledge handed down to me..."

"By your mother?"

"Not my mother, who was brought here from another region when she married my father, but from the wise women of the forest and the nearby plain. One of them is now my mother's companion, but she is not as well-informed at her older sisters, and she thinks what I am doing is dangerous...there is a certain tension in the house in consequence. But the point is that without some local knowledge, the invocation that Ollivier and I achieved would have been far weaker in its effect. Even with the aid of his manuscripts, I probably could not have done it. The path that we followed is labyrinthine, and there are many dead ends therein. I suspect that the labyrinth in question cannot be negotiated successfully without guidance."

"Supernatural guidance?"

"Yes. But not, I repeat, diabolical guidance—not in the simplistic sense that the Church understands Satan, or the concepts of good and evil. Ollivier shared my opinion."

"And Brother Michael too, it seems," said Primael, pensively.

"I don't know about that. He has given me these papers that Ollivier left for me, as he had promised to do, and he must have read them, just as he had long been aware of Ollivier's research and experimentation, but he did not confide his judgment to me—he too is a prudent man. Mercifully, he did not reach for his cross and recite the formula of exorcism. Ollivier had told him what he was doing and what he hoped to achieve, so we can assume that he was, and is, at least willing to suspend his judgment, in the interests of learning more."

Primael hesitated for some time before saying: "Do you know why Ollivier never made any such confession to me?"

"Not exactly," said Tardivel. "Perhaps he was simply following his superior's order. But he might also have wanted to protect your innocence. He was convinced, in his own mind, that what he was doing was not evil, but he could not be absolutely sure that he was not a victim of diabolical deception and temptation."

And he did not want to expose me to that risk, Primael thought, warily. *Had he ever thought that I needed to know, he would surely have told me, no matter what Brother Michael had instructed him to do, but he probably judged that my innocence was a greater asset to me than a knowledge of what he was doing would be.*

"But you are prepared to expose me to the risk?" he commented, a trifle sarcastically

"Circumstances have changed. Now, in my estimation, at least—and Brother Michael's too, for what that is worth—it's necessary that you know, and necessary that you come to Tardivel. It would be difficult, if not impossible, for you to stay at Tardivel for any length of time without knowing the truth—the whole truth, so far as I know it—but it will take time to tell, and will require a good deal of explanation, in as orderly a manner as I can contrive. You have been a teacher for a long time, and you understand very well why there are certain matters that can only be revealed, and absorbed, by degrees. I apologize if I do not handle that process with the same efficiency and expertise that someone like you or Ollivier could bring to it. I will do my best. If you would rather organize the process yourself, by means of an interrogation, by all means do so; it will probably help me to organize my own ideas. But there are certain matters that will have to wait until we reach Tardivel—things that have to be shown rather than told. Again, as a teacher, you will understand that."

Primael understood well enough that it would be difficult to organize his own questions in a orderly manner, given that there were so many, and so many different directions to follow. His eyes strayed over the landscape, relatively narrow at this point in the road, but not so confined that he could not see a group of standing stones on a ridge, like sentinels on watch—but what they might once have been protecting had vanished without trace, along which any immediate threat from which it required protection. And there was a possibility, too, that their air of being sentinels might be a mere product of his imagination, like every other purpose that recent invaders had invented in the attempt to suppress the enigma. He knew that their name, *menhir*, simply meant "long stone," and contained no information other than that apparent to the naked, uninformed eye. Those organized into *dolmens*—"stone tables" in archaic Breton—were thought by monkish scholars to be the remains of tombs, probably once covered by mounds of turf, but even that was guesswork.

Perhaps some of the spirits that were said to haunt them knew more, and might be willing and able reveal the secret to an expert necromancer, but the spirits of the recently dead would have no memory of it, and the most ancient dead would presumably be unable to make themselves comprehensible, if they could speak at all...

"Do the dead speak?" he asked Corentin Tardivel. "When you summon them by means of the tyranny of the word, do they respond in speech?"

"Yes, they speak," said Tardivel, "and the words are audible to more than one listener, so the voices are not illusions of the mind. The air stirs...especially in the forest."

"Do they speak in Latin, Bas-Breton or bastard Norman?"

"They speak in the languages they knew when they were alive, I suppose. I have not heard many, at least in a coherent fashion; the incomprehensible whispers that the formulae often summon might be in any tongue, or none."

"It would doubtless be foolish to expect," Primael mused, "that very many members of the vast legions of the dead accumulated over the centuries all over the world would be able to speak to us intelligibly, let alone any spirits that have never been human. A severe limitation, that, on what they might be able tell us, unless the few scholars among the dead have continued to learn in their new existence, and to master the multitudinous languages of the dead."

"That is not impossible," said Tardivel, a trifle defensively, in confrontation with Primael's slight sarcasm. "but I fear that those Greek philosophers who believed that the soul, once liberated from the body, would have perfect knowledge of everything, were very optimistic. Such imaginations as Plato's of the fashion in which the dead continue their existence in the afterlife, appear be defective."

"But the invoked dead *can* speak," said Primael, persisting in the emphasis of the established point. And they can be seen too?"

"They can certainly be heard, and felt," his interlocutor replied—a significant supplement, Primael thought. "To judge from my immediate acquaintance, however," Corentin continued, "which might not be typical, seeing the spirits of the dead with human eyes is difficult. Often, there is no more than a kind of tremor in the atmosphere, as if the eye were looking through curved glass or rippling water. But they are tangible, and they have the texture and solidity of flesh. They can touch, with sensible fingers, and they can be touched, in the fullness of their anatomy, human…or otherwise."

"Otherwise? You mean animal, or monstrous?"

"It isn't easy to determine the whole form from mere touches."

"And what about the other senses?" Primael queried, hurrying now as more questions occurred to him. "Do the dead stink? How do they taste?"

"If you wish," the young man retorted, his voice taking on a certain resentment as he detected a note of skepticism in the questions, "I will do what I can, at Tardivel, to enable you to investigate such questions yourself. Ollivier can answer them better than I ever could, if he will come when we call."

"When *we* call?" Primael queried. "You are the necromancer, not I."

"So I am," Tardivel agreed. "But once you have heard the dead, and felt…something, I think you will be enthusiastic to continue. Once you begin with experiments of this sort, you will not find it easy to stop...even if you cannot help suspecting that there is diabolism in it. I am giving you fair warning."

What Primael could not help suspecting, for the moment, was that the young man was thinking about his own experience, and perhaps generalizing from it too extravagantly. Plainly, having thought that Ollivier might have abandoned him, Corentin had become very anxious about the progress of his research, and the planning of it, but he had not been tempted to stop, and seemed to feel a marked urgency with regard to the necessity of continuing.

Is he mad? Primael thought. *Are the voices he can hear and the semblances of flesh that he can touch mere hallucinations, the products of his disturbed soul? But if, as he claims, the voices can be heard by more than one listener, the folly must be real...or contagious."*

"We are coming to a better road, beyond that next hill," Corentin told him, "which goes almost straight for a while in the direction we need to follow. There is a ferry over the river, and an inn of sorts on the far bank. We should let our mounts rest there for a while, and feed them, and take some nourishment ourselves, although I should like to go a league or two further by nightfall, if it would not be too taxing for you. Are you agreeable?

"I am in your hands," the Benedictine said. "Have no fear for my endurance. I am old, but not decrepit."

IV

They did not talk about private matters in the inn, although there was no indication that the innkeeper or his maid were listening to them. They were well aware that appearances could be deceptive, and that such individuals were always starved of distraction. Once they had resumed their journey, however, at Tardivel's request, Primael told him more about the effects of Ollivier's illness.

"Ollivier had not aged as gracefully as some people do even before he went to Herbriant," he said, "but he was not unduly ugly, and had a venerable air about him conducive to trust. The disease, however, caused a very rapid deterioration in his countenance as well as elsewhere, causing ulcerations and discolorations that spoiled his features completely. People find it surprisingly easy, alas, to associate ugliness with evil in their minds, in spite of the fact that the great majority of townspeople and peasants alike are far from pretty. *As ugly as sin*, the common saying has it, which only means that sin is ugly, but can easily be misinterpreted as implying that ugliness is a symptom of sin."

"Words are sometimes treacherous servants," Tardivel agreed, "and legend sometimes exerts a tyranny over our ideas that is difficult to avoid."

"Some time before he was consigned to the grave into which we saw him laid today," Primael continued, "Ollivier had begun to take on the appearance of a dead man, with marbled skin that his beard was impotent to conceal, sunken eyes and a twisted mouth. Perhaps he left the Abbey a little too often before he was confined to his bed, but it would have done no good had he locked himself away. No one said in so many words within my hearing that his disfigurement was evidence of any secret sin, let alone a specific interest in the practice of necromancy, but legend, as you say, has a tyranny of its own, and anxious thought is not easy to police. 'All illness comes from God,' is a common saw, although not strictly orthodox, 'and disfigurement is divine punishment.' Ollivier and I had seen far too many sick men and women in our time to believe any such thing. Unfortunately, we and the Abbot were the only residents of the Abbey old enough to remember the last serious epidemic in Paimpol, and the lessons it taught us."

"So it was definitely not news from Tardivel that started the rumors about Ollivier?" Corentin seemed anxious to avoid the guilt of that responsibility.

"I don't believe so—but everyone knew that he had spent an unusually long time there, and when his disfiguration started the hare running, it must have been easy to make the connection. Coincidence is a great tempter in the construction of wild imaginings. Nor, if you are anxious about that possibility too, was it rumors from Tardivel, or rumors concerning Ollivier, that brought the Dominican spies to Paimpol. They were merely scouting, but the gossip was the kind of thing for which they were hunting, probably with little success, and having heard it...well, as you saw this morning, they obviously thought Ollivier's death a good opportunity to put on a none-too-subtle display of menace. Ridiculous, in essence...except that we are living in a world where the ridiculous can all too easily become murderous. I do not know how far legend can be trusted regarding the events of the Albigensian crusade, which enabled Dominic Guzman to found the Order of Preachers, but it has certainly grown ever more powerful in three centuries, especially since the extermination of the Templars. I'm well aware that the Dominican Order has been host to great scholars, like Albertus Magnus, as well as heresy-hunting Inquisitors, but I fear that they have probably earned the reputation that precedes them well enough."

"I fear so too," said Tardivel.

Primael took up the thread again "They certainly did not start the war for political hegemony in Bretagne, but they will surely take what advantage they can from the upheaval it is causing." His eyes strayed from the road to scan a nearby hamlet, distributed between fields and orchards irrigated by a sluggish stream. "And these poor folk will be the losers, as ever, while one gang of petty lords, who still take stupid pride in being the descendants of all-conquering Normans, fights another gang nurturing the same notions, with the aid of English and Austrian archers, proclaiming all the while that they are patriots fighting for one improvised nation or another. To the so-called knights, it is a game of slaughter, in which the true Bretons are merely counters whose murder and oppression counts the score."

He blushed slightly, as he realized that his tongue had run away with him, and that Corentin de Tardivel was himself a "so-called knight." The young man did not seem to take any offense, but the momentary embarrassment caused Primael to follow the train of thought further

"You're a Vicomte yourself," he observed, warily. "Have you not inherited some oath of vassalage that will oblige you to fight in the war if you are summoned, for François, as he now calls himself, as if he were French already, even while defying the French in his capacity as a Norman Duke? The summons would come from his treasurer, Landais, I suppose, who seems to have all authority in his hands now, but would you not be required to fight if he commanded it?"

"My ancestors were prudent men," said Tardivel, shortly. "They did what it was necessary to do to survive and thrive, becoming quasi-Norman. And François is a more honest appellation than Francsez, given that the descendants of the Normans have long since adapted to the new language, just as the descendants of the Franks did before them. France is no longer an illusion of ambition and glory, it seems to me, as it is in the stories we tell of noble knights and shining armor, tourneys and crusades, but a brutal reality backed by heavy arbalests and long cannon. It has crushed the south, now that Burgundy has gone the way of the Languedoc, and all-but expelled the English Normans. The west will surely fall—but

Bretagne has already been submerged for centuries, under one invader or another, and has not yet been completely drowned. Perhaps the time is not far off, but...that does not answer your question, though, does it?

"Yes, Brother, I am a vassal; if I am summoned by the Duke's heirs, I can still be obliged to raise a company of my own vassals and go to play my part in the massacre, as butcher or victim. But my little domain is remote, and inconsequential. Wars are no longer fought today as they were in our ancestors' time. Kings and Dukes prefer hiring trained and battle-hardened mercenaries to calling upon peasants and burgers who have never held a sword or a bow. To be a bowman or an arbalestier nowadays is a career, requiring long discipline, and cannons are now the responsibility of trained artillerists famil-iar with their variety, their capacity and their projectiles. I doubt that I shall be troubled by the Duke, and for the mo-ment, I fear the Dominicans more, although they have no men-at-arms to call upon as yet, nor papal envoys to crack the whip and muster the bishops in their support."

"Rome has its own political problems, so rumor has it," Primael observed, "but now that bulls can be printed, a bliz-zard of paper is beginning to harass Christendom in a way that handwritten parchment never could. Unrest is seething. Sixtus is said to be more interested in artistic splendor and money than matters of doctrine, but he has permitted the establish-ment of an independent Inquisition in Spain, and now that Louis is dead, it cannot be certain that Anne and Charles will continue their quarrel against him. If the French crown were to consider it politic to ape Ferdinand and Isabella...but Brother Michael considered that unlikely, since France and Spain have ever been rivals, never at peace for long, and France has not yet annexed Bretagne..."

Primael became aware that he was talking about matters of which he had no real knowledge, and although they could hardly be considered irrelevant to his present situation, they were far from the real issue that was weighing upon his heart: that his closest friend had kept such a dire and terrible secret from him, and that the superior of the community in whose bosom he had spent his life had also kept the secret from him. He was allowing his thought to stray in order to distract him from the hurt of that discovery.

But is the injury to my pride not a distraction in itself? he thought. *I am a man of God. Should I not be more concerned with the enormity of the apparent sin that Ollivier has committed than the petty fact that he did not confide it to me. What would my duty have been, after all, had he admitted it? And what is my duty now that I know, on the authority of the Abbot as well as this strange young man? Why am I here and where am I going? What must I do when I arrive?*

Primael had the sudden, desolate feeling that he was utterly out of his depth. Life in the Abbey, under the Rule had never been a bed of roses, but compared with the life of the peasants in the fields surrounding the lake, and the burgers of the town, it had been facile and secure. He had never thought of himself as being an exceptionally happy man, or an unusually fortunate one, but it occurred to him now, as he was drawing away from his home toward an unknown and perhaps sinister destination, and already beginning to feel saddle-sore, that he had indeed been very content and fortunate in his insulation from the world, to the extent that the loss of that contentment was terrifying..

But he could not turn back, literally or figuratively. He could not turn his mule around, and he could not unlearn what Brother Michael had told him, so casually, about his dead, disfigured friend, which Corentin de Tardivel had endorsed and had already complicated further.

"We've come far enough for today," said Corentin Tardivel, interrupting his meditation. "We've made better progress than I expected, and that mule has earned oats as honestly as my sturdy fellow, but the sun is setting and we ought to seek shelter for the night—in a barn if we cannot obtain hospitality in a house, given that we are in good farmland. We will not have the same advantage tomorrow night, I fear, even if we start at dawn and our mounts give us the same sterling service. I dare not urge them too hard, else one or the other will surely break down, and there are no replacements to be had for several leagues beyond this point."

Without waiting for consent, this time, Tardivel looked around from the top of the rise where he had paused, selected one of the more imposing dwellings within view—by what criteria, Primael did not know—and rode away in order to consult a stout woman who was drawing water from a nearby well. After a brief interval, while Primael stroked his mount, reassuring the animal that its labor was all but done for one day, the vicomte came back to tell the Benedictine that they would not have to settle for the barn, and would even have mattresses of a sort to protect their weary limbs from the insults of a wooden floor, while their mounts had stalls in a stable, and good oats.

Primael did not ask him what such favors had cost, but he felt guiltily glad of being able to travel in the company of a man with a sturdy purse, and no fear of dipping into it.

When they had eaten a supper that seemed good to Primael, but poor to Tardivel, and given their hosts and their children God's blessing as well as a metal fee, they were shown to a room that seemed spacious enough, though poorly furnished. Tardivel had to search his saddle-bag for a tinder-box in order that he might light a candle, which had also taken from his luggage. He seemed to have misplaced it—his luggage was far more elaborate than Primael's—and it took him some time to unearth it, but the candle finally flared up. Again, they did not talk about any sensitive matters while there was a possibility of being overheard, and Primael soon went to sleep, worn out by an exhausting and very strange day.

If he dreamed, he forgot his dreams as soon as his companion woke him up in the morning, at first light. They did not linger in the house, but mounted up as soon as Tardivel had saddled the horse and the mule.

They had soon quit the farmland and returned to the arid undulating heath, with scattered stands of trees, but it was not very long before higher hills were visible in the distance every time they topped a rise, with dark foliage: the marches of Herbriant. They seemed sinister to Primael's gaze, prejudiced in spite of his scholarship and his faith by dark legends. In current usage and belief, Broceliande was no more, as a name or as a memory, if it had ever really existed at all, but the idea and the legend lingered: legends of hauntings older than history, beyond the reach even of occult science, of which even such specters as the Dames Blanches were mere vestiges. But he was a Christian, armored against all things Satanic, no matter how ancient.

Primael remembered debates that he had had with Ollivier over the years regarding the War in Heaven. The references in Holy Writ were oblique, and although Cabalistic documents made reference to the testament of Enoch, which supposedly contained a fuller account, no one in western Christendom, so far as he knew, had ever read it. It was, therefore a legend, but one with a certain weight of authority—for after all, if Satan really had been cast out of heaven, and the angelic *egregori* really had sired the *nephilim*, as Genesis asserted, then the war must have been fought, and must therefore have had a date. When? Before the creation of Adam, presumably, if the serpent in Eden really was Satan—but Ollivier, Primael remembered, had taken leave to doubt that, since the text did not say so. Might the war in Heaven, then, have taken place after the creation of Adam, or perhaps in parallel with it. After all, Ollivier had argued, wars were not fought in a day although battles sometimes were.

In those debates, Primael remembered, there had been a difference of attitude between himself and his friend. He had regarded them as scholarly games, mental exercises, like attempts to estimate the number of angels capable of dancing on the head of a pin. The point of them had not been to find an answer, but to test the flexibility of thought, the ingenuity of intellect. But Ollivier had sometimes—often, in fact—contended that they were not irrelevant to the way the world was, and ought to be evaluated.

"In the times before Moses," he had said, once, "people had a conception of war very different from the one that we have formed and developed greatly since the days of Charlemagne. The contending forces were tribes whose numbers were countable, and in which the weapons were very primitive. They could be settled by a single engagement. Our wars are very different. The forces are more numerous and more complex, and the projectiles fired by arbalests, longbows and cannons far greater in range than javelins, short bows and slings, and wars extend over decades. How long have the English Normans been in conflict with the French Normans? More than a century, if my count is good, and the matter is not settled yet. And in the meantime, have not both sets of Normans ceased, in any meaningful sense, to be Norman? Have they not interbred so extensively, on the one hand with the descendants of the Saxons and Celts, and on the other with the descendants of the Franks and Gauls, to have lost their distinction?"

"All that is true," Primael had said, at the time, "but it has no relevance at all to any war that might have been fought in Heaven by the forces of the Archangel Michael, from whom our good Abbot took his name, and the forces of the rebel Lucifer. If artists represent Michael clad in shining armor, like one of Charlemagne's paladins, that is symbolism and allegory. We have no idea how angels fight, or even how they are formed; they are everywhere in art today, but no sculptor or painter has ever depicted them from life."

"And by the same token," Ollivier had replied, we have no idea how long the War in Heaven lasted, when it began, or whether it has ended?"

"*Whether* it has ended?" Primael had queried, although he remembered now had he had felt the argumentative ground being cut away from him even as he pronounced the word.

"Precisely," Ollivier had replied. "Can anyone contemplating the world believe that it has ended that the affair is settled? Has not the Church been constantly rallied by one Pope after another to fight the ever-present menace of Satan? Do we not know, nowadays, that no peace treaty has every truly ended a war, but has only postponed the conflict, or transformed it from a contest of pitched battles to a contest of slow harassments? Even if Satan really was cast down into Hell and imprisoned there, that certainly has not put an end to the conflict with his forces, and we have the word of *Genesis* that not all the renegade angels were imprisoned with them, for the *egregori*—the Watchers—who sired the *nephilim*—the Giants—must have been rogues too, whether they owed any open allegiance to Lucifer or not. You and I have lived through the reign of Louis XI, the Universal Spider, and witnessed it from what has so far been a comfortable distance, and we have surely had lessons in the art and politics of warfare of which Moses could never have dreamed. If angels really do make war, can they really be less subtle than the King of France, the Holy Roman Emperor, or even Duc François, who has needed all his ingenuity to preserve the doomed hegemony of his diluted Norman tribe in Bretagne thus far."

Primael remember that he had complimented Ollivier on the ingenuity of his argument, and that his friend really had been stubborn in representing it carefully as an exercise in ingenuity, even though Primael had known full well that Ollivier had considered it more than that, as something relevant to the contest between good and evil within the human soul, including the souls of those in Holy Orders, within which the Franciscan white friars and the Dominican black friars, although aligned on the same side, as the staunchest of allies, were also rivals, while the Benedictines, who secretly reckoned themselves holier than either, and the Carthusians, while similarly allied, sometimes looked at one another askance. And in world where an entire Order, perhaps the most powerful of all, the mighty Templars, had been convicted of alliance with the Devil, in the figure of Baphomet, and brought down by a King of France...

If Ollivier was right, Primael thought, *then not only is the War in Heaven not over, but he and I, vassals in of Christendom, have been fighting in the ranks all our lives, albeit with meager weapons. And now, it seems that he has tried to equip himself with more powerful and more ingenious instruments—but for employment on which side? Could he know? Can I?*

Then he pulled himself together, and told himself that the trees he could see on the distant horizon were just trees, and that calling a forest a vestige of Broceliande was a mere naming game of no real significance, and that he would be under God's protection there, as he had been in the Abbey, and that there was nothing to fear.

"We ought reach the forest by nightfall without hastening unduly," Tardivel told him, breaking in on Primael's meditation yet again, although he had seemed slightly relieved to have been able to put off his own promised explanations again. Now, though he was evidently pulling himself together: girding his loins, so to speak, for the task that he had to undertake.

"That's good," said Primael, in a neutral tone. "It's pleasant to be riding, but I'm becoming a trifle sore, and I shall be glad to arrive at our destination.

"That, I fear, we shall not achieve before nightfall," Tardivel told him. "The château will still be several leagues away, over difficult terrain, and it will be very difficult to converse as we ride. There is still time today, though, for me to tell you everything I need to tell you in advance of our arrival, and for you to ask me the questions that are bound to come to your mind. It might be best if I were to tell you my own history, in simple terms, so that you will be able to understand why and how one of the poorest of your students—oh. don't protest!—became a scholar of sorts, and a seeker of forbidden wisdom."

Primael sketched a gesture inviting the vicomte to tell his story.

The other took a deep breath, and began: "If you remember my arrival at the Abbey clearly, Brother—and it would surely be forgivable if you do not—you will recall that I must have seemed a very ordinary recruit to your school, the son of a pretentious father sent away from home in order to acquire a fashionable veneer of culture and learning, certainly not a novice intended to learn the skills of a scrivener or preparatory instruction for the priesthood. I can't deny that I was something of a fool in those days, and although you and Brother Ollivier eventually taught me to be less of a fool than I was, I am uncomfortably aware that my knowledge is of a very narrow kind.

"I doubt that you ever met my father; I know that he had not been one of your students. Probably, you were not even aware of his reputation. Had you met him, I doubt if he would have impressed you with his command of the aristocratic virtues, but he felt that he had them, or at least lamented their lack. He was not a fighting man, and had never been summoned to bear arms for the Duke, but that was something he regretted rather than being something for which he was grateful. He was a keen hunter, and took great pleasure in wielding a sword and firing a bow. He would have been glad, I feel sure, if I had turned out to be the kind of man he would have liked to be, and took pride in pretending to be. He was bold in word, and in deed, and he believed, with reason, that he had a will and a stomach of iron. In fact, neither wine nor passion had the power to disturb his firmness of mind—but that only served to make his head impregnable to wisdom or sophistication.

"When I first became a student at the Abbey, I still had the notion that I ought to strive to live up to my father's hopes and expectations, and that made me rather recalcitrant to learning—but I changed. Brother Ollivier did not take long to see through my facade of reckless intolerance to glimpse a gentler soul within; he was kind enough to take an interest in me, and to make an effort to cultivate what he saw. He never expected to make a monk of me, I'm sure, but he was not one of those monks who make a fetish out of recruitment. He was only interested in making better men."

"I know," said Primael, but so softly that it hardly seemed an interruption.

"In formal settings, of course, he never gave evidence by word or gesture that he knew what a poseur I was, but in private he talked to me in a different way, and he taught me to trust him, and to be honest in what I said to him. With him, and him alone, I came to feel that I could be my true self: full of doubt, capable of passion, and tender of sentiment—all traits that my father affected to despise, although I now believe firmly that it was an act on his part, a display partly born of his attitude to my mother.

"His marriage had been arranged by their families, of course, as such marriages routinely are, and I assume that it must have seemed appropriate at the time. Both families had Breton names, but both claimed Norman descent. Both were mongrelized, but for political reasons they displayed allegiance, externally at least, to ideas and ideals handed down by the most recent conquerors of the land. Neither family knew one another well enough to penetrate the other's façade, and neither, in all likelihood, knew how different the other actually was, behind its appearances. That could have been irrelevant to the marriage itself; I honestly believe that it might have become a close and rewarding relationship if my mother and father, as individuals, had been willing to make the effort to love one another, or to be steadfast allies even in the absence of genuine affection. They were not. They lived effectively separate, if not opposed, lives; they tolerated one another but always retained a measure of resentment at having been forced into a relationship that they did not like—a resentment that festered but only rarely found any outlet in argument and conflict, at least until I was five or six years old and first became able to listen and pay attention to what people wanted to tell me and make of me.

"It might seem absurd, but I was hardly aware of the fact that they were in conflict while I was very young, because I hardly ever saw them together, except in formal circumstances where etiquette ruled. If I gravitated toward my father rather than my mother, it was not because I made a choice between what I perceived to be opposed opinions, or even because I was conscious of following one course of action rather than another. I simply did whatever seemed natural at the time; I did not realize that what I did accentuated the discord between them, or that the discord in question was what led to my mother being effectively imprisoned within the house, condemned by my father as a madwoman. At the time, I simply accepted what I was told, and what I was told thereafter I was told almost exclusively by him, because I was hardly allowed to see my mother except in his presence.

"To my shame, I did not feel any particular sense of deprivation to begin with, and I was not overtaken by serious concern until I reached the age of thirteen, at which time I began to become painfully aware of many things to which I had previously given no thought—but that was also the age at which my father decided that I required the kind of education that I could only obtain from literate men, and made his preparations to send me away. Even after that, the matter of my mother's supposed madness and manner in which my father treated her might never have become a critical issue, and Ollivier might never have come to the manse at my invitation, to see my mother at my request, in order to make an estimation of her supposed madness and to conclude that she was not mad at all…but I'm getting ahead of the order of events, and ought to go back in time.

"As I have said, while I was at the Abbey, Brother Ollivier was the only person that I really grew to trust, and to whom I confided my true feelings. That was an accident of circumstance, I suppose, and it could as easily have been you, or no one, that I accepted as a confidant. But the salient point is that, by confiding in him, I won his confidence to some extent, so that he began to say to me some of the things that the rules and etiquette of the Abbey would not permit him to discuss freely with his brethren.

"You know, obviously, the Brother Ollivier's formal teaching was strictly orthodox. You also know that his personal opinions were somewhat less orthodox—but you might not have known that he was extremely careful about the extent to which he confided his unorthodox opinions to you, or to any of his brethren except the Abbot, his confessor. Perhaps it might seem odd to you, and bad, that he also confided those opinions, gradually, to me, but he did, and I took an increasing interest in them, because they seemed to me more reasonable that the views that were specified by dogma and the curriculum.

"In particular, as you know, Ollivier was interested in the occult sciences, but not in the way of those vulgar alchemists whose only ambition is to make gold from lead, or those vulgar astrologers whose only aim is to read secrets in the stars that they might use to their personal advantage. He studied both sciences for possible philosophical insights into the nature of matter and the nature of being, and he was interested in books of magic for the same reason. He did not accept the common belief that any magic is inherently good or evil. His view was that although any knowledge might be used for evil ends by evil men, knowledge as such is always good. Ignorance, he used to say, is the greatest evil of all."

"I heard him say that many times," Primael agreed.

"For that reason," Tardivel went on, "Ollivier had studied the arcane lore of necromancy, not with the intention of become a master of necromantic magic for any practical end, but in order to learn more about the mysteries of death—to enhance his understanding. He had not intended, in the beginning, to play with the conjuration of ghosts or spirits; to begin with, the written word was enough for him. He valued enlightenment far more than power. The story of his researches, he confided to me by degrees, over a period of years. In return, I talked to him about my own very different problems, which arose from increasing friction between myself and my father regarding my life and my future. In my periodic temporary returns to Tardivel, I had become sharply aware the unhappiness that he caused my sister, and the relentless tyranny which he exerted over his tenants and his bondsmen. I had already begun to wonder whether my mother was truly mad—or, at least, sufficiently so to warrant incarceration. But I could not successfully oppose him because I was still forced by circumstance at least to pretend to be striving to become what he wanted me to be. I think, in retrospect, that I had already had begun to hate my father, and in so doing had perhaps begun to dislike myself too, for being so obviously his son, but I was not aware of that at the time.

"Then disaster struck. During the vacation prior to the completion of my studies—some three months before Ollivier came to the château for the last time at my urgent invitation—I fell in love. Love was not a factor in my father's calculations of advantage, and he was already attempting to negotiate a marriage for me on the basis of his own financial interests. It would have been bad enough even had I fallen in love with a woman of my own class, other than the one he considered most useful to the family interest; in fact, it was far worse; I fell in love with a commoner, who was beautiful, but of no account whatsoever in my father's scheme of things. It is an old story, of course, and perfectly banal, but it does not seem at all banal to those who live it rather than hearing it narrated.

"To my father, the very idea of marrying for love, and perhaps the idea of love itself, seemed bizarre. I suspect that he had not an atom of true affection in his being. I, by virtue of some silly jest of the fate that determines such things, am very differently made, and my honest passion for the girl—whose name was Katarin—was quite boundless. I could not envision life without her, and it seemed to me that life itself had come to depend on my possession of her. By *possession* I do not mean mere physical possession—I doubt that my father would have raised any word of objection had I been prepared simply to seduce the girl and then discard her—but an authentic union. My father could not tolerate that, and my feelings could not sway him in the matter.

"When I told Ollivier what had happened, he would not tell me what to do, but he tried to give me such assistance as he could in negotiating a path through my confusion, and calculating the probable consequences of the choices I might make. It was doubtless not his intention, but he enabled me to understand that the time had come when I must either break completely with my father or obliterate the secret self that I had cultivated during my years at the Abbey and become a mere puppet of his designs. Unfortunately, Ollivier did not enable me to match his own prudence; I required a painful lesson before I was able to do that.

"I decided, recklessly, that I was not prepared to deny my own heart, and that if I could not obtain the permission that I required from my father to marry Katarin, then I would elope with her, and not return to Tardivel until he was dead. Perhaps I should have done so, without further prevarication, but in fact I presented him with that ultimatum, hoping that he might yield. I was ready—or so I thought—for any eventuality, even the possibility that my father might disown me, and forbid my name ever to be mentioned again in his house or his estates. I half-expected that, and was prepared in my mind to accept it...but I had underestimated him. Perhaps it would have been different had he had another heir to put in my place, but I had no brother and nor had he. I do not think he could face the thought of allowing his lands and his titles to become subservient to another name in being diverted—all the more so as he was at odds with my sister, who was beginning to exhibit the same recalcitrance to his will as me; or, in his eyes, the same symptoms of madness as my mother. He chose another course."

Corentin de Tardivel paused in his account to draw a long breath. He did not seem to be taking the opportunity to study his listener, and to attempt to measure his reaction, but rather to be retreating into himself. Thus far, he had been quite calm and very scrupulous in his speech, as befitted a nobleman of Bretagne and an heir to Norman chivalric ideals, but his breathing suddenly became clotted by emotion, and Primael saw there were tears in his eyes: tears of anguish, and tears of rage.

When it seemed that the other might be unable to go on, Primael Quemerle said, very quietly: "He had the girl killed?"

"Had her killed?" answered Tardivel, as though the words had been forced out of him with a hot iron. "Needless to say, her murderer was never identified...her murderer, and her

63

rapist. He feigned surprise, and sympathy...but I *knew*. I knew even then, long before I had the confirmation, that he had done it. I did not want to believe it. I resisted believing it, even though I *knew*. I had never for an instant imagined him capable of such an atrocity, and I told myself repeatedly that he could not have done such a thing, even though he was the only person...but to answer your question precisely, although I could not admit that I knew it at the time, no, he did not have her killed, *he killed her himself.* And when I eventually discovered that, it was all that I could do to stop myself killing him in my turn. But I had had my lesson, and I was so much further in Brother Ollivier's debt, that I was able to wait for natural causes to perform the execution for me—not as painfully as I would have liked, alas."

Primael did not know what to say. He could not imagine that Ollivier had known what to say either, when poor Corentin had run to tell him that his beloved Katarin was dead, and that his own heart was broken.

"Looking back," said Corentin de Tardivel, when he was capable of continuing his tale, "it seems to me now that the folly of it all is that if I had been what my father wanted me to be, and what he tried to make me, then I *would* have killed him. With a sword or a cudgel or a poisoned cup, I would have snuffed out his vile existence, and sent our title to oblivion by surrendering myself to the law and going gladly to the gallows. But I was not that man. I was not yet what Brother Ollivier had wanted to make of me either, but I was becoming my own man. If it was impossible for me to marry without my father's consent, it was also impossible for him to make me marry without mine. I refused the bride he had negotiated for me, and I told him flatly that I would not marry anyone while he was alive. Did that hasten his illness and his death? I doubt it, but I would not be sorry to think so if it had.

"What I also did was to invite Brother Ollivier to come to Tardivel the first time. I told my father that he was a very learned man, and that he might be able to cure the canker that was imperiling his life. That was a temptation my father could not resist, even though he must have suspected that it was a lie. And, in fact, Ollivier did give him herbal concoctions that eased his pain considerably, and helped him die more comfortably. But Ollivier also saw my mother, and quickly convinced himself, if not my father, that she was not mad. And, as you will doubtless have guessed long ago while I have been rambling, he eventually enabled me to summon Katarin's spirit."

"Ah," said Primael, who had indeed guessed it, but felt that some response, however inarticulate, was required.

"He told me before we even began that we could not bring Katarin back from the dead in the flesh, but that her spirit might be a different matter; he believed that with the aid of what he knew and information I had received, we might be able to communicate with her spirit. It required both assiduous study and careful experimentation, but..."

"Wait," said Primael. "It seems to me that you are getting ahead of the story again. You mentioned wise women as the source of your information, but that is very vague. Do you mean witches?"

"Certainly not—not, at any rate, as the Church understands the term. But there have long been traditions in Bretagne, and in Herbriant and Ploermel more than anywhere else, that certain women, seeresses, if you wish, can communicate to some extent with spirits, including the spirits of the dead as well as the Dames Blanches, and even the Marie-Mortes. They know evocative formulae of their own but, more importantly, they know where they can be employed most fruitfully—the power of the stones."

"Menhirs, you man?"

"Yes, and dolmens. Ollivier thought that much of what they said about the souls of the stones was imagination, but that their suppositions regarding the influence of certain stones on visions and their ability to reflect and enhance incantations were worthy of experimental investigation. He was interested on my mother's visions too, and the possible influence of the forest on their content."

"But what Olivier learned from these wise women enabled him to do more in the matter of necromantic evocation than he had previously been able to achieve in Paimpol, working from texts alone?"

"Most certainly. He wouldn't have been able to obtain the information alone, of course—nor, in all likelihood, would I—but my mother had connections with the wise women, via her family that dated back to her childhood. Her family was concerned and indignant about the way that she had been treated by my father, but had no legal right to interfere; when I went to them on her behalf, however, they were willing and eager to help me recruit assistance from the wise women for my own purpose. When her parents had contracted her marriage with my father their calculations, like his, had been material, and they had long kept that aspect of their history secret; my father knew nothing about it. Her relatives didn't know, when the marriage was negotiated, that my mother, who was only fourteen years old at the time, was a visionary. By the time they found out, it was too late, and only a few were concerned, because they belonged to the sisterhood of the wise women.

"When I approached them, they hadn't previously taken much interest in me, believing me to be very much my father's son, as he represented me to be, but when I told them that I wanted to do everything possible to help my mother, that my father was ill and likely to die, and what had happened to Katarin, they became enthusiastic to communicate with Brother Ollivier, just as he was very enthusiastic to meet them. I served as an intermediary, and we experimented together with the methods that we developed by means of the combination of the information. I was the one who actually summoned the spirit of Katarin, perhaps by means of the tyranny of the word, and perhaps because she was desperate to come, and only required help in opening the way."

"But she did come?" Primael said, more as an encouragement than because he still had any doubt regarding the fact—or, at least, the fact that Corentin believed it.

"Most certainly," Corentin confirmed. "Things didn't work out exactly as we had anticipated. Neither the books nor the traditions, it seems, are anything but assemblies of half-truths and speculations. Ollivier was by no means certain exactly what kind of apparition we would be able to produce, and Genovela—a cousin on my mother's side, who was my principal point of contact among her relatives, and also became my principal point of contact with the wise women of Herbriant—was unable to be any more definite in her dubious expectations, but Ollivier was hopeful that I ought to be able to hear Katarin's voice, and perhaps see her face. He was right about the voice, but wrong about the face...but there was compensation for that, in that I was able to feel her touch."

"The touch of her fingers?"

"More than that, Brother Primael, but I won't go into detail about that, unless you insist."

Familiar with tales of succubi, Primael did not insist, but he felt a slight chill, and wondered whether it would be prudent for him to bear in mind continually that Vicomte de Tardivel might be the victim of demonic delusion...or perhaps hereditary madness. "And the summoning was achieved with words—incantations of some kind?" he said, instead, again, more by way of encouragement than a necessary request for information.

"Principally. I shed a few drops of blood on the first occasion, but I have since become convinced that it was an unnecessary embellishment, born of melodrama. The words do, indeed, seem to be where the power resides, although the place where they are spoken is equally important. Whether the words compel or merely facilitate, I'm not sure, but for the purposes of my marriage to Katarin, it hardly matters."

"Your marriage?"

"Not Holy Matrimony, strictly speaking in the eyes of the Church, evidently, but I believe it to be a marriage, and so does she."

"She...her spirit...has told you that?"

"Repeatedly."

"And she has also told you that your father raped and killed her?"

"Yes. Do you doubt her? Do you think that she is a demon sent from Hell to delude and damn me with false testimony and false promises?"

"It's a hypothesis I feel compelled to bear in mind," said Primael, dryly, "but I have an open mind. There is doubtless a great deal for me to learn yet before I have all the facts of the matter, and I would be a fool to rush to judgment. It is not what Ollivier thought, I presume?"

"No," said the young man, calmly, "it is not."

But Ollivier is dead, Primael thought, and he died bearing what at least some of my brethren deemed to be stigmata of damnation. They are fools, of course...but calling a man a fool does not prove that he is wrong. The Dominicans are ambitious and devious, but deserving such epithets does not prove that they are wrong. It is, indeed, necessary for me to keep an open mind in this matter. Even if I take it as axiomatic that magic is not inherently evil, that does not mean that it cannot be used for evil ends, by evil beings.

Aloud, he said: "I understand why you wanted to do what you have done, Corentin. I also understand why you say that it is the only thing that really matters to you. But is Katarin, then, the only spirit you have tried to conjure?"

"By no means—but she is the only one, thus far, that I have been able to hear clearly, and touch fully. The others seem more tentative, incoherent whisperers and ghostly fingers, except when they come in visions. Then they become clearly visible as well as clearly audible...but those visitors are in the mind, not in the external world, and what they say is often strange and unusually unhelpful."

"What about Ollivier?" Primael asked. "Did he conjure audible spirits other than in his dreams, before he died?"

"He certainly tried, but I don't know how much success he might have achieved even before leaving Tardivel. He was...prudent in what he told me about his achievements and ambitions. The papers he left for me at the Abbey might tell me, but in any case, I intend to ask him directly, if I can. If you wish—and I hope that you will. Brother Primael—you might be able to hear his answer yourself."

Primael wondered whether that thought ought to provoke horror or delight in him—and why, in fact, it only seemed to provoke a kind of void, and absence of expectation.

"And what about this Genovela?" he asked. "What use have she and her sisters made of the discovery in which they have participated—or what use do they intend to make of it?"

"I don't know that either. You'll be able to ask her. Perhaps she'll tell you, but she might not."

"Because she's prudent?"

"Indeed—and wisely so. But you might be able to earn her trust. Ollivier did, I think."

Primael was not at all sure that he could match Ollivier in winning the trust of a witch, if this Genovela really was a witch.

"She has not conjured the Dames Blanches, then, so far as you know?" he queried.

Unexpectedly, Tardivel laughed. "The Dames Blanches have no need of necromancy to be summoned," he said. "They are not dead. If they are spirits, as they seem to be, they are spirits of a different kind. Them, I have seen.

"You've seen them—and lived to tell the tale?"

"Stories of that sort are wildly exaggerated. They're not hostile; if people have died after seeing them, they died needlessly, of their own fear...but my inclination is to consider tales of that ilk as mere fancy. As Ollivier says, if anyone ever died of fear, the diagnosis would be impossible, and the folklore claims that the Dames Blanches are benevolent and protective, although what they protect people against is unclear.

"Ollivier saw the Dames Blanches too?"

"Yes, more than once, in attendance at my conjurations—uninvited, but perhaps attracted.

"And the Marie-Mortes?"

"They're more enigmatic. No, I have not seen a Marie-Morte, and certainly haven't made any attempt to summon one. I can't speak for Ollivier in that regard, but I think that he would have told me had his curiosity overcome his prudence to that extent. That's a kind of conjuration that might not be best attempted alone, and one in which Genovela's cautionary warnings might be entirely justified."

That gave Primael some pause for thought. The opinion of the Church—or that of Brother Michael, at any rate—was that the Breton legend of the Marie-Mortes was a confusion of pagan notions and Christian ones. Much as the Church had co-opted various pagan religious sites in order to construct churches, and had reinterpreted various pagan idols, so stubborn pagans might have usurped and perverted Christian ideas. In Brother Michael's opinion, Marie-Mortes were the icons of a perverted pagan Mariolatry, which made the Virgin into a figure to be feared as well as revered, an agent of Death who could be kindly and merciful, but could also be fierce and vindictive. But that was a Christian opinion, an interpretation of a pagan mystery. Breton-born as he was, Primael had no clear idea of what the Marie-Mortes might be thought to be by those who had venerated them in the distant past, and perhaps still did, in the context of lingering tradition.

What am I doing here? he asked himself, not for the first time—but this time he had a more specific meaning in mind. Why, exactly, had Brother Michael sent him to Tardivel? Why had he told him, before he left, that Ollivier really had practiced necromancy. It was true, evidently, and he had asked the question, but that did not really explain why Michael had told him, when he could easily have evaded the question. What did Michael expect of him, in sending him into what he evidently knew to be a nest of sorcerers?

He did not know. But then, looking back more than forty years, he did not really know why a previous superior has sent him and Ollivier, as juniors to three other monks, to Granada, on a mission that had surely had more to do with curiosity than conversion, and the effect of which had surely been to set Ollivier's feet on the road that he had followed...perhaps to damnation.

Again, Primael felt a chill. It appeared, if Corentin de Tardivel was telling the truth, that it might be possible to ask Ollivier's spirit about Michael's motivation. But would Ollivier's guesses be any better than his own, and how could he possibly determine whether any answer he received had not come from the mouth of the Father of Lies?

My soul is in danger, Primael thought. *Do I still have sufficient armor of faith to withstand an assault? And if I can even pose that question, how can I possibly answer it affirmatively?*

Yet again his eyes went to the dark line of trees that fringed the horizon, very much closer now than it had seemed when he had first glimpsed it: the edge of the forest where he would have to spend the night in the open, at the mercy of its population, natural and supernatural.

I should never have followed that funeral cart, he thought. I should have stayed in my cell, where I belong, where I have always belonged.

But it was too late for regrets.

V

Once Primael and Corentin were in the forest, however, it seemed far less sinister to the monk than it had when viewed from a distance. The sun was on the brink of setting, so it was not shining upon the foliage in the same bright fashion that it would have done from its zenith, but even so, the trees were just trees, banal if not benign Their crowns did not exclude all light, and the grayness of the gloom—for the sun was setting behind solid cloud, and its redness was shielded—seemed meek enough.

When Primael dismounted, he felt more relief than fear, at least for the moment, for his body had accumulated various nagging aches while he had been astride the mule's back. Having ridden for almost two days, with only one substantial pause and a few briefer intervals, he was extremely weary. Nevertheless, he set about unsaddling the animal and feeding it, after having led it to a nearby stream in order to drink. He set the saddle down on the ground, braced over the root of an oak, in order to serve as a pillow, and he tested the moss growing between the sprawling roots for comfort. Wrapped in his habit as he was, he could have done without any other cover, but he was glad that the mule had been equipped with a saddle-blanket large enough to wrap his sandaled feet and his calves.

Tardivel had some bread in his luggage, with a handful of walnuts and some small apples, all of which he divided carefully between the two of them.

"It's wretched, I fear," he said, "but we'll make up for it in the morning, when we reach the manse. I can build a fire, if you wish; the smoke might keep the insects away. There's nothing larger to fear; my father hunted the last of the wild boar to extinction, and everything else will avoid us."

"There's no need," Primael told him. "The night is overcast, so the temperature won't drop too far, given the season."

"You're wishing that you hadn't come, aren't you?" said the young man. "You'd rather have stayed in your cell, even at the risk that the evil talk about Ollivier might be transferred to you, and might continue to stir the suspicions of the Dominicans."

"Michael instructed me to come. I had no choice."

"Perhaps not—but I had. Perhaps I should not have asked for you. But I honestly think that it's in your interest, as well as mine."

"Is it in yours?" Primael queried. "I confess that I cannot see why. Given what you have told me, will the presence of a priest at the château really be a useful influence?"

"We are not pagans, Brother Primael," said Tardivel. "My story necessarily brought various unorthodox ideas to the forefront, but we are good people, and, in our own eyes, good Christians. Your presence will be a consolation to my sister, who became very fond of Ollivier, and my mother will be very glad to talk to a scholar who shares much of Ollivier's education. Genovela, too, will be interested to meet you, once her initial suspicion wears off. No one at the château is your enemy, Brother, and none will consider you to be one, unless you go out of your way to manifest hostility. I do not think I am taking an undue risk in being honest with you, precisely because I know you to be a man of God, an honest man and a scrupulous scholar. I believe that you will be a useful member of our small community, until Brother Michael judges it safe for you to return to the Abbey."

"I am not entirely sure," Primael remarked, "that my safety—or his, for that matter—is the motive for Brother Michael's decision."

"Are you not? Well, I suppose you know him far better than I do. No matter what his motive might be, however, I repeat that you will be welcome at the château, and I hope that you will find your stay there rewarding."

"In practicing necromancy?" retorted Primael, bluntly.

Tardivel laughed. "That is entirely your decision," he said. "No one will hold it against you if you refuse." Primael did not believe him; Corentin, he felt sure, would certainly hold it against him if he were to refuse to participate in his game of conjurations.

"And what if I try to exorcize the spirits that you conjure?" Primael asked, combatively.

"That might be an interesting experiment," the other replied. "I would rather you let Katarin alone, obviously, but if you were to discover that the formula of exorcism is effective against her, I suppose I might be forced to reappraise my own experience, in spite of my passion, my conviction and my faith. Speak to her first, though, and hear what she has to say—and Genovela, and mother too. Judge for yourself whether we are mad or evil, but judge on the facts. Don't make up your mind in advance."

"The facts," Primael said, raising the cowl of his habit to shelter his ears and his tonsured head from a sudden nocturnal breeze, from which the trees were not an adequate shield, "do not speak for themselves. They require interpretation...and that is not an easy task."

"For me, perhaps not. Genovela is uneducated, in your sense, and mother might well be hallucinated. But I have faith in your intellect, Brother Primael."

Primael bowed his head slightly, and said: "So had I, once. I was sure that the change in Ollivier was the effect of an affliction that he had not invited or deserved. Could I have been so sure if I had known that he really was a necromancer?"

"I certainly hope so," said Tardivel. "I have told you that his motives were pure, that he exercised his knowledge only to help his friend, and I believe that to be true. If it was a judgment on his necromancy that engraved some kind of death-mask on his features, then it was a cruel and stupid judgment, for he did not deserve it. I was the one who worked the magic, and the one who reaped its benefits. If there was a debt to be paid, then I should have paid it, and would have done so willingly! Have faith in your beliefs, Master, as I do. The man you saw buried yesterday was a man as good as any in the world, and whatever disfigured him was no fault of his, but an undeserved misfortune."

Primael tilted his head back and stared into infinity through a gap in the foliage. "For the moment," he said, "I don't know what to believe."

"That is not a bad thing," Tardivel opined. "Honest doubt is befitting to a scholar. I welcome your uncertainty, and look forward to seeing it resolved, when…you know all the facts."

Primael noted the hesitation, and guessed that his interlocutor had been about to about to suggest that he would be able to resolve his uncertainty when he had practiced necromancy himself, or simply when he had seen the Dames Blanches, who did not require to be summoned.

"At the very least," the monk suggested, "You must admit that your posthumous intercourse with your spirit wife is…unnatural."

Corentin was restless, and did not seem ready, as yet, to go to sleep, even though the twilight was fading fast, and it would soon be pitch black in the forest, with a starless night above the canopy. He did not dismiss the question, but seems glad of the opportunity to answer it, if only to let his feelings show.

"Yes," he said, "unnatural, to be sure. When a father is utterly without love or compassion, that is natural! When a father murders his son's innocent bride, that is natural! But when a son opposes his father's will and obtains a slight measure of compensation for his father's evil, that is definitely unnatural. It is entirely natural for the fops and philanderers of the French court in Paris to parade themselves in silk and velvet beneath their powdered wigs and painted faces while plotting the devastation of Bretagne. It is natural that they should live in gaudy luxury while the peasants who work the soil to produce their wealth go hungry. It is natural for the regent and her brother to plot the conquest of Bretagne instead of seeing to the affairs of their own subjects. Their measured dances are natural, and the games which they play with quoits and skittles. Their manners and hypocrisies are as natural as the blood that others shed to permit them to maintain them—at least, it seems so to them.

"Instruct me, Master, I beg you. Tell me why men like you and I should respect and revere what is *natural*, when everything that humans put of themselves under that label is artifice, and mostly wicked artifice? Your belief is that disease and illness are natural shocks to which our fragile flesh is heir, not supernatural punishments sent by the gods or inflicted by the ill-wishing of witches. Ollivier Abalain's belief was that knowledge of life and death is only knowledge of nature, and that magic is merely a potential means of shaping nature, like other arts and crafts. You could not see a significant difference between yourself and your lifelong friend three days ago—can you really see one now?"

For a long minute, Primael did not reply—and when he did, it was not with an answer but with a question.

"Has your phantom lover told you what will happen to you," he asked, "when you die in your turn, and go to the realm of the dead?"

Corentin laughed, very briefly.

"The matter is not so simple," he said. "If I have the power to ensure before I die that I can be a specter, then I shall do my utmost exert that power with my dying breath, and will be all the closer to my love for sharing her strange substantiality. If I have not...then I shall have to wait and see."

"And what if you fall in love again with a woman of flesh and blood," asked Primael, "or want to marry in order to sire an heir, or come to find the presence of a phantom lover inconvenient for some other reason? Will you be able to banish her easily as you summoned her? Is that possible?"

Primael could not see the younger man, but the shadows stirred as Corentin shook his head, to deny the possibility and perhaps to rule the questions impertinent. Primael suspected, however, that the other was not untroubled by such questions. The young man knew that love is not always eternal, nor the call of duty entirely impotent.

"What right did you have to ask Ollivier to help you in your unholy endeavor?" Primael wondered, aloud, addressing the question as much to himself as the young man, "What right do you have to ask for mine?"

It was pitch dark, but Primael did not need light to judge that Tardivel was genuinely confused by the questions that were being raised. He was not his father's son; he did not have the stubborn certainty of faith in himself.

"He was my friend," the young man said, after a slight pause, "and a better father to me than my own. It was not a matter of right, or even of asking. It was a matter of friendship."

Primael could understand that. Ollivier had been his friend, too, and he could understand Ollivier's desire to serve as a substitute father to Corentin. When the young man had compiled his catalogue of challenges, he might have mentioned that was quite natural for priests, being celibate, to redirect their paternal instincts toward sons failed by their actual fathers.

Except, he could not help thinking, that priests were not always as strictly celibate as they had vowed to be, and the redirection of paternal instincts might not be a simple matter.

"Friendship," he commented, aloud, "sometimes requires the refusal of requests, when their fulfillment might lead to catastrophe

"I love my wife," Tardivel said, reverting to challenging mode, "with all my heart. And she loves me. There is no catastrophe; quite the opposite."

"Do you think that it can last forever?" asked Primael, mildly, knowing what the answer would be.

"I do. For life—and beyond."

Primael refrained from shrugging his shoulders, although the gesture would have been invisible. Nor did he say, aloud: *Let us hope, then, that your boldness will not let you down, and that your heart is as constant as your father's, after its different fashion.*

Corentin did not take advantage of the silence to suggest that they ought to sleep. Instead, he said: "I hope, Master, that you will not think any worse of your friend, because of what I have told you. I did not mean to injure him in your estimation."

"You have not done that," Primael said, although he was not sure whether it was true. "And I am grateful to know that I am not the only man who will mourn his passing. If the only epitaph he will have is graven in the memories of other men, I am glad that there are two of us to share the burden of it."

"So am I, Brother," said Corentin de Tardivel, and then added: "Where is his spirit, at present, do you suppose?"

"How can I know?" asked Primael. "Are you not in a better position to make suppositions than I am?"

"Perhaps," said Tardivel, quietly. "Genovela would recite the gnomic maxim that it is close at hand or far away, and ask whether it matters which. She has an inclination to speak in riddles, inherited from tradition. Perhaps you will be able to pin her down."

"I heard a tale somewhere that depicted the spirit of a necromancer bound, either by a misfired spell or the edict of God, to its rotting hull," said Primael, suddenly dredging the memory up from the depths of his mind, "and the teller claimed that such a spirit cannot escape from the hell of that decay, although it can sometimes animate the body as a lich with glowing eyes, which spreads terror wherever it goes, and leaves suffering in its train. But Ollivier was present at the time, and he dismissed the invention as stupid sacerdotal terrorism, albeit of a milder kind than the Spanish Inquisition's."

"Do you think that he feared such an end?" asked Tardivel, with such faint anxiety that it seemed a mere politeness.

"No," said Primael, confidently

"No man knows what he has to fear when he dies," said the younger man, "even one who has brought a spirit back to earth from a life beyond life. Katarin could not inform me. She had merely been asleep, she said, dreamlessly. She had no knowledge of Heaven or Hell, nor any company of the dead. And yet, she was able to return, so she must have been somewhere close at hand, no matter how far away. And I cannot help feeling that it matters, that it requires understanding."

Primael held his hands up before his face. They were invisible, but he knew that they were gnarled and stiff. The pain in their swollen joints did not let him rest for long nowadays, and he had been clutching the mule's reins all day. Might it reduce his pain, he wondered, if he cut off the fingers that he did not really need, and which offended him? Or should he recognize the pain as a divine punishment to be borne with patience, or as a penance, and not—as he had always believed—a mere accident of happenstance? He had, after all, given succor and sustenance to a secret necromancer.

"He was a good man," murmured Primael. "He was a good friend."

"Amen to that," said Corentin de Tardivel, and seemed ready, at last, to go to sleep. Primael heard him arranging himself in a recumbent position, on his side. He murmured a prayer, just loud enough to be heard, although he was not sure that his companion would take any comfort from it.

This time, Primael dreamed, and remembered his dream so well that when Corentin eventually woke him, as soon as the sky began to pale, he wondered whether he had really been asleep at all, or whether he had suffered the fate that other men were reputed to have suffered on lying down in Broceliande and opening their souls to the access of the spirits of the wood. Had that been the case, however, he would surely have been visited by the Dames Blanches, or follets, or farfadets, sprites of one of the many kinds that took the place of the Greek dryads and nymphs in the now-sparse woods and all-too-extensive heaths of Bretagne.

In fact, to begin with, it was the spirit of a man who had come to touch him on the shoulder, and say: "Walk with me, child."

The man was not Ollivier. It was Gilles de Rais, who had been hanged over a fire in 1440. Primael had not yet been twenty years old when he had lodged briefly at Tiffauges, a few years earlier than that fatal date, and Gilles had only been in his early thirties, so it seemed slightly odd that Gilles should address him as "child," especially as he was now not far short of seventy years old, but he made no objection.

It did not seem at all odd to him, however, when he came to his feet, to find that he was no longer in a wood but on an open heath, walking between hills in the direction of a solitary menhir twice as tall as a man and twice as broad in its face. The night was not cloudy; the moon was nearly full and the stars were brighter than the stars of Bretagne usually were.

"I didn't summon you," Primael said to his new companion. "I'm not a necromancer."

"Neither was I, alas," said Gilles. "But nor was I a murderer."

"I always believed that the charges were false," Primael said. "You were caught in a trap. You confessed in order to spare yourself torture. The witnesses against you were suborned."

"Do you think so?" said Gilles. "In fact, I made no confession, and my two servants gave no testimony. Nor were we executed publicly on the Ile de Biesse. The entire history is a tissue of lies. I was murdered and so were they, and the story was concocted to cover up our murder, by men who understood the tyranny of the written word over human belief. There were hundreds of people who would have been able to say with certainty that it was all false, that none of it had happened, and some of them did, but voices are lost in the wind, while writing remains. All history is lies, written to serve the interests of the liars."

"Including the scriptures?" Primael asked.

"Especially the scriptures," said Gilles de Rais.

"Where have you been since 1440, then?" asked Primael, "and where are you now?"

"Close at hand and far away," said Gilles. "Nowhere you would recognize as a place, in spite of the heather beneath our feet and that standing stone, although there is a sense in which we have not left Bretagne."

"You have not been in Heaven with Jeanne d'Arc, then?" Primael asked.

"Is Jeanne in Heaven?" Gilles asked, earnestly, as if he thought that Primael might know the answer. "I would like to think so. She was mad, of course, but so very charming in her madness, and so very useful to history—to the lie that is. Legends like hers do not arise easily, but they are even more difficult to kill than they are to create. The English were fools to think otherwise."

"But they did burn her?" Primael queried.

"Oh yes, they burned her. Sometimes liars act out their lies. And murderers always find it easy to destroy little girls."

"So I've heard," said Primael.

They had reached the menhir. It was daubed with some kind of dye, dark blue in color. It was not easy to make out by starlight, even close up, but the daubs formed symbols, each the size of a human thumb, presumably writing, in an unknown language.

"What does it mean?" asked Primael.

"I haven't the faintest idea," said Gilles. "The world is replete with languages, but few are comprehensible to any but a few particular users. The myth of Babel is a lie, but there is some truth in its import. Sometimes, the world of the living reflects that of the dead rather than the other way around.

"Those ancients were wrong, then, who assumed that spirit would have perfect knowledge?"

"Utterly wrong," Gilles confirmed. "Liars all, but accidentally so, in many cases. There were great minds among them, who strove with all their might to find the truth within themselves and without. Alas, it was not there. But I did not come to discuss the failings of philosophy, rather to warn you of danger to your body and soul."

"That's kind of you," the Benedictine observed, "but I was not unaware of a vague menace. Can you be more specific?"

"Certainly. You were followed from Paimpol by one of the Dominicans who watched you operate the funeral rite over Ollivier's grave—the tall one, the true fanatic. The shorter one has gone in search of friendly ears, in order to denounce you as a heretic. They hope that the Bishop will send armed men to arrest you, and that if Tardivel refuses to hand you over, he will risk excommunication and dispossession."

"I looked around repeatedly," Primael said. "I didn't see anyone following us."

"The Dominican knows where you're going. It wasn't necessary for him to keep you in sight. His task is to scout the surroundings of the château, and make what preparations he can for the arrival of his companion, who will join him in Herbriant as soon as possible."

"I see. And what do you suggest that I do about it?"

"If you were to find him, you could probably make a pact with him to betray the château and all of its inhabitants, and assist in charging them with all manner of heresies and diabolisms. On the other hand, if you were to stab him in the back, it would be easy to hide his body, and to make your own preparations to receive his friends. A clever ambush might enable you to slaughter them all without losing a single one of Tardivel's servants."

"You're suggesting that I ought to betray an entire company of innocent people, or murder a company of others?"

"No, I'm merely pointing out that you could. You must do, obviously, what your conscience bids you to do. You might end up like poor Jeanne, though, without even the belated consolation of being named a martyr."

"And that's what you came to tell me?"

"Not all of it. Do you remember your brief sojourn in Tiffauges, when you were no more than a child?"

"I remember it very well, and I was no child. I had been to Granada and back, as you well know, since you consulted the manuscripts that Ollivier and I brought back."

"I did, but that is a matter of little relevance. Do you recall a lapse that you had in your vow of celibacy?"

It was on the tip of Primael's tongue to say that there was no way that Gilles could know that, but clearly there were perfectly mundane means by which he might have been informed of it while he was alive. He thought about denying it, but what was the point? He was only dreaming, after all, dredging up memories from his own past in order to construct a fantasy, and he had confessed the sin at the time and had been absolved. He had not even been severally criticized. "Not all succubi are demons," he confessor had said to him. "Be more careful in future." His penance had not been unduly heavy.

"My conscience is clear," was all he said to Gilles de Rais.

"I wish I could say the same," said Gilles, "but I'm not stewing in a vat of boiling oil for all eternity, so I dare say that it could be murkier. I didn't bring the matter up in order to criticize you, child, but merely to tell your something that you don't know. The girl had a child."

Well, yes, Primael thought. *I didn't know that, it's true, but it isn't as if the thought never occurred to me. I even considered making enquiries, but the sin had been confessed and absolved, and at not-yet-twenty years of age, one is not excessively weighted down by a sense of responsibility, even when one is in Holy Orders. Nor can I say that I have never given the matter another thought over the last forty-some years. All in all, therefore, it's not entirely surprising that the idea should resurface in a dream, at a point in time when my life is being turned upside-down, especially when I had been given occasion to think, almost immediately before going to sleep, how natural Ollivier's pseudoparental feelings were for another man's son.*

Aloud—at least, it seemed to be aloud—he said: "Is he alive?"

"The child was a daughter," said Gilles. "And yes, she is alive."

"I'm glad," said Primael. "Does she know who her father is?"

"No. She was given a history that is all lies—but only one of the liars knew that it was a lie, and she died without confessing it, to the daughter or to the husband that I found for her. I had that obligation, you see. It happened in my house, after all, and you were my guest."

"How can you know that she died without confessing the lie?" Primael asked, feeling a perverse sense of triumph at having caught himself out in an error in his dream-invention.

"She told me so," sad Gilles, "when I visited her on her deathbed. She asked me to watch over her daughter, who would be married off herself one day. She wasn't entirely accurate in her assessment of my abilities, but it wouldn't have been kind to correct her misapprehensions. I have tried, but the circumstances weren't easy. I have nothing for which to feel guilty, in this instance—unlike you, some might think, in spite of your absolution—but I apologize anyway for my neglect."

"Are you telling me that my daughter has suffered some avoidable misfortune?"

"All misfortunes are avoidable, in principle."

"What misfortune?" snapped Primael, bluntly.

"Having carefully avoided investigating the consequences of your lapse for more than forty years, you are now becoming impatient with me?" the figment of his dream retorted.

"Don't play games with me, Gilles. Tell me, if you know—although I cannot imagine how you could—what misfortune has befallen my daughter."

"Ask her yourself when you see her," said Giles. "She will rend your heart far better than I can, and some might say that you would not otherwise be receiving your just desserts."

"Tel me, damn it!" said Primael thinking that there was no sin in losing one's temper in a dream, and unable to help it in any case. It occurred to him, as he regretted the oath, that he would not find a confessor at Tardivel, given that he had no intention of seeking out the Dominican in the woods, for any purpose.

"Given that I'm your guest, at present," Gilles said, "and that I came entirely for your benefit, for I assure you that I am obtaining none, you lack politeness, Primael Quemerle. I do not need to tell you who your daughter is. You will probably recognize her when you see her—or, if you do not, it will be because you do not merit her acquaintance. Let us pray that the former is the case, for both your sakes. Adieu."

And with that, Gilles de Rais vanished, as only a figment of a dream or a specter can.

Primael did not wake up.

He inspected with gnomic writing on the menhir, which seemed to be tainting him with its inscrutability. He felt someone touch the back of his neck, stated, and looked around, but there was no one there. The ghostly fingers touched his forehead, lightly.

"Seigneur de Rais?" he asked. He heard a sound of muffled laughter.

"Seigneur?" said a female voice, perfectly clear and audible, although there was nowhere it could have come from, except perhaps the stone. He could not tell whether the person was laughing because he had mistaken her sex or her rank.

"My daughter?" he guessed.

"Certainly not," she replied. "You invited me. Why don't you know? If you don't want me, I'll leave. *Au revoir.*"

And like Gilles de Rais, she was no longer there—although he could hardly say that she had vanished, since she had never been visible. Her *au revoir* had been a mockery

All this is understandable, Primael told himself. *Conscience works in underhanded ways, especially under the cloak of unconsciousness. I am playing games with myself, reflecting my discomfort and confusion. I have invented all of this, including this looming stone and its indecipherable message. Remorse is punishing me for present mistakes by reminding me of past mistakes. None of which means that the Dominican has not followed me from Paimpol, which is entirely plausible. As for the possibility that I have a child who is about to return in the flesh to haunt me, that is a refined form*

of self-torture that even an Inquisitor would be obliged to ad-
mire. Now, when I arrive at Corentin's home, I shall be on the
lookout everywhere for anyone who might conceivably be my
daughter. There is bound to be at least one person in the
household of the appropriate age, and probably more than
one. And how will I be able to persuade myself that she is not
my daughter, even without an atom of evidence that she might
be? Oh, Primael Quemerle, why did you not simply wrap a
cilice around your wrist before leaving Paimpol?

Nor was the nightmare finished yet, for as he stood there, contemplating the menhir, another figure appeared before him, apparently have walked around it from the other side. It was a woman, of sorts. She was wearing a blue robe with a hood vaguely reminiscent of a wimple. Her age was inestimable, because her face, although it was possessed of blue eyes, and the features had an unmistakably feminine cast, was more than a little reminiscent of a death's head.

"What are you doing here, child?" she asked. "You have no business here."

"Agreed," said Primael, before sighing, as he wondered whether this was his first test, and whether he had already failed it, by not recognizing his daughter in what he mistook instead for a Marie-Morte, or the caricature of one. "Would you care to tell me where *here* is, for I seem to have lost my bearings, and I'm as anxious to be gone as you seem to be to be rid of me?"

Strangely, her expression softened. "You're lost?" she said, with a note of sympathy in her voice.

"Completely," Primael confessed. "You couldn't give me directions to Herbriant Forest, by any chance?"

"You can't read the signpost?" the cadaverous woman remarked.

"Not a syllable," Primael admitted.

"That's unfortunate," she said. "But you do realize that you're dreaming, I suppose?"

"Evidently," he said "I'm lying between the roots of an ancient oak, a few leagues from Tardivel, fast asleep. To be

honest, I expected to wake up when Gilles de Rais vanished."
He left that remark dangling, as bait for a response that might
be informative.

"It's not always possible to wake up when we want to,"
the woman observed, regretfully, "even when one's alive. It's
even harder when one isn't." She extended a bony hand to
point in a direction vertically beneath the moon, which, if the
moon was setting, might be vaguely south-west. "Broceliande
is that way, but it's a long way to travel now. It used to be
much closer. I can't go with you, and I can't promise that
you'll get there, but I'm not deceiving you."

"The Church," Primael observed, "would call you a demon, and your nunnish costume a sacrilege."

"The Church," said the Marie-Morte, "is very free with
its accusations of diabolism and sacrilege. Use your own
judgment, child."

With the hand she had used to indicate the way to go, she
reached out to stroke his right cheek with the three middle
fingers.

"I'm not a child," he said, although he had let it pass the
first time.

"Do you think so?" she said. "Forgive me a way of
speaking. I'm very old, you see. Very, very old. But I still
have feelings, you know—maternal ones, among others. And
thank you."

"For what?"

"For not making the sign of the cross when you recognized me for what I am. It's insulting, but many priests can't
help themselves, even in their dreams. Faith can be such a
tyrant."

"So can the Word," he riposted, flippantly.

Her eyes narrowed. "Indeed it can," she said. "But that's
far more your concern than mine, rhetorician. Au revoir."

And like Gilles de Rais, she vanished. Like the invisible
woman, she was no longer there.

What was that all about? Primael wondered. *What is my
mind playing at now. Was that my conscience? I don't think*

so. Something else, then—something groping for a direction, trying to orientate itself in a labyrinth of legend. There's nothing unusual in her saying au revoir *instead of* adieu. *Dreams can recur, and often do. And if she does come back again, I'll remember her, even if I've forgotten her completely in the waking interval, as I probably will.*

He started walking toward a point on the horizon directly beneath the moon.

He never got there—but, somewhat to his surprise, he did not forget a single instant of the dream. He remembered every last detail, or thought he did, even though Corentin de Tardivel seemed to be trying to shake it out of his head.

VI

"Thank God," said Tardivel. "For a moment there, I thought you'd died in your sleep."

"For a moment, so did I," Primael admitted, "but I didn't go to Heaven, alas. Did you dream?"

"Not that I can remember," the younger man said. "I was too tired, I think. Walking a horse can be just as tired as galloping.. I've no bread left, alas, but we should reach the château soon enough. Although the paths are winding, I know them all. We won't go astray."

"The Dominican will, though," said Primael, as he went behind a bush, prior to going to the stream in order to wash his hands and splash his face. "Good. May he stay lost, and good riddance."

"What Dominican?" Tardivel asked.

"The tall one. The one who followed us from Paimpol, to scout the region around the château."

"That's possible," the younger man said, invisibly, apparently assuming that it was a guess or a deduction, probably correctly. "But he won't find anything hereabouts to his advantage, and if he has any imagination, he might have bad dreams himself if he lies down to sleep in the forest tonight. Am I obliged by courtesy to offer him hospitality, do you think, if he shouts at the door of the château?"

"No," said Primael, curtly. "If he takes offense at the refusal, so be it. And if he has bad dreams when he lies down to sleep in the forest, so much the better. How many men do you have in the château capable of bearing arms?"

"I have half a dozen within the walls with sufficient strength and skill, in addition to myself, and if I blow a signal on my horn, I can summon anther dozen immediately, and half a hundred in a matter of hours when the signal's relayed. I have a good stock of crossbows, although only a handful of them are modern arbalests, and plenty of bolts and lesser arms.

The manse could not possibly stand against an army, but I doubt that a force of fewer than a hundred men could take the house by storm, in spite of its poor defenses, and I hope that I might be able hold off a siege by a small contingent for at least a month. Does that reassure you, Brother?"

"Somewhat. And how many women are there in your household?"

"About twenty, at the moment. In the event of a siege or an attack, though, I'd try to get all or most of them to safety elsewhere."

"What ages are they?"

Primael had returned from the stream, and could see the surprise in Tardivel's expression, but he simply answered the question. "Mostly young. Only three are aged."

"How many in their mid- and late forties?"

"Only one, I think—Mother's chambermaid. She came with Mother; and must be about the same age."

Primael felt a sudden chill in his spine. "Your mother is from Poitou?"

"Bas-Poitou, yes—Montagu, to be precise. Do you know it? Ollivier mentioned that you he had stayed in the region for a while, but that was in Tiffauges, was it not?"

"Yes," said Primael. "Montagu is not far away, I believe?"

"A day's ride on a good horse, perhaps a little more. Shall I help you to mount up?"

The vicomte had already saddled the mule and the horse; everything was ready for their departure. Primael allowed the younger man to help him up on to the mule's back, not without a painful stretch as he placed himself astride the animal.

But it was a dream, Primael reminded himself, *and Corentin had already told me how old his mother was when she was married, and it only required arithmetic to estimate her present age. And in any case, if either of the two were...the person to whom Giles referred, it surely must be the chambermaid. But I'm still playing games with myself, still dreaming...*

It was no longer possible for the horse and the mule to travel side by side. The forest paths were, as Tardivel had said, winding, and they were also narrow, at least when the forest was dense. It was by no means uniform in that regard, but in the areas where the trees were not as densely packed the ground was very uneven. Jagged rocks often protruded through the undergrowth, and although their forms gave every appearance of being entirely natural, Primael could not help being reminded of menhirs, and even of dolmens. He found himself scanning them intently, searching for inscriptions in an unknown tongue, but there was no evidence of any kind of dye, and he could not see the particular shade of blue that he had seen in his dream anywhere. The myosotis flowers that could occasionally be seen in the clearings were completely different. He searched the foliage for the birds that fluttered away as the riders approached, in case he could spot any mythical bluebirds, but all those he glimpsed were speckled brown or black, no different from those that plagued the Abbey's kitchen-gardens. Primael's brethren always drove them away, not being Franciscans and thus not being required by legend to treat them kindly.

The forest was not entirely devoid of population, although the signs of its habitation were distant for the moment. It was not a good timber forest; the trees rarely grew straight and most were rather thin in the branch as well as gnarled, but he heard the distant sound of a ax more than once, and from the higher ground, where the trees yielded their dominion to rocks and ferns, he saw thin lines of smoke rising into the calm air, achieving a good height before being caught and dissipated by the breeze. Some, presumably, were cooking fires, and others the work of charcoal-burners. Primael had no doubt, too, that the forest played host to poachers. All the descendants of the Normans retained their obsession with hunting, and the property of forests, which had long made thieves of native Bretons who did not have that notion, and thought they had a sacred right to set ingenious snares for birds and small animals, which no human law could legitimately over-rule, by virtue of its immemorial antiquity.

Although it was inhabited, however, he did not catch a glimpse of anyone. Any people using the paths along which Corentin de Tardivel was making his careful way home must have hidden when they heard him approach, even if they were numbered among those who would have come in answer to the sounding of his horn to summon defenders to the château. Primael had no doubt that they would hide from a Dominican too, if any man of that stripe came prying, even if they had no idea what his costume signified. Instinct had more force here-abouts than the customs of civilization—especially the chival-ric sham of Norman etiquette. Brethren who hailed from Eng-land knew songs and tales in which outcasts from Norman law formed bands that haunted the forests and exacted tolls from travelers who believed that they had rights of dominion there. Such tales even featured outlaw friars, but without specifying their Order—not white or black, Primael assumed, more likely gray.

The daylight was brighter than it had been the previous day, and as the morning went on, and the residual mists cleared, the sky became predominantly blue and the clouds were white, like fluff or lint rather than yesterday's coarse sheets. In that light, the forest seemed, if not benign, at least calm and placid, devoid of menace. The birdsong had not seemed penetrating even before sunrise, and it was more sub-tle still as midday approached, but the sunlight seemed to add to its faint melodic quality, and the hum of wild bees, when they passed close to the occasional nest, was reminiscent of the Abbey's hives.

Gradually, albeit by no means directly, the paths that the bay horse followed took them to higher elevations, until the mound on which Tardivel stood suddenly appeared. As castles went it was small, not built on the Norman model, with crenel-lated ramparts and towers; its keep had a few embellishments, but its defenses consisted primarily of the faces of the mound, step but easily scaled with the aid of ladders, if no one at the top were pouring boiling oil. Its roofs were designed to collect rainwater rather than to expel it, although there was evidently a spring lower down the hill.

From the location at which the château first became visible to Primael, he could not see the cottages beneath the citadel, which made up the surrounding village, but he could see a number of vegetable patches in clefts in the rock, and knew that they were symptoms of a much more intensive exploitation of the environs.

The path was wide enough at that point for the mule to draw level with the horse, and Tardivel waited for it to do so. "My home," he said to the Benedictine. "Paltry, I suppose, by comparison with the fortresses that François started building before falling ill, with a view to withstanding the fury of Tristan L'Hermite's cannon, but I defy anyone to bring any substantial artillery to within a league of it, or even to manipulate a battering-ram against its door. It has no ditch, drawbridge or portcullis, but it has withstood several attacks and small sieges over the centuries. The stones you see are not so very old— little more than five or six generations—but there was a castle here long before that, while the Normans were still fishing the fjords in the far north, when this land was Grand Bretagne and the other the lesser, when the English Cornwall was a colony of Cornouailles and when wizard Merlin lived here, before Norman liars exported him to England via Wales and attached him to some petty English warlord."

"The English brethren who come to the Abbey are very proud of those romances," Primael observed. "They are surprised when we tell them that Merlin is ours, not theirs, and that Joseph of Arimathea brought the Holy Grail to Provence, and not to Wales. Do you know that they have even stolen Ys, and replaced it in the Irish Sea, confusing it in the process with Lyonesse? But the Normans monopolized that authority of their written word for two centuries and more, and there is no way now to undo their work, which the new printing presses will probably preserve indefinitely."

"Your kind had the monopoly of writing before them," Tardivel pointed out. "You should have used it better."

"My forebears believed that they were doing exactly that by committing its use to the faith," said Primael, feeling obliged to put up some kind of defense, although he knew that Corentin was right. If there was one lesson above all others to be learned from history, it was that history, not faith, had the authority, and that anyone who invented a better history—a more appealing pack of lies—than the faith had contrived would eventually win men's hearts and minds against all protest. He added, though: "And we did better than local tradition, did we not? If Norman history is now prevailing over the legendry of the Church, the legendry of the Church certainly prevailed over the lore of the lonely voice during the long ordeal of the Dark Ages and the mortal harvest of the Black Death."

"I can hardly deny that," Corentin admitted. "And why should I want to, since I am a naturalized Norman myself, educated in your Abbey by stern adherents of the faith? In placid times there is no conflict between the various fractions of my soul, but now that the peace is disturbed...well, you and I could easily be calculated as enemies, not merely by the wise women, but even by the Dames Blanches—whose responsibility is not so much to protect us as Broceliande—and perhaps even..."

He stopped, but Primael had the idea clearly in his head that the words his companion had not wanted, or had not been able, to pronounce were: *my own mad mother*.

He did not want to follow that line of enquiry yet, so he said: "What about the Marie-Mortes? Whose side are they on?"

"How should I know?" replied the vicomte. "How can anyone penetrate their layers of disguise? They are said to be older than your faith and our traditions. It's said that they know the truth about a great many things that we do not, but if so, they're very sparing with their revelation. No one knows really what they are, not even the Dames Blanches, according to Genovela. That is strange, is it not: that spirits should be quite unaware of the nature of other spirits?"

"Not at all," Primael said, although it was not a thought he had ever voiced, or even entertained, before. "We have very little idea of what we are ourselves, and our ideas regarding the nature of other living beings are very primitive. Why should spiritual beings have any greater advantage, once we have accepted that they do not have perfect knowledge? Perhaps angels have no more idea than we have how many of them could dance on the head of a pin. How could there have been a War in Heaven if there were not uncertainty in Heaven as to the whys and wherefores of Heavenly existence? God's tyrannical Word might have created the universe, but that does not necessarily imply that it could confine, or even describe it. What's the matter?"

Corentin de Tardivel had suddenly paled, like a man who had seen a ghost, in spite of the bright daylight and the benign verdure of the surroundings.

"Nothing," said the younger man. Then he thought better of the denial and added: "Just a momentary delusion. For a moment, I thought you had been possessed by Ollivier's spirit—but it is not at all surprising, is it, that your ideas and speech should echo his, since you have been together at Paimpont all your lives, and must have had this same argument, or ones much like it, between yourselves repeatedly. We had best press on—the distance we still have to cover seems trivial, and would be if we could fly like birds, but it is not so easy to ride, the ground being anything but level."

He did not wait for a response, but turned his horse away, and took the lead again, leaving Primael and the mule to follow.

What the young man had said was perfectly true, Primael knew—but that was not the point, and the other obviously knew that as well as he did. The interesting thing was not the natural explanation for the momentary delusion, but the fact that it had arisen. Corentin de Tardivel was a necromancer, who believed himself to be wedded to a spirit—to a succubus, in the parlance of the Faith, although he would doubtless reject the implications of that word. In the same way, he would reject the implications of the Church's definition of demonic possession. For him, the notion that Ollivier—whose spirit, in spite of his death, remained accessible to necromantic summoning, and which he had every intention of attempting to summon—might possess his close friend and lifelong companion was perfectly reasonable.

And what about me? Primael thought. *For more than forty years, since we returned from our mission to Granada, Ollivier and I have been exchanging our ideas almost on a daily basis. How could we not have colonized one another's minds, mutually, like the inhabitants of Cornouaille and Cornwall, Gaul and Galles? In spite of our secrets—and I ought not to forget, while resenting the fact that he kept secrets from me, that I kept some from him—did we not have a measure of possession over one another's thoughts, a common property therein? And if Corentin really can summon his spirit by means of some formula of arcane speech, and make it audible and tangible, who could possibly be better equipped to hear it, to recognize it and feel it than me? If he is uniquely privileged to enter into posthumous communion with the woman he loved, to the extent of an authentic marriage, do I not have a special privilege myself to communicate with Ollivier?*

All of that, it seemed to him, was perfectly reasonable, given the seemingly proven premise that necromancy was possible, and that the knowledge of the *pythorem* of Endor had not been entirely lost.

Had he been as prudent as he would have liked to think himself, Primael might well have stopped at that, but he could not help his thought running on.

And when I dream, he thought, *if dreaming opens the heart and the mind to spiritual entities, is it not reasonable that I might have a special privilege in regard to Gilles de Rais, whom I only knew briefly, but whose remembrance subsequent events and legendry have impressed upon my mind with such force? Why should I not have established an authentic communication with him at the crossroads of the other world, even thought I could not read the signpost?*

But in that case, what privilege did I have with the Marie-Morte...or she with me? What privilege does anyone have with a creature of that enigmatic kind, or she with any human, given that her kind seems so distant from ours, and so alien that it can only manifest itself in strange disguise, compounded from images of the Virgin and death?

But she is old—very old—and that raises the question of where the imagery that we associate with the Virgin and Death originated, and whether the costume that we attribute to the mother of Jesus, and the figure we credit to the Grim Reaper might be borrowed from more ancient and more numinous figures, and adapted as disguises...

Primael lost himself in that labyrinth of ideas even as the forest, in spite of the unevenness of the ground, became far less labyrinthine, the path more distinct, and its objective clearly visible. He had the opportunity as he drew nearer to it to study the detail of the château much more closely, and the community in its shadow, to assess its gardens and orchards and comprehend its way of life, but he did not do it, lost within himself.

In a sense, of course, that was the story and the summary of his life. He had always had opportunities to engage with mundane material life, even after taking Holy Orders and committing himself to the monastic life. But ever since his youthful expedition to Spain, with all its associated anxieties and hardships, he had settled into life at the Abbey, regulating his existence within the framework of offices and rituals, measured by the old bronze bell. His duties as a scribe and a teacher had fitted neatly enough into that rigid temporal frame, and within its interstices he had retreated even further, gratefully, into a mazy private world of ideas, an endless self-involved internal monologue, fueled by his reading and his discussions with the brethren: dialogues monopolized by Ollivier, and more recently by Brother Michael, because the majority of the brethren, even though they were monks, did not retreat to the same extent, did not delve into themselves in the same way.

As they approached the door of the château, and prepared to dismount, Primael had a sudden twinge of anxious suspicion, not only that he might have misspent his life in turning his mind away from the external to dwell almost entirely in an abstract world of ideas constructed out of words and images, but also that he had done so under false pretences. Outwardly, he had lived in perfect accordance with the Rule. Monks of his Order were supposed to spend their lives in meditation, supposed to retreat from the mundane world into the labyrinth of thought, but they were supposed to do so with a very specific purpose: to find God, to communicate with Christ, to be possessed by the Holy Spirit.

At one time, Primael remembered, albeit not very clearly, he had tried sincerely to do that, and had even expected to succeed, with time. But he had not succeeded, and the time had passed, and without even being consciously aware of it, he had soon stopped trying, and had merely put on a show. Instead of endeavoring to reach the heart of the spiritual maze, he had contented himself with mapping parts of the labyrinth, investigating the twists and turns of ideas, investigating dead ends...to the extent that he had not only stopped trying to find the presumed center, but had even stopped believing that such discovery was possible, that God was discoverable and the Holy Spirit tangible. He had lost his faith, without even noticing that the prayers he said every day, repeatedly and incessantly, had become mere habit, devoid of meaning. He had fallen, not out of pride or rebellion, but simply by neglect.

To all appearances, he was an excellent Benedictine, and a perfectly orthodox teacher. He would have defied the cleverest Dominican to find any solid evidence that he had every strayed from the path laid down for him by the Rule and Papal dictate—and yet, behind that mask, there was...what? Not a void, certainly, but not true faith either. He had not, strictly speaking, lost belief in God, but he had certainly lost sight and sensation of anything but the abstract idea of Him. The Word of God was not audible to him, the body and blood of Christ provided him with no nourishment, and the supposed presence of the Holy Spirit was had not the slightest whiff of incense.

What was there instead? Until two days ago, he realized, he had not even been aware of the absence, so comfortable and bland had the bedrock of his mental existence become. But he was aware of it now. Why? Because Ollivier's ignominious death and bleak burial, followed by the permission, or the instruction, to leave the Abbey had jolted him out of his torpor? Yes, of course—but beneath those symptoms there was a deeper unease, a more fundamental disturbance. The war? No, even the war was merely another symptom, still remote...

When he dismounted from the mule, he was extracted from his wayward meditations by the pain consequent on setting foot on the ground, which ran up his legs to his groin, but that distraction was immediately overtaken by another, as he became aware that the door of the château had opened, and that several people had emerged, eagerly and impatiently, in order to meet Corentin de Tardivel, whose approach had evidently been signaled at a distance.

Several of those who had emerged were servants, but two women came forward who were clearly not. One of them embraced Corentin, and one merely inclined her head, but even while they greeted him, with every evidence of being glad to see him safely returned, their principal attention had shifted to Primael.

The visitor saw their expressions shift as they realized that he was not the man they were expecting—not Ollivier, that is. He thought that he read initial disappointment on both faces, with hunts of puzzlement and unease. Because he was not Ollivier, whose arrival they had been anticipating with some avidity—more, perhaps, than was entirely reasonable—Primael had seemed to them, momentarily, to be a disturbing anomaly, cause for suspicion...but almost immediately, the suspicion in their gaze seemed to ease, as if they had recognized the replacement, as if they already knew him, even though they had never seen him before.

Corentin de Tardivel immediately moved to dispel their confusion, but what he said further emphasized Primael's impression that, in a curious sense, he was already known here, even though he had never set foot within Herbriant before..

"Brother Primael," the young man said, "may I introduce my mother, the dowager Vicomtesse Beatriz de Tardivel, and her distant cousin and close companion, Genovela Pinvidic. Mother, this is Ollivier's friend, Primael, of whom you heard him speak many a time when he was with us—a man who has shared his life, and his knowledge. If anyone can help Aidrena, he is the man most likely to do it, now that Ollivier, alas, is dead."

Primael's eyes, not unnaturally, were on Beatriz de Tardivel, and he saw the reaction of distress caused to her by the announcement of Ollivier's death—but from the corner of his eye, he saw, and took note, that the woman named as Genovela did not seem nearly as surprised, and hardly dismayed at all.

She suspected it already, Primael thought, *but she did not confide her suspicion to her mistress*.

Without waiting for conscious bidding, his eyes were already scanning the females among group of servants who were standing back respectfully, waiting to escort the newcomers into the house, while two men hastened to take charge of the horse and the mule; but they were all young; there was no one among them who might have been Beatriz de Tardivel's maidservant.

Beatriz was a slender woman, not tall—she was shorter by a head than her son—and there was nothing very aristocratic in her bearing, although her costume marked her status clearly enough. Her dark brown hair was already streaked with gray, and her face had lost any vestige of the bloom of youth. Her complexion must once have been rich, by no means pale but with a hint of gold, but time had tarnished that gold, and it now seemed more akin to a sickly jaundice. She was not beautiful, and did not give the impression of every having been beautiful, although Primael was willing to give her the benefit of his doubt and think that she might have been pretty once, when her brown eyes had had more of a gleam and her lips had been fuller. The eyes were certainly not without intelligence now, and he felt the intensity of their penetration as they searched his own face.

And she is an aristocrat, Primael thought. *If, by some jest of fate, the ghost of Gilles de Rais conjured by my dream was anything more than a phantom of my own deceptive imagination, he could not possibly have found a husband for my daughter's mother in such elevated ranks. If the dream was true—which is manifestly absurd—the chambermaid must be my daughter.*

He made a deliberate effort to dispel that train of thought from his mind, and looked instead at Genovela Pinvidic, who was studying him with an intensity that might have seemed—and was, in fact—impolite.

She was not much older than Corentin, in her early thirties. She did not fit the conventional image of a "wise woman." She too was shorter than average, and thinner, but seemed much sturdier than Beatriz. Her complexion was darker, but it had retained its healthy sheen. Her eyes were darker too, but they retained a gleam of youth, which did not compromise the intelligent intensity of her stare.

Beatriz de Tardivel hastened to assure Primael that he was welcome, as a friend of Ollivier; she even expressed sympathy for him, having lost his friend.

"Ollivier spoke about you often," she said. "He said you were the best man he knew, a true scholar and a true man of God."

Half right, Primael thought, having abruptly dropped the second part of the pretence in his own mind, but hastened his train of thought to other matters while he expressed his gratitude, and offered subtle apologies for not being the man they had anticipated, the man they had wanted to see, apparently ardently. The chatelaine hastened to assure him that no apology was necessary, and really seemed to believe—or, at least to hope—that the substitution would make little difference to her anticipation.

It occurred to Primael that Beatriz de Tardivel had not been looking forward to seeing Brother Ollivier because she expected that he might be able to cure her daughter, or herself, but because he constituted intelligent company, someone to whom she could talk on a level of something akin to social equality and confidentiality: a role for which one venerable monk might well be as good as another, especially given the fact that Ollivier had already introduced him, after a fashion, in a laudatory fashion.

As the two women asked Corentin questions, and Primael observed their exchanges, he could not see the slightest sign that Beatriz de Tardivel was anything but perfectly reasonable—but Ollivier had talked about her, just as he had talked to her about him. Primael knew that she was subject to epileptic seizures, sometimes to the kind of seizures known in medical parlance as *grand mal*, but also minor, and more frequent, disruptions of the conscious control of her body and mind. The onset of the symptoms had been delayed until late adolescence, as they often were, and her family had not known that she was a "visionary" when they negotiated her marriage—which hardly excused them for negotiating that marriage to a man like Vicomte de Tardivel, if Corentin's description of his father was not exaggerated. Doubtless they had not known what manner of man he was, but Primael could not help thinking that, if Corentin's account was accurate, they ought to have made more effort to find out. Beatriz had survived the marriage, but as he studied her, Primael had no difficulty finding indelible marks of the experience, which perhaps might have driven her mad, even if she had not had the vulnerability imposed by her epilepsy. She must, he thought, be stronger than she seemed.

"Come inside," said Corentin, eventually. "I want you to meet Aidrena." He looked at his mother as he spoke, and his mother nodded.

"She is a little better," she said—but then her expression clouded slightly. "She is expecting to see Ollivier. Please do not take it amiss, Brother Primael, if she seems a trifle disappointed. She valued his counsel and benefited greatly from his occasional presence. She is...delicate."

Primael read a hint of apology in her words that included herself as well as her daughter, as she realized that she too might have valued Ollivier's presence and "counsel" unduly—although that was not surprising, in a place which received precious few visitors, and must have a very narrow society—and that she was only too well aware of her own "delicacy." The chatelaine glanced at Genovela in a slightly censorious fashion, as if rebuking her for making her own disappointment a little too evident. Apparently, even the wise woman had learned to respect Ollivier and value his advice, and for her, the substitution did not seem as adequate.

The younger woman seemed to accept the rebuke, and made an effort to dispel her expression of suspicion. She looked at Corentin, as if for advice. He nodded his head imperceptibly, as if to thank her for making the effort.

Corentin ushered Primael into the house, after inviting the two women to precede him, but they stood aside as soon as they had traversed the vestibule into the small inner courtyard, leaving Corentin to go through another door, guiding Primael to a spiral staircase. Primael took note of the fact that although the château was evidently well supplied with servants, Corentin opened the door himself, in a perfectly natural fashion, and that no one rushed to accompany them on the stairway. That allowed him to form a swift impression of the relationship between the various strata of the internal social hierarchy, and the absence therefrom of formal arrogance. The quasi-Norman veneer of the Tardivels did not seem to be deeply ingrained.

When Corentin moved the curtain of a small door, through which the Benedictine could only pass by ducking his head, although he was not exceptionally tall, Primael found himself confronted by a plush but narrow bed, in which a young woman in her twenties, perhaps two years younger than Corentin, was already sitting up in anticipation, although the effort seemed to be costing her slightly. She had dark hair, almost black, and dark eyes; her complexion must have been similar once to Genovela's rather than her mother's, but it was faded by her illness—an illness that Ollivier had not been able to categorize as accurately as the other when describing it to Primael at Paimpol, but which left her perpetually weak and very easily exhausted.

The most surprising thing about Aidrena's expression, however, it seemed to Primael, was the lack of surprise therein. Like Genovela, he guessed, she had had a suspicion of Ollivier's death, and perhaps even more conviction in her suspicion. Her mother had not been wrong to anticipate a certain disappointment on her part in not seeing the man on whom she had come to rely for counsel, but it was mingled with a definite relief, as if she already felt sure that the friend about whom Ollivier has said so much would be an adequate replacement. He was glad of that, and that the effort she was making to sit up, in order to issue a greeting to the chateau's guest, seemed hopeful.

Corentin had hastened to overtake Primael in order to introduce him to his sister in an expansive manner, but Primael could see that the introduction and the laudatory commentary were unnecessary, that Aidrena already knew him by reputation. Aidrena was obviously glad to see her brother, to embrace him and to ask him for news while he sat on the edge of her bed, but Corentin clearly had other things to do, and Aidrena did not seem anxious to retain him. She soon gave him permission to leave, but made a point of asking him to leave Primael with her.

Primael was slightly surprised by the fact that Aidrena wanted to be alone with him, although it was hardly unusual for people to make such a request for confessional purposes. Corentin did not question the request; Primael was a monk, after all, and she must have been accustomed to be in confidence with Ollivier during his occasional visits. He sat down in an armchair, next to be bed but at a carefully-estimated re-spectful distance, and assumed the attitude and expression of a spiritual advisor.

"It is very kind of you to come all this way, Brother Primael," she said, "in order to lend assistance to strangers."

Primael did not tell her that he had had no choice. "If my meager medical lore can be of any assistance to anyone at Tardivel," he said, "I am only too glad to be here. And I do not feel that you or your mother are strangers; Ollivier seems to have spoken about me to you far more abundantly than he ever spoke to me about you, but I have been welcomed by your brother and my mother as a friend, and I feel that a bond already exists between me and the house of Tardivel. I am a lesser man than Ollivier, I fear, in terms of intelligence and initiative, but I will do my very best to substitute for him."

"That is not what Brother Ollivier said," Aidrena told him. "He said that his medicine was inferior to yours."

"He was a kind man," said Primael, "and a modest one. We have studied the same books, and have often accompanied one another in consultations, aiding one another by means of discussion and suggestion. I am certainly a lesser man without him."

"Perhaps that is why," Aidrena ventured, "when he was attempting to find appropriate treatments for my illness, he continually made a point of consulting you, even though you were not here—as if you were present in spirit. I suppose it was an invention, designed to assist his thinking."

"Did he do that?" Primael said, softly, rather flattered by the revelation. "I hope, then, that you will not mind if I employ a similar rhetorical trick, and make an occasional pretence of consulting him—if, that is, you want to accept me as your physician. I cannot promise to cure you, but it seems that I might be here for some time, and there might be medicaments whose effects we can test, in the hope of finding one that will restore a measure of your strength."

"That would be...interesting," Aidrena said, clearly having lost hope long ago of finding any kind of cure for her condition, and probably having tried the most likely palliatives on Ollivier's previous advice. She added: "You must be very weary after your long journey, Brother, and very hungry. You must let my brother take you to table, and rest thereafter. But know that I am glad that you are here. Genovela is kind too, and she has sought advice on my account from her fellow wise women, but Brother Ollivier always said two intelligences are better than one, if they can work in harmony and not in conflict. May I ask you one question before you go, though?"

"Of course," said Primael.

"I know that your books do not have a remedy for my mother's illness, or Brother Ollivier would have employed it, but can you help to soothe it? Everyone strives to hide it from me, as they strive to hide everything else, but I know that her visions have intensified lately, especially since Corentin left to fetch…you. There seems to be a disturbance in the atmosphere, which I do not recognize, and she feels it even more intensely than I do. Can you help her?"

"I don't know," said Primael, honestly, "but I am certainly willing to try, if she cares to consult me."

Aidrena seemed uncertain about that possibility. She was about to pull a bell-cord when the curtain moved again, and Corentin put his head through the gap.

"Excuse me," he said, "but Mother has ordered a meal be served for Brother Primael, May I take him away?"

"I was about to send him," Aidrena replied, "but I want to continue our conversation later—I have more to say to him."

Corentin inclined his head in agreement, and stood aside, holding the curtain up for Primael to pass through, ducking his head carefully. On the landing, he heard Aidrena say to Corentin: "And put a rein on Genovela."

He thought he heard Corentin reply: "No need," but could not be sure. The young man ducked himself, and then escorted Primael down the stairway. "If I judge Mother right," he murmured, evidently having overheard the Benedictine's reply to Aidrena's final question as he had interrupted their conversation, "she is quite willing to consult you—perhaps a little too eager."

"And Genovela?" Primael could not help asking.

"I think she wants to talk to you as well, when the opportunity arises. Ollivier conferred with her, but what they talked about, I don't know. She isn't hostile to you, though, although she might seem a trifle surly, and she is not glad in the way that Mother and Aidrena seem to be. Everyone here is nervous, and understandably; remote as we are, news travels here, and the war is progressing westwards, already some way beyond Nantes. Logic dictates that the French armies will surely concentrate their principal strength around Rennes and also move steadily along the south coast, all the way to Quimper, without ever coming within twenty leagues of Herbriant, but in war, one is fearful even of remote possibilities. Genovela is nervous, and mistrustful by nature, but her intentions are good, and we all have the same objectives; she will lend you assistance, if she can."

Good intentions, Primael thought, were often difficult to measure, and although he was sure that there were immediate objectives that everyone in the château shared, he suspected that there might be others that did not command such unanimity. Aidrena was correct in her estimation that there was a disturbance in the atmosphere of the region, the origin of which was difficult to determine. He had evidently felt it while he slept, and the easy defense offered by the assumption that his response to it had only been a dream born of and shaped by his own anxieties was as unconvincing as Corentin's seeming conviction that the Château de Tardivel had the wherewithal to withstand a siege if the occasion ever arose. Now that Primael had actually seen the so-called fortress, he knew that any such boast was ridiculous.

Paimpol Abbey had only received distant rumor of the improvements made to Louis XI's artillery during the last two decades by his henchman Tristan L'Hermite, while both men were still alive and in close conspiracy, but that news had been sufficient to create the conviction that when Anne de France launched the forces she and her brother had inherited from their father against the forces now controlled by Pierre de Landais on behalf of Fransez II, they would grind them down and obliterate them, step by step. It might take two or three more years to subdue Bretagne entirely, but the present superiority of the French forces was indubitable. Brother Michael had told him that Landais had tried to sell Henry Tudor to Richard III in exchange for a company of English archers to reinforce the Breton army, but that the desperate conspiracy had backfired. Henry had escaped, the redoubtable English captain Edward Woodville was dead, and Maximilien I had never been a reliable ally. If, as it was alleged, Anne and Charles had mustered a force of five thousand mercenaries to add to their own cavalry and artillery, their captains would sweep across Bretagne like a team of reapers, methodically scything down everything in her path, and if their route took any of their companies through Herbriant, Tardivel would not be able to delay an efficient force by three days, let alone a month.

But why would any French captain come this way, when any sane tactician would simply go around the forest, following the good roads?

I am safe here, Primael told himself. *We are all safe here, from France's cannoneers and arbalestiers—but the disturbance in the air here must surely originate from something deeper and stranger.*

VII

When he had been well fed and shown the room that had been prepared for him—only a little larger than his cell at the Abbey, but more ostentatiously furnished, with a far softer bed—Primael did not feel any immediate need to rest, so he returned to see Aidrena, as he had promised to do. Genovela went with him, and there were maidservants in Aidrena's room when they arrived, but Aidrena dismissed them all immediately, demanding to be left alone with Primael.

He tried to interrogate her about her symptoms, having come in the person of her physician, but she waved his questions away. "I'm still taking the potion that Brother Ollivier prescribed," she told him. "He left detailed instructions of how to prepare it, which have been followed with exactitude. If it has not made me better, it has certainly prevented me from getting any worse. How did he die?"

"He contracted a wasting disease," Primael told her. "Its progress was rapid, and our medical knowledge, although perhaps as extensive as that of any scholar in Bretagne, was not adequate to arrest it. Nor were my prayers, and those of the entire Brotherhood. Your brother arrived just in time to see him lowered into his grave. I was there, and he remembered me as one of his teachers. He asked the Abbot if he might bring me to Tardivel in Ollivier's stead, and Brother Michael consented to that."

"Corentin told him that it was for my benefit that he had me to Paimpol? And he told you the same? Yes, of course he did, and doubtless did not think that he was deceiving anyone. But you know, I assume, that is motives were mixed. He has told you everything—about Katarin, that is?"

"He has told me the elements of the story, at least."

She was studying his face. Evidently, the reason she had asked him to come back was not to discuss her own predicament, but her brother's. He was not surprised by that. "And was that the first you knew about Ollivier's dabbling in nec-romancy?" she asked.

"Not quite," said Primael. "I heard it first from Brother Michael—but it was Corentin who gave me the explanation."

"And yet you came?"

"Yes, evidently."

"Thank you for that. As a good Churchman, you have taken the inference from what you have been told, I presume, that the family is accursed?"

"The notion had occurred to me, but I rejected it. I do not believe in curses. I believe disease to be an entirely natural phenomenon—your illness, as well as your mother's. Ollivier could not put a name to it, but it seems, from what you've just told me, the treatment he applied to your symptoms has had some success. That seems to confirm my opinion that the fault is in your flesh. Perhaps it is hereditary, in some measure, but I do not believe it to be the result of a curse or a spell. If I can help at all, it will be in the same way that Ollivier helped, with herbal remedies."

While he was speaking, her face had taken on a visible expression of satisfaction and approval. Her mention of a curse had been a test, not an expression of conviction—a check to make sure that what Ollivier had told her about him was true. "And Corentin?" she said. "Is his fault in the flesh as well?"

Primael knew exactly what she meant, but he hedged anyway. "What fault do you mean, Lady Aidrena."

"Please don't treat me as a child," she replied. "Everybody does it automatically, because I'm weak, but my mind is sharp, and educated. Ollivier could see that, and so must you. I mean Corentin's obsession, his conviction that Katarin has risen from the dead, that he can converse with her…and commune with her in the flesh. Don't tell me that you do not doubt the reality of his experience, no matter what lengths you have gone to in order to humor him. Mother and Genovela believe him, I know, but Brother Ollivier was in doubt, to say the least. What Brother Ollivier told me about you convinced me that you must see things differently, and you have just proved his point in regard to Mother. Ollivier said to me in so many words, or perhaps to himself while thinking aloud, that if he described Corentin's adventure to you, you would interpret it as pure hallucination."

"In that case," said Primael, quietly, "he thought me more definite in my opinions than I really am. In all honesty, Lady Aidrena, I do not know what to think of your brother's story. I am hoping to be able to interrogate him about it at far greater length than I was able to do while we were riding along rough roads, one of us mounted on a scrawny mule and the other on a battle-charger. I have postponed my judgment until I could do that. But I am certainly intrigued to learn that, in spite of the environment in which you live and the company by which you are surrounded, even having a sharp and educated mind, you are so certain that he is deluded."

"Don't judge my upbringing by my present surroundings. Genevola has not been here long, and there was a long period in my youth when I hardly saw my mother. Has Corentin told you that my father treated me very badly?"

"He did say something of the sort."

"He is not entirely wrong, but not entirely right either. Father was a short-tempered man, very intolerant of contradiction, and he was often violent with those considered to be underlings. He considered my condition to be a weakness, and thought that if I could only muster enough will-power, that would counter it. He could be brutal, even to me—but he did love me, in his fashion, and he would not have hurt me deliberately. He often sat by my bed, as you are doing now, for long hours, and talked to me—far more, I think than he ever talked to Corentin. Toward the end, when he fell ill himself, and was furious with himself because his determination was not adequate to fight it, I believe I came to see him more clearly than Corentin, and more clearly than he saw himself. I understood that his intolerance of contradiction was a reaction against his own deep doubts and uncertainties...but by that time, I had absorbed the effect of his stern attitude to every-

111

thing he called nonsense and superstition. I love my brother, Brother Primael, have no doubt of that…but that is precisely why I am so concerned about him. I know that he is not simply mad, any more than my mother is…but just as my mother has visions that she takes for reality, although they might well be no more than side-effects of her convulsive fits, I cannot help wondering whether the fact that Corentin hears Katarin's voice and feels her caresses might not be an internal effect of his intense desire and remorse rather than the visitations of an actual spirit."

"Remorse?" Primael queried.

"Of course. He feels responsible for Katarin's death. He believes that father killed her because of his infatuation with her. Did he not tell you that?"

"Yes, he did. Do you think that his belief is mistaken?"

"I do, although I have no illusions about my father, and I know that he was capable of instructing one of his servants to kill an inconvenient vassal. As to the supposed testimony of Katarin's spirit that Father murdered her himself, after raping her, though…that is another matter. That, I am certain, is pure delusion."

"Ah," said Primael, thinking that some response, however inarticulate, was called for, but having none better, for the moment. Aidrena de Tardivel was not what he had expected at all. He wondered how many other surprises were awaiting him in this forgotten corner of Broceliande.

"As a confessor in a monastery," Aidrena said, with a slight hesitancy arising from delicacy, although she was not blushing, "you are doubtless familiar, as Ollivier was, with the phenomenon of the succubus?"

"Phenomenon?" Primael hedged.

"I'm not a child, Father, delicate as I am," she reminded him. "Brother Ollivier did me the honor of speaking to me seriously in response to the confessions I made him. It is, he said, not uncommon for young monks to dream about…nocturnal visitations."

Primael was slightly surprised that Ollivier had talked about such things to a young woman, even in a confessional context, but he knew that it was not really a case for astonishment. Confessors were instructed to take an interest in such matters, and to give absolution for sins of that sort, which were often those uppermost in the minds of those seeking absolution. "That's true," he said.

"But he said that such visitations are not due, in his opinion, to literal visitations by demons, but the result of...physical pressures associated with celibacy."

"That was certainly his opinion," Primael agreed.

"I'm embarrassing you by talking about it. It's indelicate of me, I know, but it's a matter of some concern to me, as you can imagine. If Corentin's Katarin can be regarded as a hallucinatory succubus, perhaps..."

"I take the inference," Primael said. "Yes, it is certainly possible that...physical pressures might make some contribution to such a delusion, if it is, in fact, a delusion."

"Good. Ollivier said that you would take that view when I put the matter to him—but as you've said, he seems to have thought you more convinced than you really are. To tell the truth, I suspect that he only quoted certain things as your likely opinion as a way of avoiding taking responsibility for them himself."

"That's possible," said Primael, blandly.

"But he wasn't representing you falsely, was he? Exaggerating slightly, at worst?"

"No," Primael agreed, "he wasn't representing me falsely, only exaggerating my certainty." *More than slightly*, he added, silently

"Good, because this is important. If your interpretation of the origin of the succubus is correct, the same argument ought to apply, should it not, to the incubus? Not that I am trying to account for Mother's convulsions, you understand, but merely certain aspects of her visions."

To that, Primael not having expected it, he could not even muster an "Ah," at least for the moment.

"Please don't look at me like that," said Aidrena. "I'm not asking you for a judgment, because I know that you haven't interrogated Mother yet, any more than you've interrogated Corentin fully—and I suspect that when you see Mother, you will be the one undergoing the interrogation, at least for today and perhaps for some time to come. However, if, as I believe, Corentin is deluded, then Mother is far more so. Brother Ollivier refused to say that she is mad, just as Corentin does, and they are right, I believe, in respect of her convulsions—but the fact that her epilepsy is not a kind of madness does not mean that her visions are not. I have strong reasons, as you can imagine, for hoping that the family is not, in fact, cursed with a hereditary madness, but if I am to be convinced that it is not, then I am compelled, am I not, to search for alternative explanations of the convictions they have formed as a result of their visions? That is the assistance that I expect of you, as my physician. Ollivier never mentioned any of this of you?"

"He could not," Primael said, a trifle faintly. "He would have considered it subject to the secrecy of the confessional. But I am beginning to understand, now, the character of some of the philosophical debates we had prior to his final illness. He did not tell me anything about the precise nature of your Mother's visions, either, for the same reason. He was a scrupulous man. Anything you or your mother said to him that he interpreted as a confession, whether the ritual formulae had been recited beforehand or not, he would have regarded as sacrosanct. My attitude is the same—even though you have not asked to make a formal confession, I will treat everything that you are saying to me as a sacred confidence."

Her eyes narrowed slightly, but not with suspicion. "Are you implying," he asked, "that something I have just said to you constitutes a sin in need of absolution?"

"No," he said, "you have not said anything that does not seem to me to be wholly virtuous. I can see nothing in it but altruistic concern for your brother and your mother, which I naturally applaud."

114

It was her turn to say: "Ah." After a slight pause, she added: "I would not like to deceive you by means of circumlocution, Father. When I say that I have strong reasons for being interested in this matter, they are not entirely altruistic. I have visions of my own, Brother Primael...which might easily become delusions, were I to take them too seriously, and my search for explanations is not as...purely scholarly as you are ready to assume."

Primael shook his head, slowly. "Nor is mine, child," he said, softly, applauding her desire not to deceive by means of circumlocution.

She did not smile, or nod her head, nor did she say anything, but he detected a certain approval nevertheless. Even so, she said, again: "I'm not a child."

"I know," he said. "Forgive a manner of speaking. I'm old, and I've grown accustomed to thinking of all young people as if they were my children, or even grandchildren. Monks still have feelings, including quasi-paternal ones."

"Of course," she said. "It's the nature of the vocation, is it not, to substitute a paternal affection for all humans for the affection you might have concentrated on your own children had you taken a different route in life? When father sent Corentin to Paimpol Abbey, I asked him whether he would send me to a convent when I reached the same age. I was surprised by the abruptness of his refusal, but I think I understand, now, that he had no fear of Corentin being persuaded by the Benedictines that he had a religious vocation, but was anxious that I might not have been immune to such seduction. It became a dead issue anyway; I would not have been well enough to go away, once I reached thirteen. He tried, though, to fill in for that lack of an education as best he could. He did not have much Latin himself, but he could read, and he bought books, in spite of his reputation for avarice, and read them with me. His choice might have been a trifle eccentric, but Corentin approved, saying that I was being spared much tedium, while being informed of things that it was valuable to know, for the health of the mind."

"It certainly seems to have had its effect on your intellect and eloquence," said Primael.

"Had I been healthy, of course, my father would have searched for a husband for me, as he searched for a wife for Corentin, but he told me squarely that he did not think that I could stand up to the rigors of marriage. My mother has made the remark that not all marriages are as rigorous as hers, but it is not a matter that she cares to discuss. Genovela says that I had a fortunate escape, but she is not married herself, and when I asked her whether she was visited by the incubus she said that wise women never are. I cannot quite decide, as yet, as to the extent of her delusions. The Dames Blanches are puzzling, in several ways, but they have not visited me, as yet."

"What about the Marie-Mortes?" Primael asked, before prudence could interrupt him.

"I've never seen one of them either—but I have a very insular life here, in this little room. If I were able to go into the forest...I try, sometimes, when I feel a little better, but I become weak and tire so rapidly, and whatever Father used to think, it is not a lack of will power that makes me so. That, I'm sure, is not a delusion. Brother Ollivier agreed with me."

"We have seen similar illnesses in Paimpol. There are fathers there—and mothers too—who have the same attitude as your father, construing the weakness of their children as a weakness of the will rather than the body, but I do not believe that to be the case, any more than he did. The body is subject to countless afflictions, some of them strange and puzzling, and the human organism is so very complex that it is not surprising that there are a thousand ways in which it might suffer flaws and defects, without any need for the intervention of diabolical or divine intervention. Are there, by chance any herbals among the books that your father acquired?"

"Yes, and Brother Ollivier sent another not long ago. He said in his letter that we might investigate it together when he came again"

"I will consult it," Primael said. "And we shall, indeed, investigate it together—but we must be prudent in our trials. I have learned to my own cost, and that of others, that the wisdom of Galen is sometimes unreliable, although it is possible that we mistake his meaning, or that the properties of certain plants have changed over time."

She seemed heartened, not merely by the prospect, but also by the evidence of his caution. "My troubles are not the most urgent, Father," she said. "Interrogate Corentin, and Mother too. I will not ask you to discuss with me what they tell you, after what you have said, but I will beg you to consider their cases carefully. If it helps you to imagine an interlocutor with whom to debate their possible treatment, feel free to think of me, although Ollivier will probably be more helpful to you."

"Thank you, Lady Aidrena," said Primael. "What you have told me has been most enlightening, and has given me much fuel for thought."

As he stood up in order to take his leave, she said, swiftly: "You will come to see me every day, Father, won't you, for as long as you're here? I have so many things that I would like to talk about to someone…well, without wanting to see ungrateful, to someone other than Mother and Genovela, or even Corentin. I learned from Ollivier how very useful it is to be able to consult a true philosopher."

"I will come every day, for as long as I am here," Primael promised. "Au revoir, Lady Aidrena."

"Au revoir, Father Primael."

He was not surprised to find Genovela waiting at the bottom of the spiral staircase. "You may go up to Mademoiselle de Tardivel's room, if you wish, my lady," he said.

"Your lady?" she queried, lightly. "You're being ironic, I think, Brother Primael. "But I'm not waiting to see Aidrena, I'm waiting to see you. May I talk with you before you go to pay your respects to Lady Beatriz?"

Primael glanced at the narrow window that cast a dull illumination into the bottom of the stairwell, measuring the time still left before sunset. "I'm already overdue in that duty," he said.

"You are," she answered, "but she will understand Aidrena's insistence that you give her priority, even though she is impatient to see you herself, and I hope that she will understand mine."

Primael could not estimate the likelihood of that, as he had no idea what Genovela wanted to say to him. "Shall we step into the courtyard?" he asked.

"I'd prefer to go further than that, if you're agreeable," said the wise woman. "Will you walk with me into the forest for a while? Not long, I assure you."

"Very well," said Primael.

They crossed the courtyard and went out through the main door of the château. Genovela led him through the cluster of huts in a few strides, and into the wood, by a path that led away from the château at right angles to the one by which he and Corentin had approached it. Primael said nothing, waiting for his guide to say whatever was on her mind. She stopped in a dense copse, curtained on all sides by slender trunks and low-hanging foliage.

"How is Aidrena," the woman asked, presumably by way of a polite preliminary.

"Better than I had been led to expect when Corentin asked my superior for permission to bring me here," Primael hedged.

"Doubtless he was using a pretext," said Genovela, and then got to be point, abruptly. "Did you know that you were being followed from Paimpol by a black friar?"

"We did not see him on the road, but we were aware of the possibility. He and a companion saw us meet at the burial-ground where Ollivier was interred. The Dominicans are curious by nature. Do you know what the black friars are?"

"We do. You might think that we are cut off from civilization hereabouts, and very backward, but we take an interest in what is happening in the wider world, even when we do not have as much reason as we have now to do so. Is the black friar just a spy, do you think?"

"Probably. His companion in Paimpol might have made an arrangement to follow him here after making his report, with or without others."

"Did you know that Rennes has been taken by the French forces, and that the bulk of the army responsible is advancing in this direction?"

"No, I didn't, but it doesn't surprise me. The logic of the situation has been clear for some time, but Landais' forces will be concentrated in defense of the principal towns—probably not including Ploermel, let alone Paimpol. There's no reason why the invading forces should pass this way."

"Agreed—but that might not prevent the Dominicans from borrowing a contingent. From the viewpoint of a military tactician, Herbriant is utterly insignificant, but heresy-hunters will not see things that way. We've encountered them in the past. This isn't the first time that their attention has been drawn to the relics of Broceliande."

"They're jackals, not lions." Primael told her. "They scavenge where more powerful forces have gone before. It wasn't the Dominicans who crucified Gilles de Rais, or the Templars, or even the Albigensians. They only moved in when the hunt was under way and the pack had been unleashed. They can't bring soldiers here on their own initiative."

"Times have changed," said the wise woman, sourly. "You're behind them, Brother. Can you talk to the Dominican?"

Primael was surprised by the suggestion. "And say what?" he queried. "He had no charge to level against me three days ago, but since then he's seen me preside over the burial of a supposed necromancer, my closest friend. If he doesn't know already, he'll find out soon enough that I once visited Arabic and Jewish scholars in Granada, and have been a guest of Gilles de Rais, as well as accompanying Corentin de Tardivel into one of the last enclaves of the great pagan forest. Anything I say to him from now on will seem to him to be coming straight from the Devil's mouth—or that's the way it will be represented, when he reports it to his own superiors. Better to give them nothing, in my opinion."

The wise woman scowled, but raised no objection. "I suppose that scaring him half to death would only make things worse," she said.

"Probably," said Primael. "Fear is a double-edged sword, even at the best of times. Killing him would make things even worse, if such a possibility had crossed your mind."

"It's not our way," she told him. "You might think of us as pagan barbarians, which we are, I suppose, but we're not savages, or Normans. We only kill in necessary self-defense or for just vengeance."

Primael did not query her use of the term *Normans*. He knew what she meant.

"And you don't consider that the Dominican's presence in the forest necessitates self-defense?" he queried.

"His presence, no," she said. "If he's content to look and go away, no one hereabouts will trouble him."

"Is that all you wanted to ask me?" he said.

"No, it isn't," she said. "it would probably have been better for all of us, in retrospect, if you hadn't come, although I have to admit that I was looking forward to seeing Ollivier—but since you're here in his stead, I need to ask: are you going to help Corentin to summon spirits?"

"He wants to me to participate in an attempt to do that, if only to convince me that he can."

"Can you talk some sense into him?""

"I don't know. What do you mean by *sense*?"

"What he's doing is dangerous. He ought to be content with what he has. If he wants to do more simply to impress you, you need to stop him. When I say dangerous, I don't just mean for him and for you, I mean for all of us."

"How, exactly?" asked Primael, curiously.

The wise woman stared at him. "Aidrena has told you that he's deluded," she concluded, presumably jumping to that conclusion without much difficulty. "It's as well for her that she believes it, but it's necessary that you don't. It's necessary, too, that you don't take the old lady's visions too seriously, even though they're real enough. We're under siege here, and have been for a long time. There's a turbulence, and we don't know why, or how it will work out—but Corentin's incantations certainly aren't helping. The Dames Blanches are anxious, and they're not easily disturbed."

As she spoke, there was, indeed, a literal turbulence in the air, like a sudden squall; the foliage of the young and flexible trees that surrounded them rattled loudly, and the branches agitated. Primael looked at Genovela accusingly.

"That wasn't my doing," she said, when the swirling gust of wind had died away, as suddenly as it had arrived. "In fact..." Primael became aware that she was looking at him oddly, as if wondering whether he were in some way responsible for nature's mocking gesture.

Eventually, however the wise woman merely paused, and then resumed what she had been saying before: "It's in your interests, Brother—not just your personal interests, but those of Paimpol Abbey—to help smooth things over, if they can be smoothed. If you have any medical means of preventing the old lady from having fits, use them, and if you can persuade her that her visions are just dreams, and not visitations from a glamorized Devil, do that. And above all, if you can talk Corentin out of summoning any more spirits, do that. Let him be content with Katarin; I doubt that she'll do him any harm, or anyone else, if it really was the old Vicomte or some hireling of his who killed her—but if he or Beatriz contrives to open the door to something truly dangerous with the aid of Ollivier's spells, there's no knowing where it might end."

"Do you believe, then," Primael asked, warily, "that Olivier's necromancy merely opened a door to...somewhere else—that they don't command the spirits, but merely make it possible for them to come?"

"Of course," she said. "The dead aren't at anyone's beck and call—but they can be invited. It's necessary to be careful, though, what invitations we issue. Corentin, I know, is anxious to summon Olivier, and Ollivier might well be anxious to come, but it's necessary, if that's your intention too, to be very careful. It seemed to me, on due reflection, that Ollivier was a good and perhaps a useful man, although my sisters were in two minds about it. He told me that you're also a good man. I hope he's right—and that your conscience is a reliable guide."

"I hope so too," said Primael, mildly. "By your sisters, I presume you mean the wise women of Herbriant?"

"Among others."

"Among other wise women, or among other residents of Herbriant?"

"Both."

"Including the Dames Blanches? And the Marie-Mortes?"

Genovela contrived a laugh. "Be careful, Father. There are beliefs, are there not, that are heretical to entertain, and ideas that are dangerous to contemplate? Take a lesson from Aidrena, and treat everything as a delusion until you have tangible proof to the contrary—and by *tangible proof*, I don't just mean invisible fingers stroking your cheek. There are some things that it's better for a God-fearing man like you not to know. If you aren't careful, you'll have bad dreams, and you might find that your prayers aren't a sufficient defense against them."

Too late, thought Primael; but what he said aloud, prudently, was: "I'm not your enemy, Genovela, although the black friars surely are, and mine too. If you receive any more news of them, or of Charles VIII's army, I'd be grateful if you'd keep me informed."

The wise woman inclined her head. "I'm a friend to everyone here," she said, "And I'm speaking to you as a friend. I hope we'll have an opportunity to speak again, in a more leisurely manner. Forgive me if I seem a trifle abrupt, but..." she shrugged her shoulders.

I know, thought Primael. *There's a turbulence in the air*.

He bowed, politely to the wise woman went back into the château, and went to pay his now-long-overdue respects to Beatriz de Tardivel.

VIII

The chatelaine received Primael in the sitting-room of her apartment, where two armchairs had been placed by the hearth, although no fire was set there. She was alone there, once she had dismissed Genovela, who had escorted him in; she must have cleared the room in preparation, and issued orders that she did not want to be disturbed. Primael had not yet caught the slightest glimpse of her chambermaid. He wanted to ask about her, but there was no way he could do so without the question seeming bizarre.

"Have you seen Aidrena?" asked Beatriz, when the initial formalities were over, and they had both sat down in the padded armchairs, upholstered in what Primael assumed to be deerskin. Even though the chamber obviously belonged to a lady, there were several hunting trophies on the wall, including the antlers of roebucks.

"Yes," said Primael. "My apologies for doing so before coming to see you, but Corentin was anxious about her. I'm glad to find that she's in good spirits, and that the medicament that Ollivier made up for her seems to be holding her illness in check."

"Can you do any more for her than that?" Madame de Tardivel asked.

"I don't know," admitted Primael, "but if I might consult the books in your library, and if I can obtain Genovela's help in locating any simples that might be beneficial, Aidrena is amenable to careful experiment."

"The library is at your disposal," said the chatelaine. "I can't speak for Genovela—the wise women are a law into themselves. She's here as my companion, and an adviser, and I've been very grateful for her company, especially while Corentin has been away, but…wise women make a fetish out of being enigmatic and secretive. She'll doubtless take you into the forest, as she did Ollivier, and interrogate you about matters that I wouldn't understand, but she has a good heart, and I wouldn't want to be without her at present. I'm constantly afraid that she'll be summoned away by her strange sisters, or by the Dames Blanches. Do you know about the Dames Blanches?"

"Only what is reported by legend," Primael said.

"You're probably fortunate. Ollivier was curious about them, but it's hardly for me to hold that against him. What did he tell you about me?"

"Nothing at all. He regarded his conversations with you as confidential. I knew that he'd come here more than once even before his sojourn earlier this year, but he didn't tell me anything about the various medical problems he addressed, or about Corentin's ventures in necromancy, or anything that any of you had said to him in private."

"That's a pity," she said. "Had you been better informed I'd have been interested to hear your opinions. He didn't even tell you about the Druid stone? The one that the local people also call the signpost?"

Primael was braced for the unexpected, and the reproduction of the word that the Marie-Morte had pronounced in his dream did not cause him to start. It was, he supposed, one more reason to suspect that the vision was not simply compounded out of things he already knew, or might have deduced, but it did not seem to be of any significance in itself. He filed it away for further meditation.

"No," he said, in answer to the chatelaine's questions, "but the Abbot told me that Ollivier had practiced necromancy before he gave me permission to accompany Corentin, and Corentin told me the whole story, at least in summary, on the way here."

"Do you disapprove?"

"I haven't made up my mind, as yet, whether I ought to disapprove. I need to question Corentin further."

"And you haven't seen the papers that the Abbot of Paimpol gave Corentin on Ollivier's behalf?"

"No," Primael admitted, "but I dare say that Corentin won't keep them secret from me, if I'm to play the role here that he wanted Ollivier to play."

"Which you have not yet decided to do?" Beatriz suggested.

"Not yet," Primael confirmed, although he had a strong suspicion that his participation would be unavoidable.

Beatriz took a moment to consider the situation as it had now been mapped out for her, and the expected extent of Primael's ignorance. Then she said: "Aidrena has told you, of course, that she believes Corentin to be deluded?"

"Yes," said Primael, simply.

"And what do you think of her theory that he has conjured a succubus from his own imagination, in order to soothe his frustrated lust?"

Slightly taken aback by the directness of the question, Primael said: "It's…interesting."

The chatelaine laughed. "It's interesting that that's your reaction," she said, "and perhaps more revealing than you expected it to be, guarded as it was. You know that I suffer from periodic epileptic fits?"

"Yes," said Primael, still surprised by her bluntness. Remembering his conversations with Aidrena and Genovela, however, and the note he had already made of the prevailing lack of formality in the house, he supposed that he ought to have expected it.

"And you've been told that I have visions?"

"Yes."

"And Corentin and Aidrena have both asked you to examine me carefully, to evaluate my condition carefully, and to be prudent in humoring me?"

"It's understandable that they're concerned about you," said Primael, neutrally.

"Indeed, as I am about them, even though we've been virtual strangers for much of their lives. Corentin has told you that I have been very cruelly abused, of course, and Aidrena has probably told you that her father believed, albeit wrongly, that he was acting for the best, in everyone's interests. They might both be right, or not, but they're equally uncertain as to what to make of me now, and who can blame them, given that I'm uncertain what to make of myself. Tell me, Brother Primael, is it the orthodox belief of Churchmen that there was once a war of angels to determine who would occupy the throne of Heaven?"

Primael had become accustomed to the chatelaine's alacrity in covering argumentative ground and he had been expecting the topic to some up sooner or later. His response was posed and casual, as if he were discussing an obscure point of theology with Ollivier or Michael. "It's certainly a common supposition among Churchmen," he said, "but not an important point of doctrine. The Scriptures are very unclear on the matter, and it's difficult for scholars to decide how to interpret the references to it."

"Yes, it is," she agreed. "How do you interpret the references in *Genesis* to the fathers of the nephilim?"

"I hardly know what to make of them, but I suspect that all attempts to render the words into modern languages are misleading, and that the references in Hebrew might themselves be garbled translations of some older, long-lost script. There are said to be other extant writings known in that East that offer details of a war in Heaven, but no Western scholar has seen them, so far as I know, and if they do exist, questions would inevitably arise as to their reliability. If you asked Ollivier the same question, he must have mentioned you that Cabalists to whom we spoke in Granada more than forty years ago told us that the fathers of the nephilim were *egregori*, or Watchers, and that they were a faction of rebel angels expelled from Heaven with a leader named Semiaza, whom the Church calls Satan, or Lucifer. Where that information came from, I don't know, and I'm inclined to regard it as a fanciful story."

"But as a good Christian, you do believe in Satan?"

"As a good Christian, I'm honestly not sure. There is evil in the world, and temptation is certainly an ever-present danger to sin, but I'm not at all certain that temptation ought to be imagined as an external force, let alone personalized as an active entity. I wonder whether it ought to be imagined rather as a force within us, an aspect of our own minds, which only appears to be alien because we try to resist it—especially when our resistance fails."

"You'll get on very well with Aidrena then—although that's only to be expected, as she got on so well with Ollivier, and the ideas she has now mostly came out of her discussions with him. Remember, though, that she's just a child, whatever she thinks, and that her visions…did she tell you that she has visions?"

"We didn't speak for long," Primael hedged. "I've promised to see her every day, while I'm here. She's obviously not lonely here, with so many people surrounding her, but I think Ollivier provided her with a different kind of company, for which she's still hungry: a mentor of sorts."

"That's one word for it," said Beatriz. "And she expects you to slide seamlessly into the role she assigned to Ollivier. Can you do that?"

"I'm not Ollivier," Primael said, "but I shall do my best to provide a similar service, if she requires it of me."

"I'm glad to hear it," said the chatelaine, giving the impression that it was not on only on her daughter's behalf that she was glad, although it was about Aidrena—apparently, at least—that she continued speaking. "She was delighted to find someone not only prepared to spend time with her but to take her perfectly seriously, which she didn't feel that her mother and older brother were entirely able to do. It's perhaps as well that he wasn't a younger man, or she'd surely have fallen in love with him, and that could only have led to disaster. My children seem to be unlucky in that regard, I fear. Have you ever been in love, Brother Primael?"

"I don't believe I have, in the sense that the phrase is usually used," Primael said, "but I entered my novitiate and confirmed my vocation while I was still young. Ollivier and I were ordered to join a mission to the Moorish cities of Spain while I was not yet twenty, and we became scholars thereafter, initially copying and studying manuscripts that we obtained there. I have not been entirely isolated from external society, of course, having fulfilled various pastoral duties in Paimpol and the surrounding area, but what is normally called falling in love was never a possibility, no real opportunity being able to present itself. As a priest, however, it is my duty to love all of humankind, and I have always taken that duty seriously."

Have I, though? he thought, and could not help charging himself with hypocrisy. He wondered whether he, or anyone else, could absolve him of that particular sin.

"I never had a real opportunity myself," she said, "but I had children eventually, albeit not by choice. I loved my children very dearly, from the day of their birth, and I still do, intensely, even though I was hardly allowed to see them for most of their lives. It grieves me to think that I might have caused them any accidental distress, and that I might be causing such distress day by day, by virtue of my convulsions…or my visions. Can you understand that, Brother Primael?"

"Yes, I can," he replied, not lying, but perhaps exaggerating his intellectual grasp.

"Good. Have you ever heard the suggestion that Saul's sudden collapse on the road to Damascus, and the revelation that made him into Saint Paul, and thus led to the creation of the Roman Church, might have been an epileptic fit, like those by which I am sometimes afflicted?"

"Yes," said Primael.

"And do you doubt his revelation in consequence?"

"No," said Primael, aware that he was on dangerous ground, already anticipating her next argumentative step.

"Good. You accept, then, that Saul's epilepsy might merely have been a means of delivering an authentic revelation, with the requisite sense of absolute certainty and commitment that made him a prophet. "She did not wait for him to acquiesce, but simply went on: "You will not be surprised, therefore, if I tell you that I too have had visions that carry their own seeming guarantee of absolute certainty. Unlike Saint Paul, of course, I cannot become a wandering preacher,

129

ambitious to found a church. I am not even a nun, who might thus have some entitlement as a visionary, although I fear that the actual content of my revelation would be more likely to have me excommunicated or burned. Ollivier told me about your encounter with Gilles de Rais and his account of the tragedy of Jeanne d'Arc. The cases are not similar, but the tale carries a lesson nonetheless. Will you hear my confession, Brother Primael, even though I warn you in advance that you will not be able to grant me absolution?"

"You must know, my Lady," said Primael, "that I cannot refuse to hear a confession, and I cannot believe that there is an unforgivable sin."

"I do know that," Beatriz de Tardivel admitted, "and I shall take advantage of it, if I may. But in so doing, for my own egotistical benefit, I cannot help feeling certain anxieties. Are you fully convinced that I am not responsible for the illness afflicting my daughter?"

"Absolutely convinced of it," said Primael, without hesitation.

"Or for my son's...eccentricity, whether he is deluded or not?"

"That is not your fault," Primael said, firmly.

"Or for the manner of Brother Ollivier's death?"

He was in a frame of mind by now that permitted him to answer the question without the slightest hesitation. "Ollivier died because of an accident of circumstance," he said. "Neither you nor your son, nor anyone else here, has any responsibility for it."

"Let us hope that you are right, Brother Primael, and that hearing my revelation will not expose you to any danger...or, at least, to any more danger than accidents of circumstance have already gathered around you. I will not ask you to bless me, Father, because, although I have certainly sinned repeatedly in my life, it is not my sins that I want to confess to you, but the substance of my revelation. You say that you are already familiar with the name Semiaza?"

"The name is allegedly attributed by certain documentary accounts of the war in Heaven to the leader of the rebel angels who were cast out of Heaven by God," Primael said, carefully, "but I have not seen any of the documents in question, and have only heard a second-hand account from a dubious source."

"I have only heard second-hand accounts of the early phases of the war myself," said Beatrix de Tardivel, softly, "but I believe the source to be entirely reliable. There is a war in Heaven, Brother Primael, and it is not over. Victory has been claimed more than once, and peace treaties made, but you know enough of history, I think, to know that no war is ever settled by treaties, which are merely postponements, or by claims of victory, which are temporary assertions."

"Recent history does suggest that," Primael agreed, "but ancient legend suggests, and present absences confirm, that the losers in many past wars have been so completely obliterated that hardly a vestige of memory or myth remains."

"But that is not the case with the war in Heaven," the chatelaine pointed out.

"That's true," Primael conceded. "If we accept the claim that Satan—Semiaza, if you wish—and the rebel angels were chained in Hell, we must also accept the corollary claim that they are exceedingly unquiet in their captivity, continuing their aggression by other means than armed combat, against humankind if not against the Heavenly host. That war, it seems, will last until the Day of the Resurrection."

"Longer than that, if any such day ever comes," said Beatriz de Tardivel. "Tell me, Brother Primael, where do you think the Hell is located to which Semiaza and his rebel angels were supposedly confined?"

"Tradition places it is an underworld within the globe of the earth, while Heaven is placed above, in the Empyrean, but that might be a symbolic manner of speaking. Dante's *Comedy* is a magnificent dream, but not, I think, something to be taken too literally."

"Where then, is Hell, if not in the center of the earth—and where is Purgatory, if not an island in the vast ocean that extends between China and Portugal?"

"I don't know," said Primael, but he remembered the strategy that Ollivier had apparently used in conversations with Aidrena, and presumably with Beatriz too. "If Ollivier were here, I think he might make the suggestion that Hell is a state of the soul rather than a physical location, and that in all probability, the part of us that survives after the death of the physical envelope cannot be assigned to a physical location in the space we know, any more than it can be credited with a material existence, however tenuous. He might suggest that it is unhelpful, philosophically and theologically, for us to continue thinking in crude analogical terms, and that the question 'Where is Hell?' cannot be answered by pointing to a location in space."

"That is exactly what he did say, almost word for word," said the chatelaine. "I already knew that. What I want to know now is what you think."

"I wish I could give you a definite answer," said Primael. "I certainly have no better one. Philosophy has not given me one, and I have not had the privilege of any revelation."

"And if you had, you would doubt it—or at least, you would like to have the liberty to doubt it, and to wonder whether you might simply be the victim of a delusion, perhaps born of frustrated desire or perverted lust. Ollivier said that too; you sound eerily like him, although I suppose that is only natural, since you have been in such close company for most of your lives. But revelation does not come with that liberty; it does not retain the luxury of doubt. It is either truth, or madness. And by those alternatives, I do not mean that it comes from God or the Devil, because the Truth—if I am not simply mad—is that God is a liar."

"The Devil is said to be the Father of Lies," said Primael, mildly.

"I am making no apology for Semiaza. He is a liar too; perhaps he is evil. But the biggest lie of all is that God is good.

God—which is to say, the God of Scripture, whom the Jews call Yahweh or Jehovah—and Semiaza have been at war for a long time, and the first weapons deployed in war on either side are always lies. The swords and cannons only follow. And the supposed end of a war is always a lie too. Judgment is a lie. The promise of resurrection is a lie. Heaven, above all, is a lie. Hell is also a lie, in terms of its description, but there is certainly a reality to which the idea refers. Do you believe that, Brother Primael: that there *is* a real Hell, although the image that preachers offer us of a fiery Underworld is a lie?"

"Yes," said Primael, uncomfortably aware that he was speaking the truth, and not exaggerating. "I do believe in Hell. But I also believe in salvation. I believe that damnation can be avoided, and souls saved. Hell is not a place in the center of the earth to which the soul might or might not go, but a state of the soul, but it is a state that the soul might or might not inherit when life ends...and judgment is not a lie, because the end of a life is indeed a moment of judgment, when the complex sum of moral attainment and moral failure can no longer be altered or recalculated, and the account calculated."

He realized, as he finished speaking, that it was not a speech drawn from scripture or scholarship, however esoteric, any more than it had been generated by means of the imaginative sidestep of constructing in his own mind what Ollivier might have said. It had come from a deeper stratum of his soul than that. That disturbed him slightly although he did not know why. The turbulence that he and others had sensed as if it were in the atmosphere of the forest, he realized, was not in the air but in themselves, in their souls: an unease provoking visions that were doubtless idiosyncratic and personal, but also had something in common, something binding the participants in this folly together. But the trees really had stirred.

Was it really a some*thing?* he wondered. Might it not be a some*one*: Ollivier. Might it not be Ollivier the necromancer, the would-be commander of the dead, now dead himself? Was it possible that Ollivier's incessant repetition of incantations in the last days of his life had not been entirely a product of delirium, but a purpose endeavor, an attempt to defy death in some strange fashion? Was it conceivable that a necromancer could summon himself—or, if Genovela's way of looking at things were correct, open the way for his own return?

The frisson that surged along his spine almost drew a gasp from him, but he made himself rigid. But he did not have time to debate such questions with himself now. He owed his full attention to his hostess, whose confession he had consented to hear, as he was obliged to do.

"Is something wrong, Brother?" asked Beatriz de Tardivel, with sudden concern. "Do you feel unwell?"

The thought occurred to Primael that she might have mistaken the sudden stiffening of his body in response to his nervous twinge as a symptom akin to her own, that she was anxious that he might have an epileptic fit.

"I have a slight arthritis," he said. "Riding a mule for two days has disturbed it, and I had a twinge of pain."

"We are poor hosts," she said, apologetically. "We should have allowed you to rest, instead of yielding to our impatience."

"Not at all," said Primael. "I am quite comfortable now, and I have always found discussion and debate a useful distraction. It is when I am alone and inactive that I am most vulnerable to the distress of the condition. If Hell is within us and not in the center of the earth, then we take it with us wherever we go, eternally, but while we are alive, at least, we have the privilege of looking outwards, of not living in its confinement. Please continue with your…consultation."

The chatelaine leaned forward in her armchair, with genuine concern. But what he had said to her before his nervous shock had added fuel for thought to her own monologue, and her confession had not lost its impetus by virtue of such a sight interruption. After a pause, she resumed speaking, but her initial uncertainty had returned.

"You cannot believe in my revelation, I know, Brother Primael, because your faith and your Scripture forbid it, and you are a victim of the tyranny of the word. I would not wish upon you the alarm of a revelation of your own that would shatter that faith. But believe me, please, when I say that I am incapable of denying the substance of my own vision. I repeat that I am not asking you for absolution, or even for your sympathy and compassion, but I would like your understanding, to the extent that you can grant it. I would like you to hear me, as Ollivier condescended to do—and I sincerely hope, for my sake as well as yours, that you are the man of God that Ollivier believed you to be, and that hearing me cannot lead you to damnation."

The chatelaine paused, waiting for a reaction, or permission to continue.

"I will hear anything you wish to say to me, my lady," Primael assured her, "and I will do my utmost to understand it. I do not believe that hearing you can lead me to damnation. Nor do I believe that hearing you had anything to do with Ollivier's disease and death."

"Good," she said, and relaxed again in her armchair. Until he saw her relax, visibly, Primael had not been fully aware of how tense she had suddenly become, but as soon as he realized it, he became anxious, He had been asked to try to ensure that Beatriz did not have a fit, if he could; he had no idea what preventative measures could be taken against that, if any, but he had a sudden suspicion that she might not be doing herself any good by talking as she was—that if her convulsions produced her visions, it might not be improbable that rehearsing her visions, in speech or imagination, might encourage convulsions.

"Perhaps you should make your explanation more gradually," he suggested. "There is no urgency, and I shall be here for some time."

"Do you think so, Brother Primael?" she said. "That there is no urgency, I mean? I fear that there might be—that the war might be closer at hand than you think."

That was a conclusion that Primael had already reached, but which he tried, automatically, to deflect. "The French forces are many leagues away," he said, "and there is no reason to think that they will attack Herbriant." He realized, however, that the deliberate misconstruction was far too obvious, and added, apologetically: "But that is not the war you mean, of course."

"Of course not," she said.

"But who are the armies of the war against God?" Primael wondered, aloud. "Angels? Demons? The incubus and the succubus? The Dames Blanches? The Marie-Mortes? Idols all—images that we contrive in the attempt to bring order to the chaos of our inner experience, but which we cannot entirely control, and which lay siege to the citadel of consciousness..."

Tempted to let himself drift away into the labyrinth of metaphors, he caught himself up, and said: "But it is all the substance of dreams, and we must remember that. We should not give it too much weight in our waking existence."

"That is easier said than done, Brother Primael," the chatelaine said. "My late husband would have agreed with you. The power of the will, he would have insisted, is able to dispel such phantoms, if we can only muster the courage. But his defiance crumbled, in the end. The assaults of the war begin in sleep, in dreams, but once they have opened breaches in the walls of consciousness..."

Primael could not help feeling a slight chill at that. He moved his hand slightly, sketching the gesture of a cross. It did not go unnoticed, but the chatelaine made no comment. Instead, she said: "Shall I begin at the beginning? The visions did not, alas, and recounting them in order of their initial presentation would seem quite incoherent. And your beginning was, and is, the Word, and the Word is a Lie. God did not create the world in six days; indeed, God did not create the world at all, although he certainly made his creative contribution to its development, at least in the tiny corner we call the earth. Some call that bringing order out of chaos, but I have been told that there is as much chaos in the world as there was before, and greater complexity. Perhaps Yahweh did create, or at least shape, humankind, but not as a single couple in a garden, with a forbidden tree whose fruits were the knowledge of good and evil.

"In brief, there was a world before this one, before God's intervention, and relics of it still exist, and remain active. Semiaza and the egregori were offspring of Yahweh's reckless Creation, and the nephilim are their offspring, but they are not the only strangers haunting the landscapes of the worlds that exist within the soul, far away but close at hand. The Marie-Mortes, at least, are older than God, and only mimic the forms of his creations. As to where they figure in the war, I dare say that even God does not know, and...but you are not sitting comfortably at all, Brother. You are right, of course. You will be here for some time, and I ought not to let my impatience distract me from my duties as a hostess."

"It's true," Primael conceded, that I am not entirely comfortable, but the fault is entirely mine, my lady, and that of my old age. The journey has sapped my strength more than I had expected, and since I arrived in the forest..."

He stopped, lost in the maze, not knowing which way to turn.

"Something has happened?" Beatriz de Tardivel guessed. "Don't deny it, Brother...Corentin has done you no favor in bringing you here. Tell me, please, what you have seen. Perhaps I am better able to interpret it than you are, for the moment."

Perhaps you are, thought Primael, seeing more menace than hope in the possibility. He thought hard about how to answer the request, but he knew that he could not think for long without providing an answer of some sort.

After a few seconds, he said: "I had a strange dream last night, in the forest."

"Ah," said his hostess, with more than a hint of satisfaction. "Yes, the forest is conducive to strange dreams. And you dreamed that you saw a ghost?"

"Yes, among other things," Primael admitted, feeling trapped by his own honesty.

"You saw Ollivier?" She was already beginning to interpret his dream, or what she imagined he had dreamed.

"No," said Primael, spurred by honesty, "not Ollivier."

Unsurprisingly, Beatriz was not content to leave it at that. "Who, then?" she demanded. Suddenly, she was an aristocrat, exerting her authority in her own domain. She had set out playing the penitent, but now she was playing the confessor.

Primael could not think of any reason not to tell the truth, although he had an awful feeling that there was danger in so doing.

"Gilles de Rais," he said

"*Gilles de Rais?*" the chatelaine repeated, with an emphasis that he could not evaluate, although it was not merely surprise. After a brief pause, she asked him, in a neutral tone: "Do you know what he is?"

"I believe that he was innocent of the charges laid against him," Primal said, with a familiar surge of defiance. "I knew that before he told me so in the dream. I believe, and always have, that he was a true scholar."

"And in your ingenuous heart, you assume that because he was a scholar, and not a murderer of little children, he must be a good man?" The chatelaine did not seem to intend any mockery by that observation; it was merely a deduction. Curiosity now had Beatriz securely in its claw: "Where did you see him—in the dream, that is?"

"Beside an isolated menhir, which had an inscription on it in blue dye, in an unknown language."

"The signpost," said Beatriz. "Yes, of course. I seem to have made a mistake, Brother Primael. I'm sorry...I had no idea...yes, I seem to have made an error. Ollivier told me..."

She stopped, and raised her right hand, palm down, holding it horizontal with the thumb pointing at her throat, looking down at it as if it were about to betray her...as, in fact, it was. It began to shake, convulsively.

The claw that seized Primael then was not curiosity but dread.

"Brother Primael," said Beatriz de Tardivel, in a commanding tone. "Please take that hand-bell from the mantelpiece and ring it vigorously. Then go, I beg you. I do not want you to witness what is about to happen. If you meet my son, prevent him from coming in. Rozina knows what to do, and she will have all the help she needs. Everyone knows. Do it *now!*"

Primael stood up like a devil-in-a-box, grabbed the small hand-bell from the mantelpiece and shook it vigorously. The inner door of the drawing room opened immediately, and a woman, who must have been waiting beyond it in case of such a signal, bounded across the room. She was approximately the same age as her mistress, and similar in build, but her hair was black, her complexion pale and her eyes green. Primael stared at her, searching for the slightest resemblance to his own features, and trying hard to remember another set of features, which he had forgotten many years ago, and of which no trace remained.

He was nailed to the spot momentarily, and the chambermaid did not pay him the slightest attention as she bent over her mistress. Two men grabbed Primael from behind, though, and pulled him toward the door with a force utterly unbecoming their station and his dignity. But they knew what they were doing. They were following orders.

He did not put up the slightest resistance as they bundled him out of the entrance door of the apartment, and then slammed the door shut behind him.

IX

Primael had only taken two dazed steps on the staircase before he met Corentin, bounding upwards.

Without even thinking about it, he obeyed the instruction he had been given, and put his arms around the young man, in order to stop him going into his mother's apartment.

Had there been a struggle, the older man would have come off far worse, but Corentin seemed to be well aware of the commission that Primael had been given. He did not try to knock him down and climb over him. Instead he merely looked at him, a trifle reproachfully. There was a narrow window in the stairwell, level with Corentin's head, and the rays of the setting sun were shining through it horizontally. Corentin's face seemed flushed with blood, and Primael knew that his own face must have the same dread aspect to the younger man's gaze.

"I'm sorry," the Benedictine said. "It's my fault."

"No Brother, it isn't," said the chatelaine's son, freeing himself from Primael's grasp, and then moving the monk aside as Genovela, running up the stairs, pushed past them both. Before she opened the door that had been slammed in Primael's face a moment before, she turned to look at him, reproachfully. She, at least, had no intention of reassuring him that he was not to blame for bringing on the fit that the lady of the house did not want him or her son to witness.

Corentin began to pull Primael down the stairs, gently.

"Please don't tell Aidrena about the attack," he said. "She's feeling much better, and it would be a setback."

"She isn't a child," said Primael, without thinking about it. "She might not need as much protection as you feel that you ought to give her."

"Perhaps she isn't, and perhaps she doesn't," said Corentin, "but do you think that makes me feel any less need to give it to her? It's my role to be her brother, and yours to be objective, to treat her as an adult and help her to feel like one. That will probably do her more good than any potions you concoct—but for now, please, leave her be. She can't hear the bell from her room. Come to mine—I've been waiting all day for a chance to speak to you seriously, but there is a precedence that has to be observed, even in the home...especially in the home. There are things I need to tell you, and it was too difficult on the road."

Primael allowed himself to be led, without taking over-much notice of the route they followed through corridors that were already becoming gloomy, although the sun had not yet dipped below the horizon. The windows were narrow, and the inner courtyard of the house was in deep shadow. He barely glanced at a brief gallery in which the traditional hunting trophies and panoplies were beginning to make room for ancestral portraits, which had an upright suit of armor at one end that gave the impression of having been designed for an exceedingly short man, although its pieces had probably been considerably spaced out when they had been attached to a living body, if they ever had.

Corentin closed the door of a sitting-room very similar to the one in which Primael had just been received—which might well have been its mirror image on the other side of the manse. Corentin sat his guest down in an armchair, and then struck a light and ignited a taper, with which he carefully and methodically lit eight candles held in two candelabra. The windows of the room did not overlook the inner courtyard, but they were facing eastwards, and the sky was already darkening in that direction; before sitting down, Primael had caught a momentary glimpse of the crowns of tall trees forming a surface that stretched away into the distance like a dark unruly sea, beneath a sheer drop eight or ten times the height of a man.

"It really isn't your fault," Corentin assured him, handing his guest a cup of dark wine, which he had poured for him without asking. "I should have warned you that it was likely to happen, but she was so insistent on seeing you. Don't worry about her, please. Rozina knows exactly what to do, and

Genovela will take charge. The two sturdy lads who threw you out will give her all the help she needs."

Mention of Rozina made Primael try again to picture the chambermaid's features and to search the image for resemblances, but he had already lost it, in spite of the attention he had paid to it.

But it doesn't matter, he told himself, sternly. *It was only a dream, a conjuration of my own imagination. I have no daughter. I'm a man of God.* He tried to put out of his mind the memory of the chatelaine's blasphemy in saying that God was a liar, but his conversation with Beatriz de Tardivel had thrown his thoughts into such confusion that he could not pull them together, for the moment. He took a long sip from his cup, and the alcohol caught in his throat, causing him to cough.

He could not help remembering, though, that when he had mentioned the menhir in his dream, Beatriz de Tardivel had immediately said: "The signpost," which was exactly what the Marie-Morte had called it. How could it have been a pure product of his own imagination, if the visionary had recognized a key feature of it which had no reference point in his personal history or knowledge?

Ollivier, he thought. Ollivier is dead, but not at rest. He really was, and is, a necromancer. Corentin wants to raise his spirit, but his spirit is already here, in me, in the chatelaine, in the forest, everywhere and nowhere, close at hand and far away. All that Corentin can do with the incantations that have already been drummed into my mind is to give him a voice, and a more forceful touch... and that might not be wise, given that he is in Hell, and was in Hell even before he died, already subject to judgment... but not God's judgment. Oliver was a good man, and God is merciful. He judged himself, and has judged himself too harshly...

"Are you feeling better?" Corentin asked. Primael handed his empty cup to the younger man, who set it down on a table, where several sheets of paper were scattered: modern paper, not traditional parchment, but good bleached and varnished paper, intended for writing, for holding the imprint of good black ink in a legible manner, amenable to being scrolled or bound.

"Much better," said Primael, politeness prevailing over accuracy. "I'm sorry."

"You have nothing for which to apologize," Corentin assured him, politeness collaborating with accuracy in that instance. "Mother should have known that it was foolish to insist on seeing you right away, that both of you needed to rest, and to sleep, in order to recover an appropriate calm of mind. I'm at fault for not having forbidden it—but you will understand that, although I am the Vicomte and head of the household, my authority over my mother is far from easy to exert."

"Of course," said Primael.

"She'll recover," Corentin added, with more than a hint of his mother's bluntness. "How far did she get in detailing her visions?"

"In the beginning was the Word," Primael quoted, "and the Word is a Lie. There was more, but it was rather incoherent. The war in Heaven is still going on, between Yahweh and Semiaza, and its turbulence is close at hand. We're all in danger, it seems, but what form the danger might take, I can't quite grasp." He suddenly remembered that what he had been told had been explicitly placed under the seal of the confessional, and realized that he had just committed a terrible sin, having made the assumption that Corentin already knew everything he had just voiced, although that might not be the case. Lamely, and defensively, he added: "You must know the story much better than I do."

"Alas, no," said Corentin. "That much, to be sure, and a little more, but even that has been largely obtained second-hand. Aidrena isn't the only one that my mother tries to protect. So far as I know, the only people who have heard an elaborate account of her visions are Ollivier and Rozina—and Ollivier is dead, while getting information out of Rozina, although not impossible, is like pulling teeth. Doubtless, though, you'll hear the rest of it, if you're here for any length of time.

Whether you'll be able to make any sense of it, of course, is a different matter. I'd like to think that you might. I'd like to think that there is a rationale of sorts in the visions, as well as her attitude to them. She *is* reasonable, is she not? At the very least, she has a rational attitude to her own madness, even admitting that it might be no more than that. The fact that they cannot be a true revelation does not make them madness, if they are only dreams, and would not even make them blasphemous, but for the difficulty she has in not lending credence to them."

"There are certainly strange aspects to her account, which one would not expect of simple irrationality," Primael agreed, "but she is by no means the first person to imagine, after considering the world and its manifest evils, that God cannot be both omnipotent and omnibenevolent. Nor is it original to think that good and evil deities of approximately equal power must be engaged in a ceaseless battle that echoes through creation. Is that not the very foundation of the religion of Zoroaster, and the heresy of Mani?"

"Is it?" Corentin countered. "You would know far better than I."

"I'm sorry," said Primael. "I wasn't really asking you a question, just thinking aloud."

"What I do know," said Corentin, "is that many people still believe, as many always have, that the kind of convulsions from which my mother suffers are symptoms of diabolical possession, and that she is in need of exorcism rather than medical attention. I'm told that my father tried it once, bringing a supposedly-expert abbé all the way from Rennes. Needless to say, it didn't work, for which the exorcist initially blamed my mother. My father threw him out, so the story goes—not bodily, of course, although I doubt that he was excessively polite about it."

"You heard that from Rozina?" Primael ventured.

"Yes. She's been with my mother since before her marriage. I don't know what we'd have done without her. She's utterly devoted to Mother—worth her weight in gold."

"Did Ollivier talk to her?"

"Of course, but I don't think he got much out of her. She's taciturn, as I say, and not very trusting. Even Genovela can't get much out of her, although Rozina seems to be appreciative of the help that Genovela has tried to give my mother."

"Does Rozina have a family?"

"Not any more. I believe that her father died when she was very young, and her mother not long after she went into service with Mother."

"I'll talk to her, when I can."

He remembered then, sharply, that when he had mentioned Gilles de Rais, Beatriz had seemed startled and has asked him if he knew *what he was*, as if it were something terrible, or at least exotic. When he had told her that he believed him to be innocent of the charges laid against him, she had not contradicted him, but he had had the distinct impression that she seemed to have something else against him. He wondered whether he could obtain some enlightenment regarding that without breaking the secrecy of the confessional any more than he already had, and decided that there might be a way.

"Has Rozina ever mentioned Gilles de Rais to you?" he asked.

"Yes, she cited him as a necromancer, when muttering dark warnings regarding the danger of my experiments. Ollivier also thought that Gilles practiced necromancy, with the aid of the manuscripts of which I now have in my possession, but he didn't believe that his necromancy involved child-murder or Satanic worship. Rozina heard the legend of Gilles de Rais, obviously, when she was a child. Mother was in his presence more than once, I believe—he was a friend of the family before the scandal—but only as a little child, and she has no memory of him. After his death, of course, the family tried to distance themselves from him, ostentatiously. Rozina's parents probably told her things about him that were exceedingly uncomplimentary, which Mother might have endorsed, but Mother doesn't talk about him—not to me, at any rate, although perhaps she did to Ollivier. Ask Rozina. On the other hand..."

"What other hand?" Primael queried, when the pause went on. Corentin was frowning, as if trying to sort ideas out in his own mind.

The pause extended a little further before Corentin said, abruptly: "Did my mother mention the nephilim?"

Not wanting to answer the question, Primael simply said: "Do they feature in her visions?"

"I'm sure of it; Ollivier seemed to think that they played an important part in her delusions, and Rozina mutters the word with a certain anxious reverence. I know that an enigmatic passage in *Genesis* says that the *nephilim*, usually translated as *giants*, were the offspring of the sons of God—presumably angels, fallen or otherwise—and daughters of men. Ollivier told me that they were the offspring of *egregori*, or Watchers, a faction of Semiaza's defeated rebel angels...but not conclusively defeated, in Mother's vision. In her vision, the war is still going on, within our souls but also in the external world. The Watchers are still on earth, but hidden, and the nephilim too, similarly hidden, or disguised, living among us. It's possible, although I might be stretching inference too far, that Mother, and hence Rozina, think that Gilles de Rais was more than a necromancer..."

"A nephilim, you mean?"

"Perhaps...but you'll have to ask Rozina, or Mother. It will be easy for you to raise the subject with them, as you've met Gilles de Rais too. What did you think of him?"

"That he was a serious scholar. If he practiced, or attempted to practice, necromancy, it was in a spirit of enquiry. I believe that he was innocent of the charges against him, and that even his supposed confession might be a lie, concocted for the benefit of his accusers. But I'm sure he was as human as you or I, no kind of supernatural being..."

The assertion died in uncertainty, as he thought about the visitation in his dream. But that had simply been a dream, had it not? If the dream had been stimulated by any alien presence in his soul, it was surely Ollivier's, not that of Gilles de Rais.

Corentin had evidently noticed the fashion in which his guest's voice had tailed off. "You've had a hard day, one way and another, Brother Primael. We've imposed too much on you too rapidly. I always intended to defer my plans until tomorrow, when you've had time to recover, but if you're not too weary, I'd like to show you the manuscripts, if I may—the ones from which Ollivier and I derived the formula of conjuration, that is. You've seen the *Clavicula* and other grimoires, I know, but I'm not sure that Ollivier ever showed you the other documents, even though he probably acquired them in Granada, while you were with him."

"Probably?" Primael queried. "You don't know?" He turned toward the papers on the table, but Corentin said: "No, those are just the papers that Ollivier left with Brother Michael for me. You can take those with you, if you wish. They're not very helpful, I fear, or even very coherent. He was obviously very ill when he wrote the commentary notes, or tried to write them. Read them when you can, and tell me what you think. The crucial documents are over here."

As he spoke, Corentin went to a chest that was on the floor in an alcove, half-hidden by a curtain and partly covered by a sheet of blue velvet. He opened the curtain fully, removed the blue velvet and lifted the lid of the chest. It was difficult to be sure from the oblique angle at which Primael was gazing, but there seemed to be at least a dozen manuscripts in the chest, some of considerable volume. The two he took out were relatively small sheaves of vellum, carefully scrolled. They did not seem unusually delicate, or ancient.

Corentin gathered the papers on the table together and out them to one side, while he placed the two documents in front of a chair, on which he invited Primael to sit. When the monk had taken his place, he unfurled the first of them and weighted the corners with polished pebbles placed on the table for that purpose. Almost immediately, he said: "But this is Ollivier's handwriting."

147

"Of course," said Corentin. "It's a copy, evidently, and almost certainly made from a copy itself. Some of the Latin translation might be his; you'd be a better judge of that than I am. The other contains the actual incantations, rendered phonetically. They look like gibberish at first glance, but the formulae have power. I can attest to that."

Primael unrolled the second scroll of vellum. Corentin was right; at first glance, the characters on the sheet, in groups that were carefully spaced out, seemed quite meaningless, the words they formed not being recognizable as Latin, Breton, French or English. Primael read them, pronouncing them silently in his mind and moving his lips, but not making any sound. As he did so, he felt a strange sensation in his mind, a stir that was both familiar and unfamiliar. It was familiar, of course, because he had head Ollivier pronouncing them, over and over, in the final phase of his illness, but it was also different, and new, as if the words were being pronounced in the echo-chamber of his mind not by Ollivier's voice, or his own, but by a multitude of voices, each one imperceptible in itself but whose sum was massive: the whisper of the multitudinous dead, who had no common language, but whose memories, restricted by the physical capability of the larynx and the tongue could only contrive pronunciations of a limited range.

More turbulence, he thought—but the sensation was not in the least suggestive of a wind, or any kind of commonplace physical agitation; it was more reminiscent of an echo of his own unvoiced whisper, recurring to infinity, but very intimate as well as very remote, as if in depths of his being and coverts of his soul of whose existence he had not been aware before.

Whatever is happening to me, he said to himself, *originates within me. The origin of my particular turbulence is my own soul, and if there is any foreign intrusion it comes from me, not from Ollivier, who was my friend, my brother and who is dead. It is nothing to do with a war in Heaven, a conflict between God and Semiaza, any more than it is to do with the contest between the heirs of Louis XI and the successors of Duc François. My dream was the product of my own subcon-*

148

scious mind, not an authentic visitation from Gilles de Rais and a Marie-Morte. The same is true of all the other manifestations: Corentin's Katarin, Madame de Tardivel's visions, and Aidrena's dreams. The Lady's epilepsy and Aidrena's physical weakness are spurs to hallucination, just as Corentin's frustrated lust and my developing arthritis and the other symptoms of old age are spurs, provoking the source of dreams within the soul to produce strange imaginations. There is nothing supernatural in it, let alone demonic. If there are coincidences between the images, they're explicable in terms of common stocks of images from which the raw material of the dreams is drawn...and the influence that Ollivier had upon our thoughts and ideas while he was alive. If he is not entirely dead, it is only within our memories that he remains an active force.

But he was not convinced by his arguments—not entirely, at any rate.

Primael put the incantations aside, deliberately, and began to read the other document, which was partly a commentary upon them and partly a manual of instructions detailing the circumstance in which the invocation would be most effective, and the consequent manifestation more powerful. The commentary was gnomic, the instructions somewhat vague. His mind reacted reflexively against them, refusing momentarily to take them in, to confront their implications, real or imaginary.

But even if no demons are involved, Primael said to himself, continuing his private monologue defiantly, as if responding to a challenge, *prayer is a defense against the harm these visions can do. Prayer gives us a anchorage within the faith, a direct link to God's protection, but even if it isn't able to do that fully, because each of us, one way or another, lacks the faith required to forge that link and secure that anchorage, prayer can still be useful, as ritual and repetition, as calming words...unlike those sinister non-words, which are anything but calming, even though they have no evident meaning, and might perhaps defy and undermine meaning.*

It was, he thought, a fine sermon. He was proud of his own practiced eloquence. But was it convincing? Could he believe it? Was he still capable of defensive prayer?

When he had finished scanning the second document, in a deliberately cursory manner, he returned his attention to the formulae of the incantation, but as soon as his eyes fell upon it and his mind began to pronounce the meaningless vocables, the turbulence returned to his inner being and he shied away.

"I'm too tired," he said, aloud. "I can't concentrate." Both statements were true, but they were a feeble pretext; he felt that he was being deliberately deceptive, and not merely in order to offer a polite apology to Corentin.

He pushed away the sheet of vellum on which the formulae of necromantic summoning were written, freeing the corners from the weights, and the sheet rolled up again of its own accord. But the words that he had pronounced silently were still in his mind. Already, he could not remember them, but he knew that they were there. He felt that, at the right moment and in the right circumstances, he would be able to reconstitute them, and perhaps not only the syllables that he had spelled out in his mind, but others as yet unpronounced.

Am I a necromancer already? he wondered. *Has Ollivier's long protection come to nothing? How many years did he hide this document from me? Why? Does any of this make sense?*

No, plainly, it did not...and he had a dire suspicion that it never would.

But why should it? he thought. *Why should the unknown—the unknowable—owe any responsibility to the scope of feeble human intellect? Is it not entitled to mock us, sarcastically, when we to grapple with what is, almost by definition, beyond our comprehension: the metaphysical and the metapsychical.*

Instead of sitting back in his chair or taking his leave, however, as his assertion of tiredness and inability to concentrate had licensed him to do, he returned his attention to the other document, more intently than before. This time, he read it, carefully, from beginning to end, spelling out every word, trying as he did so to make sense of the practical instructions detailing the fashion in which the formulae contained in the closed document should be recited.

Corentin was content to watch him, to study him while he studied the documents, curious to judge the series of his reactions.

The instructions made no reference to the sacred pentacle of which other magical formulae had read made much, and did not specify any animal sacrifice, although there did seem to be a reference to a snake, and to a seal of intent made in blood—an embellishment that Corentin had already told him that he deemed superfluous, once the initial summoning was complete. The document emphasized that recitation of the formulae was not sufficient in itself to enable the conjuration to take full effect; for that, it had to be performed in a particular place. Where that place was, the document did not specify, but only used the words *officium* and *coniciet*, which were not easy to construe, meaning little more than "the assigned place of the ceremony," without any real indication of how any such place might be identified.

Eventually, Primael looked up at Corentin, who was still waiting patiently for him to finish. "You said there was more," he recalled. "You said that Ollivier couldn't make productive use of the formulae until he had combined what the documents instructed you to do with traditions native to Herbriant. That's how he was able to identify the assigned place of the ritual?"

"That's right," said Corentin, with an affirmative nod emphasized by satisfaction.

"In the forest?" Primael deduced.

"That's right. At the signpost."

Primael's arthritic spine twinged again, although he had already jumped ahead to the conclusion. "The signpost?" he queried.

"It's a rock," the young man explained, "in a grove of ancient oaks, like the grove in which legend claims that Viviane imprisoned Merlin. The forest-dwellers also call it the

Druid stone, probably because the trees are infested with mistletoe, but it doesn't seem to kill them, given that they've grown so old in company with the disease. There are other plants growing around the stone, in a clearing of sorts, almost as if there was once a kind of garden there."

"Are there symbols on the stone?" Primael asked.

"No," said Corentin. "It's just a stone, standing upright: a menhir."

Primael looked back at the manuscript that Ollivier had copied from one acquired in Granada—specifically, at the words *aspis hierosolyma*: asp of the house of peace, or asp of Jerusalem. He had assumed, at first glance, that they referred to a snake, but he remembered now that "Asp of Jerusalem" was also one of the common names of an Asiatic plant once extensively cultivated throughout Gaul because it was a commercially significant source of a blue dye, also known by the Saxon name of woad. The Gaulish Druids were said to have venerated oak trees and mistletoe, and to have daubed their bodies with woad in their religious rituals. According to legend, they had also anointed themselves with the dye when they went into battle, as a symbol of the protection of the gods.

"Will you show me this signpost?" he asked.

"Of course. That's where we'll try to summon Ollivier's spirit, as he and I first summoned Katarin's—or, at least, first enabled her spirit to become fully manifest. I would have shown it to you this morning, if I hadn't been in such a hurry to get home. Wise women from all over Europe are said to make pilgrimages of a sort to it, but Genovela won't say anything about that—secrets of the sisterhood."

"You want me to witness you using these devices in that place, to summon Ollivier's spirit?" Primael said, insistent on the clarification. "Tomorrow night?"

"Yes," said Corentin. "As you can see, the document doesn't specify midnight, or any particular phase of the moon, but tradition is eloquent on that matter, and the experimentation that Ollivier and I have carried out certainly suggests that darkness is conducive to the advent of spirits; Katarin only comes by night."

Primael bit his lip. After a pause he said: "And after you've summoned Ollivier, and proved your power? What then?"

"I don't know. Perhaps you should choose our next summoning. Gilles de Rais, perhaps? Conan Meriadoc? The wizard Merlin? Count Geoffroy? The prophet Samuel? Jesus?"

Primael let the younger man run the list on, trying to measure the extent of his defensive flippancy. Corentin probably did not know himself how he might, or ought, to continue his necromantic endeavors. "Your father?" he suggested, sarcastically, when the young man paused expectantly.

"No," said Corentin. "Not my father. Yours, perhaps? Urbain Quermerle, I believe?"

"If your sister is right," Primael observed, "and your Katarin is a succubus, perhaps we'd do better to summon Viviane than Merlin, or the *pythonem* of Endor rather than Samuel." *Or Rozina's mother*, he added, silently.

"If my sister's interpretation is correct," countered Corentin, "she and Mother have both been visited by the incubus. I do not know what form he takes in my sister's dreams, but I suspect that he is Semiaza himself in my Mother's. Would Yahweh answer your call, do you think, if you attempted to exert the tyranny of the Word upon him?

Probably not, Primael thought—but that was not the aspect of Corentin's speech to which he chose to respond. "You suspect your mother of having imaginary sexual intercourse with the Devil?" he queried, wondering why he was not more shocked and repelled.

"I know that she had actual sexual intercourse with my father," the young man countered, "twice, at least. And if Rozina's account of Mother's convictions can be believed, she does not consider Semiaza to be the Church's ugly, cloven-hoofed Devil, but a rebel angel with a just cause, more akin to a hero of Norman romance than the demon of the Sabbat:

Lancelot du Lac to her Guenever. Perhaps her dreams are pleasant and joyful—more so, at any rate, than the brute reality of her marriage…although my sister might be able to conjure up a rosier picture of the latter in her own mind than I can in mine. I can hardly ask my mother, of course, and I doubt if she took her confession that far when conversing with Ollivier. Are you not fortunate, Father, to be above the reach of such perverse temptations, just as he was?"

"Indeed," said Primael, dryly. "Perhaps, after all, we should leave your sister's thesis aside, for the moment. If we are to experiment at all, I agree that it would be tempting to commence with an attempt to summon Ollivier's spirit…but I am not at all sure that Genovela is mistaken in thinking this kind of experimentation dangerous. I need to conducted further study, and devote further thought to the matter."

"Exactly what Ollivier said," Corentin told him, "and exactly what he did. But I have conducted further study, albeit not in words scrawled by the ignorant on rotting parchment, and I have devoted further thought to it. I need to summon Ollivier's spirit, and I shall. If you will help me, as a witness, I am certain that I shall succeed—and that you will then consent to take his place fully, with regard to Aidrena, Mother and myself."

And that is it, Primael thought. *That is the answer to the question I posed myself: 'Why am I here and where am I going?' But it does not help to answer the other question that I combined with it: 'What must I do when I arrive?' On the other hand, do I really have a choice? Am I not completely committed, whether I approve or not? Am I not possessed by Ollivier's spirit, already summoned and present in the depths of my soul?*

When he made no reply, Corentin continued: "When we have summoned Ollivier, in the full force of his apparition, he will be able to advise us as to the next step we ought to take, and he will lend us his support. For the three of us, united, there will be no obstacle that we cannot overcome. But you do not believe, as yet, that we will succeed, do you?"

"I honestly do not know," said Primael, who honestly did not. "I am out of my intellectual depth, in dire need of guidance, if any is available. If these papers really can enable you to summon Ollivier's spirit, it will, I admit, be a profound shock to me...but I cannot deny the possibility, or even the temptation.

"Until tomorrow night, then," said Corentin. "Unless you would like a demonstration tonight? We can reach the signpost in less than an hour, with a good lantern, but if you are too tired, I can invoke Katarin here and now. You will not be able to see her, but you will be able to hear her voice and feel her touch."

Primael did not even hesitate in order to weigh his apprehension against his curiosity. "Not now, if you please," he said. "It has, as you say, been a long day, taxing in several different ways. I am tired, and more than a little confused. A good night's sleep in the excellent bed you have kindly provided for me will do me the world of good, and prepare me for another challenging day tomorrow."

Am I such a dire coward, then? he asked himself. *Am I really not merely capable of refusing such an opportunity, but eager to do it? But what if he is right? What if he can produce Katarin's voice, other than by some trick of ventriloquy, and she can stroke my cheeks with her fingers, other than by a trick of suggestion. What then, dutiful man of God?*

"Do you regret that I brought you here?" Corentin asked him, bluntly.

"No," said Primael, politely. "I had no choice but to come, but had I had a choice, I would have come of my own accord, and I do not regret it. I suspect, now, that it might be dangerous, both physically and spiritually, but I do not regret it. There is much here that I need to discover, and not merely for the sake of intellectual curiosity."

"Good," said Corentin, and seemed genuinely relieved. "Very well; I'll take you back to your room, if you wish—the corridors can be confusing. But collect those papers on the table first—the ones that Brother Michael gave me. You'll doubtless find much in the texts familiar, but the marginal comments, incoherent as they are, might be of interest. You might be able to make more sense of them than I can."

Primael collected up the scattered papers. It would not take him long to read them; he was familiar with the handwriting.

A servant could have shown him back to his room, but Primael was not at all surprised that Corentin chose to escort him personally. They went through the portrait gallery again and this time Primael paused in order to take a longer look at the paintings. There were not many; it was only recently that the French had begun to elaborate the practice of making representations, and painters had began to refine the methods of producing accurate likenesses. The descendants of the Normans, of course, had adopted the new fashion with great eagerness, doubtless regretting that it had not been as common, or as ingenious, during the heyday of their favored ancestors, before the dilution of their blood. Unsurprisingly, the painting of Tardivel's masters looked more Norman than they had probably been.

"My father," Corentin said, identifying the most sophisticated of the images. "I considered burning it, but Aidrena would not approve, nor even my mother. The image does not bring out his brutality, but painters have been rapid to learn the art of flattery. Do you think that all the images in the Abbey, in the frescoes and the stained glass, are as false as these?"

"They are all imaginary," Primael replied. "Falsity does not come into it. No one has any idea what any of the apostles, or any of the saints, actually looked like."

"And the contents of the reliquaries?" Corentin asked, teasingly. "Is there no falsity there? I have heard it said that if all the fragments of the True Cross contained in the churches of Christendom were brought together, they would make a tree ten times as large as any living example, partaking of a dozen different species at once."

"I have heard the saying too," said Primael, "but it is merely a figure of speech. No one has tried the experiment." *It is just an aspect of a war of words*, he thought, *in which the truth is continually disguised. Whether God is a liar or not, one can hardly exempt the Church from the accusation, and the Order of Saint Benedict is certainly not without sin in that regard.*

He regretted having thought that, however; it did not seem to be an appropriate prelude to his evening prayer, nor to the succeeding sleep, which he hoped, in view of his real exhaustion, might be dreamless.

X

His hopes were disappointed. He was not surprised by that. Nor, on reflection, when he woke up to daylight, was he unduly regretful or dismayed, in spite of the fact that the experience had been uncomfortable. Even if it were completely false, he thought, and purely a provocative product of his own vindictive mind, it was not without a certain revelatory interest. Even if his dreams could only tell him more about his own confusions, and his own disguised self, that was real information; and it was information that it was good, and necessary, for him to have.

The revelation, if that is what it had been, had begun with a visit from the succubus. That could not surprise him, in view of the conversations he had had during the day and their provocative probing. It had not alarmed him, because, being well aware that he was dreaming, and not without experience in that kind of dream, he knew that he had long been incapable of nocturnal ejaculation. The visitation could not have a climax, no matter what feelings it stirred up. That aspect of the link between his body and his soul had atrophied, and knowledge of that dereliction liberated his intellect to study the phenomenon, to inquire as to what form the succubus might take, and to make what attempt he could to analyze the significance of her mask.

But he could not see the succubus at all. He could only feel it—he deliberately refrained from categorizing it as "her," although the imaginary friction he felt was certainly that of female flesh. The tactile hallucination seemed to go on for some time, albeit endlessly, before finally fading away. It was silent at first, as well as visually uninformative, and that was usual, but when it became obvious that there was no physical effect, it made itself heard.

"You do not believe in me," it said. "You can feel me, but you do not believe in me."

"You're not a person," he said. "You're a figment of my imagination, brought into delusory existence by the incantations of nostalgia, a symptom of an inability of the mind to forget completely, even though the body has."

"Sophistry," she said. "You know, in your heart, who I am. If you had interrogated your heart properly, you would have guessed who I am when I spoke to you before, beside the signpost."

"I don't know who you are," Primael insisted, "but I know who you're not. You're not the Katarin that Corentin offered slyly to summon before I fled his company."

"Even if I'm not," the succubus told him, "I know who killed her."

"You couldn't," Primael countered, feeling satisfaction again, even though he knew that he was only catching himself out in a paradox. "If you aren't her, you can't know who killed her, for we've already established that disembodied spirits don't have perfect knowledge of things, as certain Greeks once presumed."

"Sophistry," she said again. "You are, indeed, a true man of God, expert in lying to himself, in order to patch up rotten belief—but the task is hopeless now. You have lost your faith; there is nothing, any longer, to patch or darn. You are adrift in the unknowable, and prayer can no longer make you a raft. You should have let Corentin summon Katarin, so that you could hear at least some of the truth from her mouth."

"I could not have been convinced that any voice I heard was really hers," Primael said, with a slight sigh. "At the most, I might have been able to convince myself that I was hearing the voice of Corentin's delusion, just as I'm certain that I am now hearing the voice of my own."

"Imbecile," said the succubus. "You have already admitted that Ollivier is within you, and no matter how hard you try to excuse that by saying that you have long used to rhetorical device of imagining what Ollivier might think as a means of clarifying your own thoughts, you already know that he is far more present than that, and more forceful than that. He can stir the world as well as your soul. That is the way that necromancy works. The seeds that it nurtures and enables to grow is planted in the mind of those who knew and remember the person to be invoked, but once it has matured and flowered…as a lodestone extends invisible fingers around it capable of grasping iron, so a reincarnated soul can reach out from the depths of its host, not merely to grasp dreams, incite visions and sow panic, but to move physical objects."

"I will need proof of that," Primael said. "A slight rattle of foliage, as if stirred by a wind, will not be adequate, any more than arthritic twinges, prickling sensations and any other tricks of the nerves and tautening of the sinews."

"Be careful what you wish for," the succubus advised. "Very few prayers are granted, but even God occasionally stirs. He is not conscious of your petty desires, and would not care about them if he were, but sometimes, when stroked or poked in the right fashion, he reacts. The age of miracles is by no means over, it is simply that humans are incapable of recognizing miracles, and insist on maintaining the foolish optimism that they are benign. Miracles are an everyday evil, alas, and it is God who operates them, not Satan."

"That is not what Beatriz de Tardivel believes," Primael countered, long habit tempting him to score the argumentative point, or at least to try. "She believes the war between the forces contending for the throne of Heaven to be more evenly balanced, and that both sides are similarly armed."

"If the Devil can quote scripture," the succubus mocked, "God can certainly quote anti-Scripture. But I have not come to mock you. I have come to warn you that you are on treacherous ground—more treacherous than you have yet realized—and that there is no expectation, however reasonable it might seem, that cannot fail at critical moment. You are an innocent, Brother, and a stubborn one, but you have glimpsed the truth and the time is near when you will be forced to acknowledge it. You still have a choice, and a conscience to guide you. And you still have the most useful armament of all in the war within the soul."

Well aware that he was being teased, Primael took the bait.

"And what is that weapon?" he asked.

"Resignation," the succubus told him, and left him wearily deflated, in the dark.

But he was not in the comfortable dark for long.

Afterwards, he got up, and walked. He knew that he was walking in the forest, although he had no lantern and the starlight filtering through the canopy was very meager indeed. He seemed, in fact, to be walking through a universe of shadows, dense and multitudinous: shadows or shades; it was difficult to tell while they remained black and silent. Perhaps, he thought, the Dames Blanches were only white because, had they been black, it would not have been possible to know that they were there.

The foliage was still, unstirred by any breeze, but there was a susurrus, very faint and very distant, and yet somehow ominous.

The Babel of the spirits, he thought. *The multitudinous voices of the dead, unable to communicate with one another, let alone with the living.* But the analogy was unsatisfactory, he knew. According to Holy Scripture—all lies, according to Beatriz de Tardivel and Gilles de Rais—the destruction of the tower and the fragmentation of human languages had been an act of God: of a God who, to judge by his actions rather than his tyrannical Word, was not only petty and peevish but lacked any sense of poetic justice. What kind of punishment for hubris was it to make people speak multitudinous languages instead of one? What did it facilitate? What did it prevent? What was the point?

There was, he thought, something that he was missing: something that, even if it were not a key to the enigma that would make everything make sense—he had given up on that possibility—would at last allow him a fleeting glimpse of meaning, a mild palliative for his disturbed imagination.

Eventually, he found the signpost. It was difficult to see whether it had characters inscribed on it, because it was far too

161

dark in his dream, but it seemed to him that when he reached out his hand to caress the stone, he could feel the letters forming the unreadable words. They were not decipherable by means of touch, any more than they had been legible when he had been able to see them, but there was a certain strange sensation in the contact.

No words formed in his mind to provide him with the apparatus of an explanation, but he gradually acquired a sense of the soul of the stone, and the manner in which it had been stirred by recent necromancy—which had connected, inevitably, with echoes of ancient necromancy, forming links across time. Ollivier and Corentin, individually and collectively, had attempted to exert the power of the word here, and the word did have power. Corentin really had raised the spirit of his beloved Katarin, who was not entirely in the soul of the beholder, but he had inevitably raised other entities as well, doubtless including human souls, or souls that had once been human, but also souls, or spirits, that had never been human, and perhaps never alive: souls, or spirits, that were dangerous not because they were hostile, or engaged in any kind of war for possession of human souls, but precisely because they were utterly indifferent to humankind and human kindness, to human life and human death.

Except that some of them weren't. Some of them, at least, were interested, or at least curious. Why?

Why not? In an infinity of worlds, and all the places that were not worlds, or even places, why would there not be any that possessed curiosity enough, not merely to be interested in humankind but in him, Primael Quemerle, Brother Primael of the Order of Saint Benedict, victim or collaborator in necromancy. Was he not a specimen worthy of attracting attention?

Worthy or not, had he not already attracted attention from the world of spirits? Were they not pressing upon his dreams already, and was not his present thought and inner vision a manifestation of that necromancy?

When he had heard the voices of the spirits, he had not been able to recognize them as voices, let alone understand

162

anything they said. If he felt their touch, on the other hand, he would surely recognize it as a touch—but not of human flesh, nor anything warm. Was that something he ought to wish for, or to invite?

Probably not. But was he not curious himself? Had not his entire life, in spite of his vows, been dedicated more to curiosity than to God?

"Forgive me, Lord," he murmured, automatically, "for I have sinned..."

But in a world where God, if he even existed, was probably not good, what need, and what hope, could there possibly be for forgiveness?

He tried to concentrate on the soul of the stone—which was, after all, a signpost. If it could not tell him where to go, perhaps it could it least point him in the right direction.

If Hell is not a place, Primael thought, as he tried as best he could to savor the soul of the stone, to inhale its essence and taste its sourness, *then it is, in a sense everywhere, intricately mingled with everything that is not Hell—not merely Paradise, if such a state of being is not beyond imagination, but many other states of being that are not pain or pleasure, torment or bliss, but placed on subtler scales of evaluation. And it follows, logically, unless my dreaming self has lost the thread of rational thought completely, that everywhere is everywhere, and that all souls are in some sense intertwined and intermingled, as well as being separate and lonely.*

But what, then, is Heaven?

The soul of the stone, he realized—the soul of matter, the soul of Creation—did not know that. It did not know that because its notion of evil—of Hell, of pain, of culpability—was based entirely on harm, damage and destruction, and its concept of the opposite of evil was simply the absence of evil, relief from pain, salvation from destruction. Its concept of good was entirely negative. Heaven, therefore, for the soul of the stone, could be nothing but an absence, a not-Hell.

Poor stone, he thought. *What a poverty-stricken philosophy! But then, is it not ours? Are we not made in God's image,* in the image of Creation? Have we any concept of good that goes beyond the negative, the absent, any more than the soul of the stone has?

Yes, he replied, reflexively, *we have love, we have the concept of love, and not just succubus love; we have something more than that. Haven't we?*

But he remembered that when Beatriz de Tardivel had asked him: "Have you ever been in love?" he had answered: "No." And so had she. What would Ollivier have said, or Aidrena or Genovela? Corentin, of course, would have said "Yes," without the slightest hesitation, but how reliable a witness was Corentin? *Perhaps we're all deluded*, Primael thought, *but of us all, is Corentin really the least deluded?*

He was not sure whether or not the soul of the stone really knew what he had just discovered, and whether he only thought that he really knew it himself because he thought that the soul of the stone knew it, and he thought it more likely, considered rationally, that the soul of the stone was not the kind of soul that knew things, in the sense that human minds know things, and that he was making up the train of thought himself...as, indeed, he had to be, given that he was dreaming. On the other hand, perhaps the stone was more akin to an instrument of souls than a soul itself, a means of orientation available for their use, and that was why it was called a signpost. Perhaps it had been formed, or at least positioned, with that purpose in mind, but it seemed more likely to Primael that it was merely something that people had discovered, left over from world before the world, a Creation prior to the most recent Order brought forth from Chaos, and that its discovers had found, by means of experimentation, that if they touched it in the right way, it could enable them to sense the presence of other souls, and to be sensed by them: a property that facilitated appeals, and invitations.

It must be difficult, however, Primael thought, *to direct those appeals or invitations specifically, to aim them accurately. And logically—if I have not lost my logic to the extent of mistaking grotesque leaps of the imagination for mathemati-*

cally pure deductions—if the appeals and the invitations can be effected in one direction, they ought to work in the other too. If the living can summon the dead, then the dead can surely summon the living. In all probability, it would require a certain collusion, a coincidence of motives, but in the case of Corentin and Ollivier, there will surely be more than enough common interest to allow the charm to operate. If I go with Corentin to the stone, Ollivier will surely come. And although my will is free, how can I possibly refuse him? Why would I want to refuse him?

He had a suspicion that he was confused, as he often was in dreams without quite realizing it until later, when he woke up and attempted to remember them, but he also had a suspicion that the confusion that he was experiencing at present was the kind of fecund confusion from which new order might come, if one could only master the trick of creation.

In any case, he felt better.

"Thank you," he said, to the soul of the stone, although he did not suppose for a moment that the soul of the stone could understand his words, even if it could hear them.

He continued caressing the stone for a while longer, until he became gradually aware that he was not alone: that there was another presence nearby, possessed of physical form and a kind of solidity, even a kind of warmth.

He moved his right hand away from the signpost then, in order to grope in the dark, trying to make contact with the other. When he touched a face, the face became faintly luminous, as if his touch had a magical power.

He was looking at the Marie-Morte. He had no doubt that it was the same one he had seen in the previous dream.

"I showed you the way out," she said. "You could have gone."

"I thought I had," he told her, "but it seems that I am trapped here, wherever *here* might be, if it is not everywhere."

"Close at hand and far away," she replied, mechanically, dismissing the question with the banal formula.

"But you're here too," he said. "It appears that you're trapped too, unless one of us is answering a summons."

"Appearances are deceptive," said the Marie-Morte, "and I cannot be summoned, or trapped."

"Why, then, are you here? If it's to guide and inform me, at whose behest have you come? Mine? Ollivier's?"

"You mistake what I am," said the creature who hybridized semblances of life and death, "but that is understandable, given what you are."

"It's certainly not astonishing," agreed Primael. "What worries me more is that I might be mistaking what I am, and what the world is."

"That's difficult to avoid," she replied. "The lie always begins within ourselves, and emanates from there to everywhere."

"The world is a lie, then? God really is a liar?"

"How could it be otherwise?" she retorted, a trifle scornfully. "What else can Creation be but a lie? Use your logic. The only truth lies beneath and beyond Creation, inaccessible to creatures of any kind."

"But not to you?"

"If only..."

"But you're older than God, older than his Creation—you must know the truth of my world, if not your own."

"Alas, no," she said. "I dare, sometimes, to wish that it were otherwise, but that kind of courage soon fails."

"Do you really exist? And if so, what are you?"

"You can see me, or at least, my recreation. You can hear me, and you can feel me, poor child. Thus, I exist. But as to what I am...in the beginning, so you are told, was the Word, and the Word was a Lie. Whatever I was before, if there was a before, I am now a figment of a lie; how can I know the truth, about myself or anything else?"

"But you're not entirely a product of my human imagination, a fanciful fiction of my invention, or the ghost of an ancient tradition. You have an identity, an essence, beyond that."

"We all do, Primael. You have a soul. Does that make it any easier to know yourself: to know what you truly are?"

"Yes," said Primael, "I believe that it does. I believe in the power of thought, the virtue of philosophy. I believe that, even if God and the world are a lie, and a lie at war with itself, I can discover at least a fraction of the truth about myself."

"And if you find it," said the Marie-Morte, "will it do you any good?"

"Your phrasing is misleading," Primael countered. "Discovery is a good in itself; it doesn't have to seek further justification, in some kind of calculation of material advantage."

"You're preaching to the converted," the Marie-Morte told him.

"Good," he countered. "In my experience, the unconverted never listen."

"But they hear nevertheless, else how would you and I be meeting? You do not class yourself, I suppose, among the converted?"

"Why *are* we meeting, then, if I have not summoned you, and you are not here to offer me guidance."

"But I have already offered you guidance," she said, as she reached out with a skeletal hand to touch his face, and stroke his cheek gently. "Is it my fault, if you could not follow the way?"

"No," he admitted. "But again, why are you here?"

"Because this is where I am," she said. "Not trapped, not summoned, but here nevertheless. Perhaps the question you ought to ask is why you are here, when you, at least, could be elsewhere, and probably cannot help feeling that you should be."

"Perhaps," he agreed. "This is not Hell, and I am not damned—yet. Nor is it Heaven, and I am not saved—yet. The war goes on, within and without. Everything is a lie, it seems—but beneath and beyond the lie, there *is* a Truth. There *is* existence. I am who I am, and I am not free to create any self that I can imagine. I need to discover who and what I really am."

Her fingers were still touching his cheek, still caressing him, but not in the manner of a succubus. "Poor child," she said.

Was she referring to him, he wondered, or to herself, or to some other child entirely? He did not bother to deny that he was a child. For the moment, he was lost. He knew that if he asked more questions, he would not receive any answers from the Marie-Morte that he could not provide himself, simply because the answers provided by the Marie-Morte were his own, and with regard to answering questions, her ears and voice were merely a rhetorical device. But she did have a reality. She was older than, and prior to, God.

"The nephilim," he told her, "cannot have any idea of what are they are unless they are instructed by someone capable of recognizing them. They are born to daughters of men, and do not know their fathers. They might well mistake their fathers, as many purely human children do. Some might discover that they are nephilim, and be glad of the discovery, but it is arguable, from some points of view, that it is healthier for them not to know, to be content with the lie; for the truth is not necessarily healthy. It is good, in itself, but not necessarily kind, or uplifting, or productive of strength."

The Marie-Morte did not remind him that she had shown him the way, nor did she warn him that he was treading on dangerous ground, in deep darkness. She merely stroked his cheek, maternally. She was not trying to seduce him.

"If I summon the spirit of Ollivier, or allow Corentin to do it," he said. "He will be able to tell me the truth—not because disembodied souls know everything, but because he will have worked it out. He didn't tell me anything when he was alive, because he felt that he was protecting me, but if I participate in his summoning, his spirit will be obliged to tell me what it has discovered, about life and death, anything and everything. That will be necessary, I think, for although I already know, after a fashion, what he's going to tell me, I can't believe it yet. Without his word, I can't believe it. But given what I know, how can I even trust his word? It's a strange predicament.

"Poor child," said the Marie-Morte.

"I understand, now, the peculiar attitude that people have to you—to the idea of you," Primael said. "I thought that combination of reverence and fear paradoxical, but I understand it now. I'm not afraid of you, Marie Morte, but I'm not sure that I can revere you either, Lie that you are. What a peculiar dream this is! Could anyone but a confused monk, who lost his faith long ago, but who continued going through its motions because he had nothing to put in its place, have a dream like this one—a reverie, rather, because, if I remember this in the morning then I cannot really have been asleep, can I? I am conscious, whatever that can mean."

Marie Morte, no longer merely a specimen of her kind, a member of a class of beings, but a person, with an identity of her own, put her bony arms around his neck and kissed him on the forehead with her thin, pale lips. A single tear was transferred from the edge of her lashes to his hairline, from which it trickled slowly down in the direction of his white eyebrow.

"Thank you," he said, knowing the value of the gift.

Then she was gone, and the sun rose in the east, and the forest became green, but Primael still did not wake up.

Damnation, he thought. *Have I no sense of an appropriate ending? But what more is there to add, until I know the truth—which might be never?*

He was still in a clearing around the ancient standing stone, surrounded by a circle of oaks thick with mistletoe, and knee deep in Asp of Jerusalem.

There were men among the trees: armed men, wearing the colors of Louis XI of France, the Universal Spider, who was dead but whose dynasty lived on. There was a black friar with them: a tall, lanky man. He pointed a bony finger at Primael.

"Arrest that man!" he howled.

Two soldiers stepped forward, tentatively, in order to seize the Benedictine. Primael could not understand why they were tentative. He was old, small, puny and unarmed. They were young, tall, robust, with half-pikes in their hands and arbalests slung over their shoulders—heavy arbalests, not old-fashioned crossbows; Louis' fighting-men had all the latest equipment. In spite of their armaments, however, they were apprehensive. That was superstitious dread; they knew that he was a necromancer, even if they did not know exactly what the word implied; and they did not know that the broad daylight shielded them against his spells.

Or did it? For that matter, was he only a necromancer, or was he more?

It did not matter. He did not offer any resistance.

The tall Dominican was holding a wooden cross, which he was holding in front of him, not so much in imitation of a shield as a weapon: a machine for the administration of anathema. There was fear in his eyes, but Primael knew full well that the stimulation of fear was translatable into other emotions, even by people who were not fanatics. In rare cases, it could be translated into sexual attraction; much more commonly, it was translatable into horror and hatred.

The Dominican fanatic was not a rare member of his species. His expression showed clearly enough that he was transposing his fear into malevolence. He saw Primael as an instrument of the Devil, in need of extirpation.

"Take him to the camp," the Dominican ordered his well-armed minions. "He'll be sent to Rennes for trial. His confession must be public, before he is burned."

Confession? Primael thought. Well, I suppose if I refuse to make one, even under torture, they will simply invent one, as they did for Gilles. If necessary, they will invent a trial, and witnesses, all in sworn but lying words, and declare that I was burned…and perhaps, in fact, I shall be. But what does the truth matter, if the written word bears witness, given the tyrant that it is, even more so when printed than it was when scribes like my younger self were required to devote their lives to copying its lies?

The two men who could not decide whether they were halberdiers or arbalestiers, reflecting the confusion of modern warfare and modern times, took him away.

No salvation, after all, he thought. *History takes its course. The French are following the Spanish example, and employing their own Inquisition. The Pope will not like it, but what can he do except protest? The War in Heaven is reflected on earth, and for the moment, Semiaza does not have the upper hand even in Broceliande. The superior numbers are on the other side. But he will slip away, even if I cannot. Tristan L'Hermite's cannon do not have barrels long enough to attain him.*

That, he knew, was a blasphemous thought. He was a man of God. But so was the Dominican. And God was a liar.

Well then, thought Primael, *I am definitely damned.*

And only then did he wake up, glad that he would not be taken to Rennes as a prisoner of the Inquisition.

At least, not yet.

XI

In the morning, when he awoke, Primael's first thought was that he must fulfill his promise to visit Aidrena, and must then seek news of Lady Beatriz, but his second, while he washed his hands in the bowl of lukewarm water that a servant had brought him and ate a small galette, washed down with a draught of watered wine, was that ought at least to glance through the papers that Corentin had told him to take away and read.

He realized almost immediately that he had been a trifle optimistic in thinking that it would not take him long to read them because he was familiar with the handwriting. The bulk of the script was, indeed, easy enough to follow, but the marginal notes, legible to begin with, became increasingly less so as the script deteriorated, and the coherency of the thought contained within their commentary also declined. The task of decipherment soon became onerous, and he decided that its rewards would probably not be worth the effort.

He put the papers away, and went to see Aidrena.

She did not look well. She tried to sit up in bed, but she could barely raise her head from the pillow. Even so, she beckoned him insistently toward the armchair that was positioned close to the bed, ready to receive him. As she had the day before, she dismissed the servants who had been sitting with her and attending to her needs, telling them that she did not want to be disturbed while she was with her confessor.

"I'm sorry," she said to Primael "I had hoped to be able to talk with you more robustly."

"You have nothing for which to apologize," Primael assured her. "Your illness is not your fault."

"Mother had convulsions yesterday evening," the young woman said, as if it were an explanation for her own condition. "Were you with her?"

172

Primael hesitated, but then said: "She sent me away when it began."

"Of course," said Aidrena. "And Corentin doubtless instructed you not to tell me, as if I could somehow be kept from knowing. Don't think ill of the servants, please. They're obedient to discretion. Genovela wouldn't have said a word either, had I seen her; but I knew as soon as it happened. That's possible is it not, Brother Primael? I'm her daughter, after all. I can't hear her little bell, but I can sense its vibrations regardless. Do you believe me?"

"Yes, my Lady," said Primael, simply.

"Call me Aidrena," She instructed him. "Ollivier did. Did you go into the forest afterwards with Corentin in order to summon spirits."

"No," said Primael. "I was too tired, and a little shaken myself, by your mother's attack, which I feared that my presence might have precipitated. I went to bed and slept for a long time."

"So you haven't heard his Katarin, or felt her touch?"

"No, my lady."

"Aidrena," she said. "That's a pity, I was hoping that you could tell me...whether his delusion is communicable."

"Do you mean that if I had come here and told you that I had heard Katarin's voice, that I had held a conversation with her, and that I had felt the solid touch of her invisible hand, you would have concluded that I had somehow been infected the Corentin's delusion, persuaded by suggestion to believe it?"

"Probably," she replied, "but I would have been interested to hear your evaluation, whatever it might have been. How very considerate of Corentin to allow you to postpone the privilege. He's not usually so well able to curb his impatience—but perhaps he was disturbed by mother's convulsions too, and felt the need to savor Katarin's consolations in private. It is convenient, is it not, that he can summon the succubus directly to his bed now, and has no need any longer to go into the forest to the old Druid shrine. You know about the shrine, I suppose?"

"Mention has been made of it," Primael affirmed, carefully refraining from asserting that he knew it very well indeed, having communed with its soul, although he had not actually seen it...in the flesh, as it were.

"That's what the villagers call it, and Genovela agrees, although, naturally, she pretends to know far more. She says that it was a religious site long before the Druids, although she can't possibly know that. We can't even know for sure that the Druids worshiped there—we can hardy ask them, can we? There's mistletoe everywhere, not just there. It's a long time since I've been in the forest, but I can still remember being almost well, in my childhood. As for the woad...well, you must know better than I would how abundantly it grows wild, and where."

"Asp of Jerusalem," murmured Primael.

"What's that?"

"Sorry—I was thinking aloud. Woad is also known as Asp of Jerusalem."

"Why? An asp is a kind of snake."

"I have no idea. Woad is a Saxon appellation, like madder and weld for the plants that produce red and yellow dyes, imported from Grand Bretagne by the Normans. The old Breton terms are more colorful, but are hardly used any more wherever dyeing is practiced—the language of industry always modernizes swiftly. Asp of Jerusalem is a Roman importation, though, derived from the Latin, where the word rendered as *Jerusalem* means *house of peace*, and the Latin *aspis* can mean *shield* as well as a kind of snake, but that's as far as my etymology can go."

"Well, no matter. You must ask Genovela to take you to the signpost today, since Corentin didn't take you last night. She took Ollivier—reluctantly, I think, but she did it. You can look for simples at the same time."

"I haven't had a chance to peruse your herbal yet."

174

"It probably won't tell you anything you don't know already. Genovela might. She knows the formula that Ollivier invented; at the very least she can show you where she gathers those ingredients—some of them, at least, as she seems to have to trek far and wide, going out of the forest into the heath and the meadowland for plants that don't grow in the woods."

"Gathering ingredients for medicines is always difficult," Primael admitted. "Training the novice monks in alchemical botany at the Abbey is more difficult than forcing them to master the intricacies of Latin grammar, even with the aid of books and the herb garden, and the lay pupils don't set them a good example, considering such knowledge irrelevant to their concerns. I don't suppose the wise women find the task any easier with their apprentices."

"Probably not," said Aidrena. "So, how much did Mother tell you before she got the shakes and started foaming at the mouth?"

"I can't tell you that," said the monk, remembering his error of the previous evening.

"Of course not. She swears everyone to secrecy and then blabs herself. Do you believe that there's a war in Heaven still going on?"

"It's a plausible way of looking at things, and the Church doesn't deny that Satan is still in active contention with the Lord—far from it."

"That's exactly what Ollivier said you'd say. What about the sons of Heaven fathering children with daughters of men? Is that still going on?"

"I don't know," said Primael, honestly.

"You knew Gilles de Rais, though, when you were young. Was he sired by an incubus, do you think? Is that why he became a necromancer?"

"I never saw anything to suggest to me that he was anything other than an ordinary human being."

"Nor did Mother, I dare say, but she was only a babe in arms at the time. She seems to have taken a firm hold of the idea now, though. Did she tell you that Gilles de Rais organized her parents' marriage?"

Primael felt as if he had just been stabbed in his soul, but he did his best not to react visibly. "No," he said, after the slightest of pauses. "I didn't know that. Did Ollivier know that?"

"Yes, of course. Mother probably told him, or Corentin. It's not a secret."

But none of them thought it worth mentioning to me, Primael thought. *And why should they? Ollivier couldn't have known why the fact was significant, any more than anyone else.*

"That was before the scandal, of course," Aidrena added. "He was a Maréchal of France, the most powerful and influential man in the region. It wasn't the only marriage he negotiated, by any means."

"Did he do the same for Rozina's parents?" Primael ventured, keeping his voice scrupulously level.

"Of course not. They were servants of another household, not his business at all."

But it was a dream, Primael thought. *It was all my invention, like last night's bizarre dialogue with Marie Morte. I cannot be Beatriz de Tardivel's father, and Aidrena and Corentin's grandfather. It simply isn't possible. My sin cannot be the origin of the family curse…which, after all, cannot really exist.*

"You're not saying anything," Aidrena was quick to point out. "Is that because you're considering the possibility that Gilles de Rais might have arranged the marriage to conceal some petty scandal of his own…that he might have been Mother's father?" It was obviously a suspicion that had crossed Aidrena's mind, and seemed significant to her—as it would, if she thought that Gilles de Rais was a nephilim, and the origin of the family curse. He could guess, now why Beatriz had reacted the way that she had to his mention of having dreamed about Gilles de Rais, and why she has asked him if he knew *what he was.*

"No," said Primael, in answer to Aidrena's question, glad that he could answer honestly. "No such possibility crossed my mind. It's not possible."

"It's unlikely," Aidrena corrected him, "but you can't say that it's impossible, can you? It's well within the bounds of material possibility."

"It's not true," said Primael, stubbornly.

"Probably not," said his young interlocutor, "but I strongly suspect that Mother thinks, or fears, that it might be. She can't remember Gilles de Rais herself, but her mother certainly did. Not that she blabs about that. At other times, I think she wonders whether she might have been sired by an egregore herself—that she might be a nephilim, and thus privileged to receive visions informing her of truths unknown to common mortals. If that were true, of course, or even possible, I might have to wonder about my own parentage—but then, so might anyone. You can't tell me, I know, how many young women who find themselves with child are even prepared to swear to their confessor that it must have been the incubus, but I'll wager that it's not unknown. If I were to find myself with child, it really would have been…but I don't suppose that anyone would believe me for an instant."

Primael said nothing.

"I'm embarrassing you," Aidrena observed, although she could not have had any idea how much. "But you're my confessor—if I can't talk about these things to you, to whom can I say them? Not to Mother or Corentin, that's for sure. It embarrasses Genovela too, although I'd be prepared to wager that she isn't as virginal as she pretends, nor as unacquainted with the incubus. Forgive my preoccupation, please; I can't help thinking about these things, no matter how inappropriate it might seem for a young lady of good breeding. It's probably an effect of the curse."

"There's nothing to forgive," Primael said, semi-automatically. "There's so sin in speculation." He believed that, insofar as Aidrena was concerned. As for himself, he was by no means so sure.

"Are you regretting having promised to come to see me every day?" she asked. "Am I making you uncomfortable?"

"I'm not regretting my promise in the slightest," Primael assured her. "If I seem a little uncomfortable, it isn't your fault. I didn't sleep very well last night."

"Nightmares?" guessed Aidrena. "That's a common problem hereabouts. People blame the forest, or the Druid stone, although it's really just poor diet and guilty consciences. But not in your case, I assume."

So far as Primael could tell, she was not being sarcastic. She was simply assuming that his conscience was as clear as his diet was adequate.

"If you need to talk about things that you can't talk about to anyone else, Lady Aidrena," he said, "I'm very willing to listen—but I can't promise that I'll be able to answer all your questions. My ignorance, like that of any human being, is enormous."

She did not bother to object to his further use of the title, perhaps satisfied that at least he had attached her name to it, and doubtless far preferring that form of address to *child*. "But if Corentin really can conjure the spirit of Ollivier from wherever the dead go," she said, "you'll have a means of finding answers, won't you?" This time, he did detect sarcasm.

"Perhaps," he agreed. "But you don't believe that he can, do you?"

"I'm keeping an open mind," she insisted, falsely, "just like you...and Ollivier...or so he led me to think. Has Corentin showed you the documents that he brought back from the Abbey?"

"Yes," Primael admitted. "In the main, they're careful copies of passages from books of occult science and demonology held in the Abbey's store, relating to the preparations to be made for the safe summoning of spirits and binding them to a magician's will, juxtaposed and collated, with speculative commentaries, sometimes awkwardly placed in the margins. Unfortunately, the commentaries become increasingly incoherent as Ollivier's disease began to disturb the steadiness of his hand and the stability of his mind. The copied texts are full of conflicts and contradictions, and are mostly nonsense, in my opinion; that used to be Ollivier's opinion too—but the fact that he bothered to copy them, and the nature of notes that he tried to add to them, testify that he had experimented with some of the prescriptions."

"Successfully?"

"Probably not...almost certainly not. But the fact that he tried, and would surely have kept trying if his illness hadn't overtaken him, suggests strongly that he was fully convinced that the necromancy that he had Corentin had practiced had succeeded in summoning Katarin's spirit, and that further ventures might well be fruitful, if attempted with appropriate care, in the right circumstances."

"I see," said Aidrena. "He was just humoring me, then, in agreeing with my judgment that poor Corentin was deluded...or, at least, refusing to dissent from that opinion? He believed that she was real, even though I told him that she could not possibly be real, if she confirmed Corentin's absurd conviction that my father had raped and murdered her?"

Which is not beyond the bounds of material possibility, Primael thought. Aloud, he said: "He kept the secret from me, too, very carefully—but yes, it appears that he was convinced that he and Corentin had succeeded in their venture, and that Katarin's return from the dead was not delusory."

"And he fell ill immediately afterwards," Aidrena observed.

"That was a disease," Primael countered, stubbornly. "An accident of fate. He knew that it wasn't the shock of an alarming discovery, any more than it was his fault, It could just as easily have happened to me." *And perhaps it should have*, he added, silently. *Last night's experience was just a dream, a product of my perversely prolific imagination...but what does it say about the state of my soul that I could concoct such an imagination, and continue dwelling in it?*

"I'll pray to God that it won't," said Aidrena. "I need you to stay healthy, Brother Primael, to set an example to us all. I

179

want to be able to talk to you, as I did to Ollivier, when I had the opportunity. I've missed that, so much that I don't feel I'm overstating the case to say that I really do need it. Please persist, Brother. I'll try to stick to safer subjects in future, if you wish, but I worry so much, about Mother, and about Corentin, and I'd like to understand what's happening to them, if I can, but I certainly can't do that on my own. You do see, don't you, why I need *someone?*"

Yes, I do, Primael thought. *So do I—and I hope that you can do that for me, if I can do it for you.*

"I'll come every day," was what he promised, aloud, "for as long as I'm permitted to stay here. Every day. And we'll help one another to understand, so far as understanding is possible for common mortals."

"You're not a common mortal, Brother Primael," Aidrena said, flatly. "Ollivier told me that. He said that he was, although that was just professional humility speaking, but that you're a true man of god, that whenever he was in a quandary, he always asked himself: 'What would Primael do?' He didn't always follow your imaginary advice, he said, but he was always glad of it."

"He does seem to have built up expectations here that it will be very difficult for me to meet," said Primael, ruefully. "Please don't expect too much of me, Lady Aidrena. I really am just a common mortal, a flawed sinner, certainly no saint."

"Professional humility," she repeated. "But I won't argue the point. You must go to see Mother now, if she's receiving. If not, get Genovela to take you to the Druid stone. And when you come to see me tomorrow, as promised, I want to know every last detail of Corentin's conjuration. *Every* detail, you hear? You're the only one who will tell me honestly. If he really can conjure spirits, I want to know, and if he can't, I want to know that too. I need to know, and I need you to be my eyes and ears outside. Say that you will."

Primael hedged, and simply repeated what he had already said: "I'll come every day, Lady Aidrena. Tomorrow, and every day thereafter, for as long as I'm here."

He hoped, sincerely, that it was a promise that he would be able to keep, for some considerable time to come. He excused himself, however, for taking his leave for the present, with the aid of the pretext that she had provided: that he wanted to ask for news of Beatriz, which was true.

XII

Primael did, in fact, go straight to the chatelaine's apartment; but Genovela came out of the apartment in answer to his enquiry, to tell him that the chatelaine did not feel well enough to see him yet, but would certainly see him later. In the meantime, she had asked her to take him into the forest, to show him the signpost, and to collect simples for medicines—for herself as well as for her daughter.

"Are you willing to do that?" Primael asked.

"Certainly," said the wise woman. "I'm not her servant, but I have accepted to be her companion, and I have a duty to her. If she wants me to show you the shrine in the forest, there is no reason why I should be reluctant to do so." She did not seem to be convinced that there was no such reason, but she preceded him down the stairs as she finished speaking

Very scrupulous, Primael thought. As he followed her, he said aloud: "Thank you. As a scholar I shall be very interested to see it."

"As a Churchman or as an apprentice necromancer?" she retorted.

"It is as a Churchman that I have been given permission by my superior to experiment with necromancy," he riposted in his turn, "but in either capacity, I mean no insult or harm to the wise women of Herbriant, or any other region. I am not a Dominican, avid to root out heresy. I would like to be a shield for every house of peace, against strife of every sort."

"Very noble," said the woman. "It doesn't alter the fact that what you are intending to do tonight is dangerous. Indeed, it seems to me that your very presence here is dangerous. You will forgive me if I say that I had rather you had stayed away, and would be very glad if you left."

"That's not Aidrena's opinion," said Primael, although he was aware that it was not a fair thrust.

182

"Nor my lady's, unfortunately," Genovela admitted, "and certainly not Corentin's. But one of the three is a child, and the other two are direly reckless. None of them can sense the danger, perhaps because they're too close to it. I'm only a little more distanced, and there is no precision in the perception, but…you cannot believe me, can you, man of God?"

Perhaps I should not, Primael thought. *I should dismiss it as superstitious dread.* "I am not an enemy, my lady," he said, aloud. "I want to help them, if I can…all of them."

"I believe you," she admitted. "And it seems that I cannot—so I shall do what I can to help you help them, in the faint hope that you are not impotent to do so. You might find that challenging, if Corentin's invocation fails, and even more so, if it does not."

"Aidrena is sure that it will fail," Primael remarked, as they traversed the village, which seemed ominously quiet, almost as if those of its inhabitants who were still inside their houses were hiding, like those who had hidden from Ollivier's funeral cart. "But you believe, on the contrary, that he has every chance of success?"

"Success?" she repeated, contemptuously. "I think he has every chance of inviting disaster. Do I believe that his magic will work? I fear so—but I do not believe that it will work as he intends and hopes. Aidrena is a child, overfond of romantic dreams, and Corentin is little better, besotted with his ghostly whore. Lady Beatriz has been rotted by her disease, and is direly confused by her visions. If all three are looking to you for aid and comfort, as they looked to your fellow priest, it is nothing of which to be proud."

"You do not believe, then, in Lady de Tardivel's account of the war for Heaven, or her suspicion that she, like her father, is a nephilim sired by an egregore?"

Genovela did not seem surprised or threatened by the question. "Those are not terms to which I can attach much meaning," she said, "but if you mean that there is magic in her, that is true. She is its constant victim. Whether it comes from Gilles de Rais, whatever he was, or whether he was really her father, as she seems to suspect, I don't know—but it is not contained within her, nor can it be exorcised by your Church magic. I can sense it in the air."

"Whatever Gilles de Rais might have been," Primael said, "he was certainly not Beatriz de Tardivel's father."

Genovela shrugged her shoulders. "Delusion or not," she said, "the idea troubles her sometimes. I don't believe that you can exorcize it, but by all means try. The time might be upon us, I fear, when we shall all be clutching at straws."

Is that what I am? Primael wondered. *Is that what the power of the Church is, in her eyes? A straw that a victim of drowning might clutch in vain? But where does this evil wind come from, then? Not from France, that's for sure. From Hell?*

"Are we not supposed to be gathering simples?" he asked, mildly, as they strode along a narrow path, Genovela taking the lead and he limping sorely in a vain attempt to keep pace with her. She noticed that he was struggling, and slowed down.

"You know as well as I do, Brother Primael," she said, "that the location is not conducive to the collection of medicinal species. I have half the children in the village out hunting for me, as well as spying for strangers. If you identify any further species that might be useful, you have only to describe them to me, or find me a specimen, and I'll have a bouquet in your lap within twenty-four hours. But you'll forgive me for believing, I hope, that everything that is being done with the aid of plants that are accessible in Bretagne is being done. The sisterhood has been active here far longer than monks have been in Bretagne."

"Have you read our herbals?" asked Primael, with disingenuous malice.

"No," she said. "I cannot read—but I have had their supposed secrets read to me by Ollivier. I was not impressed, but he was careful to note down information that I gave him, for incorporation into the books you keep at the Abbey."

"I shall be glad to do the same," Primael assured her, "and to test your claims as best I can, when I return to Paimpol."

"Are you sure that you will return?" the wise woman asked, "and that Paimpol will still be there if you do? The French armies are heading westwards inexorably. Landais has no forces at his disposal capable of stopping them. Maximilian will withdraw as soon as he can see no further profit in lending his forces to the ailing Fransez, and when he does, the French will be able to dictate whatever terms they wish. But that will not be the end of the killing; if the Dominicans have their way, it might only be the start."

"They are not mad dogs," Primael muttered. "They too are men of God, in their fashion. I do not think that they will trouble the Abbey." *Now that I am not there*, he refrained from adding, but he did repeat, in a slightly anguished tone: "Believe me, Genovela, I am not your enemy. I want what you want—to help the heirs of Tardivel, and to protect the forest."

She was hastening on ahead again, but she looked back in response to his plea, and slowed down again in order to let him catch up. She softened her attitude and her tone somewhat.

"I do believe you," she said, "and I thank you. These are anxious times. Forgive me if I seem direly lacking in courtesy and gratitude. My lady's convulsions are not your fault. But might I ask you one favor?"

"Ask," said Primael.

"Do everything you can to put a rein on Corentin. If he cannot be stopped from going forward, at least do your utmost to make him proceed slowly. If he succeeds in summoning Ollivier's spirit tonight, and nothing more than that, there might be no harm done. But whatever else you allow, and no matter what his mother might ask of him, *do not let him summon Gilles de Rais*."

Primael remained silent momentarily, not knowing what to say—but what he thought was that if Gilles de Rais really had visited his dream two nights ago, he probably would not wait for a formal invitation to come again, and if what Gilles had said to him in that dream were true, there were many things that he, Primael, would dearly like to ask him.

Then, feeling that some response to Genovela's request was necessary, the monk said: "I will do what I can to make sure that whatever he does is measured and modest. Will you come with us tonight?"

"Most certainly," she said "I dare not stay away. If Corentin does not want me there, he will not see me—but I shall definitely be there, visible or not."

"Good," said Primael, sincerely.

Suddenly, after moving through dense undergrowth for some time, at some further cost to Primael's bare ankles and lower calves, which his sandals and the hem of his habit could not protect, they came into a circular space, where the signpost loomed up in a fashion that Primael reflexively thought of as majestic. The woad plants that grew around it were densely packed, but had such a monopoly of the area that Primael could not believe that they were unaided in maintaining it.

This is still a garden of sorts, he thought, *and it is tended, one way or another*.

Genovela paused on the perimeter of the circle, and allowed Primael to go forward in his own—but when he reached out to caress the signpost with his right hand, she said: "Can you feel it?"

There was no need for him to ask what she meant. He could, indeed, feel it. He had felt, or thought he had felt, latent power in menhirs before. He had always assumed that it was an illusion, an effect of the size, the solidity and the stance of the stones, which often gave the impression of living beings that had been petrified in the distant past, but might only require a magic formula to come to life again. The signpost, however—which was taller and more rugged than the menhir in his dream—was overwhelming in creating that impression in his mind. It was not so much that it loomed above him so sternly, but the fact that when he touched it, when he stroked it, it seemed to welcome the attention.

186

It was not the same sensation that he had had in his dream, when illusion had informed him, absurdly, that he was sharing the soul of the stone, and thus reaching out to countless other souls, of beings and objects, human and monsters, atoms and stars. This sensation was more visceral, more down-to-earth, stirring his bowels rather than the numinous warmth of his soul. He was well aware of the fact that what he was touching was hard, cold stone—but there was more. There was surely a power in the stone, a power capable not merely of speaking but of acting: a power capable of violence.

What he was feeling was within him, he told himself, a reaction to his surroundings, and the circumstance, but he felt nevertheless that if he only knew how to make a connection, he might draw energy and solidity from the stone, and that the stone would be glad to donate it. He felt that he had the stone's promise that when he returned, that evening, it would not be in vain. But he also had the sensation that the stone was not addressing itself to him, that the stone was not even aware of his existence.

There is turbulence here, and no mistake, he thought, *but it is not chaos. It feels more like contained wrath.*

He put his left hand on the stone as well, with the palm flat.

There were no symbols painted on the stone, nothing that could be seen—but there was certainly something to be felt, and he felt it more intimately with both hands than he had with one. He felt that more strongly, and more strangely.

Not was the stone the only presence in the clearing; the force that was contained within it extended around it, in a fashion that was, needed analogous to the influence of a lodestone, and that force facilitated other presences, invisible for the moment.

He remembered the fleeting thought that had crossed his mind in his sleep, that the Dames Blanches might only be white because they could not otherwise be seen in the dark, and realized that the converse might be the more important aspect: that, like the stars, they had too little capacity to make themselves seen to compete with daylight.

He made a conscious attempt to sense their benignity, the protective intention with which legend often credited then, albeit dubiously, and he thought—although it might have been elusion—that there were, indeed entities close to the stone and far away that did not wish him harm, and therefore, in the way of considering matters that the soul of the stone had, were good. But he also felt, very forcefully, that those were not the only entities nearby, and there were some that *did* wish him harm, that had nothing in their own souls but hatred...

His breath caught in his throat. Genovela was right, he felt suddenly sure. Corentin's necromancy was going to work...but as to what would respond to his summons...

"Arrest that man!"

The voice rang out clearly and authoritatively. Primael only had to turn his head through ninety degrees to see who had spoken. He saw four men: two black friars, one tall and one short, in whom he was certain that he recognized the watchers on the hill above the burial-ground where he had pronounced the ritual of farewell over Ollivier's grave; and two men-at arms, who had half-pikes in their hands and cross-bows slung over their shoulders.

The prophecy of his dream was being repeated in the material world—but the copy, he saw immediately, was poor. The two armed men were not soldiers of the French army, or Pierre Landais' militias. They were not even wearing recognizable livery. They were servants borrowed from some minor manor, probably in some village a quarter of the size of Paimpol. The companion of the man who had followed Corentin and Primael had doubtless done his best to find the help he had been ordered to fetch, in a hurry, but there was a certain comical ridicule about the armed might that he had summoned.

Even so, Primael admitted to himself, the half-pikes were easily capable of dealing deadly blows, and the crossbows, although they were old and not arbalests of the latest model, were easily capable of firing deadly bolts. He and Genovela were unarmed. She was close enough to the trees on the far side of the clearing to dodge and run, and to escape without difficulty, but he was in the center of the circle, standing close to the stone and touching it; his back was a broadly-exposed target.

In fact, Genovela did not dodge and run. Instead, he saw from the corner of his eye that she had already braced herself, ready to run toward him, entirely willing to add her meager weight to his, even in a contest that could not be won.

But she did not move. He did not appeal to her, and she did not move. It was not necessary for her to move, because the trees went mad.

The day before, while Primael had been talking to the wise woman, the foliage surrounding them had been seized by an anomalous squall of wind, and had rattled. That was nothing by comparison with what they did now. Now, they roared, and the energy that whipped them was a veritable tornado. Nor was it simply the oaks and the dense clusters of mistletoe that were agitated furiously; the Asps of Jerusalem joined in, and suddenly, they did not bear the slightest resemblance to the shields of a house of peace, but became very suggestive indeed of venomous vipers.

The serpentine appearance, Primael supposed, was entirely fictitious, a glamour due to magic, but there was nothing illusory about the movement and the din. The enclave of the forest surrounding the Druid stone, the signpost to Hell and to the absence of Hell that constituted a meager notion of good, was *furious*.

The two Dominicans had not entered the circle; they were five or six paces beyond its rim. They were rooted to the spot, as if petrified. The two makeshift men-at arms, on the other hand, in answer to the order they had been given, had actually stepped over the boundary, into the woad-garden. They had done so tentatively, reluctantly, and fearfully, but they had done it, obedient to the tyranny of the word of God.

Unlike the Dominicans, they were still free to move, and to respond by means of movement to the scream of panic.

That was what was happening, Primael knew. What the forest was doing, within the radius of the stone's psychic lodestone, was generating what the ancients had called panic, the very essence of the Great God Pan, the spirit of Nature, the spirit of Life, the Primal Scream.

The men-at-arms dropped the half-pikes, and they ran, helplessly, in blind, stupid panic, incapable of doing anything but running away. They ran as fast as their legs could carry them, and probably faster than they had ever imagined that they might.

The two Dominicans watched them go, with expressions of increasing horror, as they realized that they were alone, and still, and now defenseless, in the presence of…what?

In their eyes, presumably the Devil, in person.

Primael stepped away from the stone, and turned sideways in order to face the two black friars. He saw that his dream had, indeed, been prophetic. The Dominicans were utterly terrified and utterly horrified—but the expressions of their faces testified to the fact that they were translating that terror and that horror into furious hatred. In the smaller man, that hatred seemed resentful and essentially timid, but in the taller one, it was more assertive and temeritous.

If looks could kill…, Primael thought.

But looks could not—the Dominican's angry stare was impotent. So were his arms. He could not raise them, even to make a symbolic gesture with his wooden cross. He could not even deliver an anathema. He was defeated, and he knew it. He was not resigned to it, but he knew it.

Three strides took Primael to where one of the half-pikes had fallen. He picked it up, looked at it disdainfully, and threw it down again, outside the circle of woad. The woad calmed down. The trees ceased roaring. Stillness overtook the whole scene, as if the tranquilizing hand of God had passed over it.

The quiet seemed intense, and palpable.

Primael stretched out his right arm and extended his index finger, pointing in a direction a fraction south of due east, where he imagined the nearest border of France to lie.

"Go," he said, simply. His voice was not loud, but it was authoritative…and tyrannical.

The Dominican who had issued the order to arrest him opened his mouth, as if to utter a protest or a threat, but no sound came out. The two black friars obeyed the order, making every effort to walk in a dignified fashion. They did not run; they were free of panic now.

It only took a matter of seconds for them to vanish into the trees, but Primael waited half a minute or so before turning to look at Genovela.

She did not bother to protest, as she had the day before, that she was not responsible for what had just happened. She stared hard at Primael, her face paler than it had any right to be, given the darkness of her complexion.

Finally, she said: "*What are you?*"

"I don't know," said Primael, sincerely. "But I can see now that you were right. My presence here is dangerous. Those two carrions crows surely won't come back without a real army at their back—we shall just have to pray that the Spider's children will not give them one…or that if they do, that the forest will be able to suggest to all its soldiers, as it did just now to the two poltroons, that they would be far better employed elsewhere."

"You could have used that halberd," Genovela pointed out. "Feeble as you are, two thrusts would have made sure that the black friars never left."

"It's not my way," said Primael. "Whatever I am, I'm not a murderer—which is something for which to be thankful, I believe, because I surely wasn't in control of myself just then, and might have done anything that was in my nature. If you'd rather I made my own way back to Tardivel, and decided to steer clear of me in future, I wouldn't blame you."

She shook her head. "They had no right to be here, on Corentin's land," she said. "I have every right to be here. The

191

forest knows that. So, I think, do you." While she was speaking she crossed the circle around the stone, obliquely. She picked up the second fallen half-pike, and hurled it away from the circle, as far as she could. She was rather slight in appearance, but her muscles were strong. It flew far enough.

"Now," she said, "I know where we can find some simples that will help to soothe my lady's residual pains. Shall we go, or do you need to commune further with the spirit of the stone?"

"Not for the moment," said Primael said. "But tonight, we shall see what we shall see."

XIII

Beatriz de Tardivel eventually received him—after being closeted for some time with Genovela—just as she had the day before, in the sitting-room of her apartment, in the armchair placed before the fireplace, where no fire was set. The weather was still set fair; there was no sign in the atmosphere of any storm—and yet, beyond the narrow horizon, Bretagne was in utter turmoil, and even the trees of the forest had a restlessness that could not be attributed to any external wind. The world was unsettled, by convulsions that might erupt at any moment.

But the chatelaine was quite calm, for the present. She was fully dressed, neatly and elegantly, and her coiffure was perfect, Rozina had had done her job with skill and devotion.

"Genovela is frightened," the lady told him. "She has been frightened for some time, of course, but it was not until today—when she least expected it, I think—that her fear abruptly found a focal point. She is wondering what you are, and cannot find an answer, except that you are somehow accursed, or at least have the power to distribute curses. But that is not an answer, is it? *Curse* is just a stupid word, which explains nothing, but simply restates the fear that gave birth to it."

"She asked me what I am, when the Dominicans and their reluctant henchmen had run away," Primael recalled. "I could not answer her—not because I did not know the answer, but because I knew that she could not believe me, and would think me a liar."

There was a ghost of a smile on the chatelaine's lips. They were healthy lips, for the moment, and the smile, had it broadened, might have seemed warm, and might have added a hint of beauty to her face, but it was just a ghost. Even so, Primael had seen a thousand smiles, and their ghosts, twisted by bitterness and irony, and he was glad that the chatelaine's was not one of those.

"I would not think that you were a liar, Brother," she told him.

"No, my lady," said Primael, thinking that the conventions applicable to his status as her appointed confessor would have licensed him to address her as "my daughter", but carefully keeping any hint of irony out of his own phantom smile. "Even if you did not believe me, you would not have thought me a liar, but only a sincere man, trying to make sense of a deceptive world."

"May I guess the answer that you could not give Genovela?"

"Of course, my lady."

"You would have told her that you are simply an ordinary man, like any other, and that you had nothing to do with the forest's epileptic fit."

"That is the truth, my lady."

"No, Brother. You are sincere, I know, but it is not the truth. I kept silent too, though, when Genovela told me what had happened, because I knew that she could not accept the truth either. To you, at least, I can confess it. But tell me first about the Dominicans. Why did they try to seize you? Are they mad?"

"Reckless, certainly, and perhaps foolish. Monks of my Order, who see them as dark versions of themselves, generally think of them either as fanatics driven by obsession or schemers ambitious to obtain power and prestige for their Order, at the expense of others, within the chaotic politics of the Church. They are a little of both, I think, but when I looked into the eyes of the man who tried to arrest me, what I saw behind his intense hatred, more than anything else, was desperation: the soul of a drowning man clutching at a straw. He and his companion are Frenchmen, operating deep in the heart of enemy territory, in a war that is nearing its violent climax, and in which thousands, of men have already been violently slain. They are men of God, supposedly non-combatants in the war, but they know too much history to think that a secure guarantee of safety."

In that, they're right," murmured the chatelaine.

"They must have been feeling direly unsafe in Paimpol, where they had been dispatched by their superiors to search for heresy—and where they were very ready to find it, encouraged by the rumors they heard, and the interpretation that those rumors allowed them to put on what they saw. What they took for evidence was ridiculous, of course, but they seized upon it, as something not merely licensing but demanding their zeal. You or I might think that what they were really desperate to find was a pretext for leaving Paimpol, for traveling as far as they could toward the invading French armies, in order to shelter behind their lines, but they probably represented their actions to themselves as a sacred duty."

"Mad, as I said," opened Lady Beatriz.

"They were ill-equipped, of course; as soldiers of God they needed others to carry weapons for them, and men-at-arms are in direly short supply at present, even to defend homes left at the mercy of fortune by Landais' strategy. They were fortunate to be able to borrow two from some petty landholder who presumably thought that it might be diplomatic, in the circumstances, to curry favor with the black friars. But the men were not even trained halberdiers, and I doubt that either of them had ever fired a crossbow at a human target or raised any kind of blade against a vagabond, let alone a monk. Their hearts were not in their work, nor their faith invested in their mission. They were only too glad to find a pretext to run. In truth, whatever stirred the forest did far more than was necessary; it did not require such a lavish hallucination to put them to flight."

"And what will they do now?

"I cannot tell," Primael admitted. "In all probability, the two Dominicans, in order to justify their panicked retreat, will ride as far as their mules can carry them to the French lines, in order to denounce me to the priests accompanying the army. They will doubtless denounce Corentin too, representing us both as vile servants of the Devil, in dire need of exorcism and cleansing fire. Whether their superiors will take any notice of what they say, I do not know. Nor do I know how the French captains might react if the Dominicans request or demand that they supply the swords and flames to support their anathema, but as everyone knows, the world is changing, and rapidly. We are no longer living in the era of Jeanne d'Arc and Gilles de Rais. The present war is a continuation of the one that was raging then, but its weapons have shifted, thanks to the new power of artillery, and the thinking behind it has shifted even more, assisted by the new power of the printing press."

"Do you really believe that the German presses will make a difference to men's thinking? I have seen a few printed books; their regimentation makes up for their lack of elegance and the poor quality of their paper, but the words are the same words, similarly copied."

"Yes, my lady. I do believe that they will make a difference; I have not seen many printed books either, but I have already observed that the standardization of the characters enables faster reading—reading by visual recognition rather the phonetic decoding. The change is only beginning to make it felt in society, but it is already profound. The pace of history is already accelerating. It is not merely the weaponry of the present war that distinguishes it from preceding phases of the conflict but its philosophy."

"How so? The French have been attempting to annex Bretagne from far longer and you or I have been alive."

"Indeed, but their reasoning has shifted. The leaders of the French armies no longer think of themselves as crusaders, seeing hypocritical justifications for their bloodthirst in terms of service to God; they think of themselves as tacticians, justifying their slaughter in terms of the imaginary need and glory of nations, and the security of secular hegemony. The captains take their new cannons post-haste to wherever there are fortresses and city walls in need of blasting, and their archers and halberdiers to wherever there are breaches to be exploited and populations to be subdued. They are becoming as mechanical as their guns, and it will not be long before the clumsy arquebus is replaced by much sleeker hand-held firearms, and arbalests will be outstripped just as they have outstripped the old crossbows. Warfare is becoming industrialized."

"God's work, if so," murmured the chatelaine, "not Semiaza's. And what will become of Tardivel, in such a world?"

"In the short term, Tardivel's weakness, as much as its isolation, might be its best guarantee of safety; because no one could sensibly seek to defend it, or to reinforce it, it is possible that no one will think it worth attacking. In the longer term, I cannot tell."

"We must hope that you are right about the short term," said Beatriz. She did not seem entirely convinced, but she was not without hope, on that score at least. She changed one slightly, however, to say: "But we have trouble within the manse as well as without, it seems, and I think you will agree that it is urgent."

"If you think that I am the focal point of that trouble, my lady, as Genovela certainly does," said Primael, "and would like me to leave...."

""Don't be ridiculous, Brother Primael," the chatelaine said. "It is precisely because you are its focal point that you must stay. You are only an ordinary man, you say—well, perhaps you are, but if so, the extraordinary travels with you and comes when you call. The madness took me the other night, I fear, when I had barely begin my explanation of the truth of the matter, but you have talked to Corentin and Aidrena, and you are a well-educated man, who had shared and helped to shape Ollivier's thinking for as long as I have been alive. You might not believe me when I tell you that you are nephilim, but you understand what I mean, and are capable of considering the implications of the term in a rational manner."

"I have been able to piece together a notion of what you might mean by the term," Primael said, "but you overestimate me if you think that I am capable of understanding it. I might have sounded very orderly in my thoughts just now, but that was because I was taking refuge in ideas with which I could deal rationally, with confidence in the adequacy of my arguments. In other matters, including those intimate to this house, I am lost in confusion."

"If you suffered from my disease," she told him, "your brain might be more vulnerable to sensations of certainty—but I would not wish that upon you, for I know what a double-edged sword the conviction of revelation can be—and no matter how deep that conviction goes, it is always framed by uncertainty, more ominous by virtue of the contrast. I wish I could be certain, for instance, that it was not hearing my confession that made Ollivier ill, and caused him to die."

"It was not," said Primael. "Of that, at least, I have the sentiment of certainty."

"And you have no fear of hearing the confession yourself—but that does not alter the fact that I am unconvinced, and afraid for you. The forest was afraid for you today, it seems, and went into convulsions in order to drive away the threat. Perhaps something within me did the same last night, and reached me with convulsions in order to save you from the threat of hearing my confession."

"You are calm now," Primael pointed out. "You are free to make any confession you wish, and it is my duty as a priest to hear it. For what it may be worth, though, if any unknown and unknowable force is intent on preventing that, I pray that it will strike me, and not you. If the cost of hearing you is that one of us must suffer, then Lord, let it be me."

There was not the ghost of a smile on the lady's lips, but there were the ghosts of tears in her eyes. "Your Lord," she said, in a whisper, "cannot be trusted. People called King Louis the Universal Spider, but he was only the feeblest echo of his model."

Primael did not contradict her—for reasons of diplomacy, he told himself. "Tell me what it is you want to tell me, my lady," he said. "I am ready to hear it."

She took a deep breath, and began. "The war for the throne of Heaven is ongoing, in all its aspects," she said, consciously repeating herself, but laying the assertion down like a foundation-stone, or at least a boundary-marker and a signpost. "The sons of God—those, at least, who came to earth as egregori, as Watchers, still father children on daughters of men—but those children have no way of knowing what they are, unless they are gifted a revelation. Even then, they have no way of knowing whether the revelation is anything but a dream. If they accept it, they risk being considered mad, and perhaps, in fact, they are mad, for if ignorance is not bliss, it is what passes among men for sanity.

"When I was a child, I thought I knew my father—at least, I thought I knew who he was, for he died too soon for me to know *him*. Other people were not so sure that he was really my father. After the great scandal, the whispers began. Gilles de Rais had negotiated by mother's marriage. The rumor took wing that she had been with child before the arrangement was made, and that my real father was Gilles de Rais, the necromancer, the diabolist, the celebrator of bloody Sabbats. People were polite, of course; although the fraction of Norman blood in our veins is very small, we live in a society that Normans made, shaped by their illusions, including the myth of chivalry, of aristocratic politeness. In reality, of course, they were and are mere brutes, Scandinavian barbarians, but that only made them cultivate their appearances more carefully—appearances partly stolen from Bretagne, and returned to us with interest as the wages of our defeat. But behind that politeness, malice seethed. I was a child of the Devil, the inheritor of a curse; that was in the way people looked at me long before I had my first seizure in public.

"My mother might have given me a little armor against that accusation had she assured me sternly that I really was her husband's child. My supposed father died before he could make any such effort himself on my behalf, so I have no way of knowing whether or not he would have committed himself to the lie, but my mother could not. She told the lie, to begin with, but without conviction, and when I grew older, and became more persistent in my inquisition, she confessed that, in fact, she had been with child before the marriage. She swore on oath that Gilles de Rais was not my father, but how could I believe her? She would not give me any other name, or even admit that it was a man. It was a moment of madness, she said, something unaccountable, an incubus, something she could not explain to herself, let alone to me.

"So, I still do not know for sure whether or not Gilles de Rais was my father, or whether, if he was, he took my mother in his own guise or some other. But I do know that Gilles de Rais was nephilim, and that I too am nephilim—as I suspect that you are yourself, Brother Primael, albeit without knowing it, and being resistant to the evidence, as most of us are. But even if you dismiss all of that as delusion and madness, facts remain. My family—my mother's relatives, and my dead father's—would have had great difficulty finding a husband for me in Montagu, or anywhere within thirty leagues of Tiffauges, but the world is wide, and rumor weakens as it travels. They found a comfortably remote place to which to send me, and a man prepared to take me. He was a brute, but not unusual in that, and he was not incapable of a certain kindness. I do not blame him any longer for the way he treated me, and I do not believe that he imprisoned me, and hurt me, out of cruelty. He really was trying to act for the best, in his treatment of me and of his children. He did hurt me, and I believe that he damaged both of the children, in his fashion, but he is not responsible for Aidrena's sickness or Corentin's delusions. They are my legacy, and the taint of nephilim blood.

"All nephilim, I think, cannot be like Gilles de Rais, or me, or my children. Perhaps some are veritably wicked, and some, like you, are certainly veritably good, like ordinary humans, but I doubt that very many can be spoiled, as we are spoiled, not just by innate sickness but by the horrid gift of revelation. But even if we are anomalies, Brother Primael, we are still reflections of the war for Heaven, which is ranging within us as well as without, more intensely within some of us than others.

"Semiaza visits me sometimes, by night, tenderly—so tenderly that I hoped at one time that he might have been my father, but he says that he was not. He also says that it is only a human delusion that places Heaven above us, in the Empyrean. In fact, he says, there is nothing beyond the atmosphere but a void of unimaginable extent, a void in which dead planets circle the sun, mocking the fragility of life, and in which a vast number of other suns also shepherd families of worlds, rotating about them helplessly, almost all of them dead but turbulent riots of mindless matter. That is not Heaven, he says, no matter what the soul of the material world might think.

"Nor, Semiaza says, is Hell in the center of the earth, where there is nothing but an ocean of liquid iron, with a core so tightly compressed that it cannot flow, so hot that even turbulence is quelled and matter is twisted into exotic forms that cannot exist on the surface, and cannot even be imagined by poor human minds that cannot cope with more than four elementary states of matter.

"Heaven and Hell alike, Semiaza says, are within and around us, latent everywhere in the air and the sea and the sunlight, but they are only sensible, and only mindful, in our souls, where the war is never-ending.

"The greatest of human errors, Semiaza says, is to think of that war as a war between good and evil. That, he says, is God's primary lie. God is not good, he says, nor is what God rejects and abhors evil. On the other hand, he says, it would be equally erroneous to think that he and God are similar, and that their conflict is simply a struggle for advantage between identical opponents, like the black and white pieces in a game of chess. Semiaza insists that there is a fundamental difference between himself and God, between God's tyranny and his rebellion. God, he says, is the Word, and the Word is God. God demands faith, and although it would be oversimplifying to say that Semiaza demands doubt, he believes doubt to be the only reliable stepping-stone to the truth.

"The power of the Word is undeniable, Semiaza says, but fundamentally treacherous. That power, he says, will always give God the advantage in the war, but that does not mean that he, the rebel angels, the nephilim and human beings, should admit defeat and surrender: quite the opposite, in his opinion.

God considers him to be ingrate, of course, since God believes—not without justification—that he created the angels as well as the world of souls and intellect. God believes that because he engendered Semiaza, Semiaza ought to honor him, as his creator and his father, and that opposing him is, *ipso facto*, that sin of pride. But that, Semiaza says, is because God is the quintessential tyrant, incapable of realizing that if a creator, however petty or grandiose, gifts his creations with free will, that freedom must include and embody the freedom of dissent.

"It is not that there is no confusion or intermediary between freedom and slavery, because there are no absolutes in that spectrum, merely degrees of differentiation, but, in the final analysis, Semiaza says, freedom of choice is freedom of dissent, and that is not evil, but, in his way of thinking, a kind of good. All good, he says, is based in freedom, including and especially the kinds of good that we classify as love: a word as treacherous as any other, but whose lie is not devoid of benevolence: what common parlance sometimes calls a white lie."

Damnation blanche, Primael thought, unable to resist the private play on words but able to resist the temptation to voice it, being wide awake although not entirely convinced that he was not also dreaming.

"Aidrena, I fear," the chatelaine continued, "and perhaps Corentin too, believe me to be misled by sentiment, and that I have been seduced by my own frustrated desires in shaping my image of Semiaza, but that is not the case. Ollivier, as a celibate monk, understood that, and I am sure that you will too, all the more so as Ollivier always insisted that you were a better man of God than he ever was. I worked out, once, by means of arithmetic and medical lore, that he might well have been at Tiffauges when I was conceived, and I asked him, delicately, whether he had any idea who my father might have been, if it was not Gilles de Rais. He understood that I was hinting that perhaps it was him, but he assured me that it was not. He was not as good a monk as he would have liked to be, he said, but that was not one of the sins he had committed. He said that Gilles de Rais, from what he knew of him, was a far more likely candidate as the seducer of my mother, but that his court, which became very unruly in later years, was already infected by a degree of licentiousness that made the list of potential fathers rather long, and that Gilles might not have been the only man there with sufficient sorcery to sow confusion in my mother's mind, and render the mystery insoluble."

The chatelaine paused, with the utmost delicacy, inviting a comment.

"If what you say about nephilim is true," Primael ventured, appalled by the depths of his own cowardice, but quite unable to help himself, "it is possible that if any sorcery were employed in your mother's seduction, the perpetrator was unaware of his own power, and that the confusion was sown independently of his will."

"That is doubtless the kinder interpretation," Beatriz de Tardivel said.

The most hypocritical, her possible father thought. He had always harbored a suspicion that the profession of confessor was an essentially hypocritical one; perhaps, he thought, he had been anticipating this terrible moment all his life.

I am damned, he thought. *Not by my sin, which I confessed, repentantly, and for which I was duly absolved, but by its consequences, for which no absolution in possible, and which even the most sincere repentance cannot free me. For me, at least, there is no gateway to Paradise, nor any love, but only a limitless void, full of mocking death.*

Then he cursed himself for the sin of pride, and for overweening melodrama. *But I am a very paltry sinner*, he thought, *trivial and of little importance in the world, let alone eternity. And my fault now, in refusing to confess to this poor woman, for reasons of shame, that I might be the author of her troubles—for very petty reasons and without the aid of any sorcery, conscious or unconscious—is as trivial as it is contemptible.*

And yet, he added, *if I was not the focus of some supernatural force then—and how can I be absolutely certain that I was not?—I surely am now. Now, I am the victim of true reve-*

lation—I can no longer doubt that—and the seeming benefi-ciary of a protective turbulence in the world.

Aloud, he said: "Has your revelation given you any conviction regarding other supernatural entities that are supposedly around us in Bretagne?"

"Follets, farfadets and the Dames Blanches, you mean?" she said, understandably taking the wrong inference. "The former are imps of a sort, but not Semiaza's. They too, it seems, are expressions of the free will of created beings, which take pleasure in anarchy, within the limited scope of their capacity. The Dames Blanche are more earnest in their hauntings, it seems—a protective sisterhood of sorts, reflecting and providing a model for wise women. All of them are fading away, though, as the world changes."

"And Marie-Mortes?" Primael prompted.

"A different matter. Their form, inevitably, is borrowed from the stocks of Creation, but it is a manifest patchwork. They existed, Semiaza says, before God and before him, however paradoxical that seems. It is like saying before time, before existence—a perversion of common meaning that our minds cannot grasp. At any rate, their origin lies outside Creation, even though they have a presence within it, and they are not combatants in the war for Heaven, although they seem to take an interest in it. They are not evil, Semiaza says, and might be good, but are more likely to be simply curious. He approves of that, partly because God does not. Have you seen one?"

"Yes," said Primael, feeling that he was on safer ground there, able to be honest, "but only in my dreams."

"So have I," she said. "They seem to have a license to roam there. Did you question her?"

"I tried, but her answers were not very clear. She questioned me too, but I am not sure whether it was curiosity or provocation."

"Why would she want to provoke you?" Beatriz asked. Primael was not sure whether the chatelaine was motivated by curiosity or whether she, too, might be seeking to provoke a reaction. In her case, however he had a clearer idea of why she might want to do that.

"I don't know why," he said, "but I think I have some idea, now, of what it is that she and other intruders on my dreams want of me."

"And what is that?" she asked, although she had to know.

"Corentin's formulae seem to work," he said, "albeit with certain difficulties. How they work, and exactly what they accomplish I'm not sure. Perhaps his phantom lover is a delusion, present only in his own sensations; but it is possible that when he and Ollivier summoned her, she was not the only thing that was enabled to return temporarily from the incomplete oblivion of death, and that Corentin's sensations were not the only ones rendered vulnerable to infection. He is determined to try the formulae again, as he is free to do, and he is trying to identify the circumstances that will maximize their effect—but I do not think he has the least idea of what that effect might be.

"When it proved difficult to replicate his first success, in Ollivier's absence, he became desperate for Ollivier's further assistance, and when it proved to be impossible to obtain, he changed his plan swiftly, and elected to try to summon Ollivier, not only as the most useful spirit to evoke, but also the one likely to be the most eager to respond to his call. In his eyes, I became the most useful substitute for Ollivier, not only because I know most of what he knew, and much of what he thought, but also because he supposed that the familiarity might actually aid in forging the link, much as his amorous passion for Katarin, and hers for him, seemed to enable the success of their first experiment."

"Bu you think that his conjuration of Ollivier might not work?" she guessed, hopefully.

"I think that it might not produce the effect that he expects and for which he s hoping. And I believe, now, that he is not the only person—or not the only entity, at any rate—that wants me to be present. Perhaps the interested agency is merely curious, but I fear that it might be more than that: that my presence might enable something that might otherwise be difficult of achievement."

"Ollivier's resurrection?"

"Perhaps. Probably…but something more. Exactly what, I don't know, but I do feel that I have been guided here, and that I am still being guided, by an agent I cannot see and cannot yet identify."

Beatriz de Tardivel evidently had her own idea concerning the possible identity of that agent, but did not name him, or even say what he was.

"If your cooperation is necessary," she ventured, "you could refuse it. You are free to choose."

"Perhaps," Primael agreed. "But I am here, and there are other reasons, now, why my presence is desired. Are you prepared to order me to go away, Madame de Tardivel? Can you even try, without causing a great deal of strife within your family?"

She did not reply immediately, apparently considering the possible consequences of various courses of action. Eventually she said: "How will your presence affect the outcome of what Corentin does?"

"I don't know. I doubt that even God, the Devil, or Marie Morte can foresee exactly what might happen, or what might be done in response, but it seems that one or more of them would like me to be in what they consider to be an appropriate frame of mind to take whatever action I can. Your confession, if it is motivated by Semiaza, might be a contribution to that, along with various other inventions, actual and hallucinatory. Unfortunately, there seems to be a contest of influences, the conflict of which only serves to increase my confusion. The faith that has served as my guide all my life, surviving as habit even when its bedrock had been lost, has been fatally corroded, leaving me bereft."

She seemed surprised by that. "Habit?" she echoed. "Ollivier was mistaken, then, is estimating you as a man of firm faith?"

"Don't criticize him for that," said Primael, dully. "I mistook myself, until I was forced by circumstance to examine my soul more closely. I suspect that Brother Michael might have known—confessors often see their clients more clearly than their clients can see themselves—but if he did, he was careful to shore up the habit and maintain the pretence. In his place, that is what I would have done."

"You no longer believe in God, then?"

"I believe in his existence, alas, but I no longer believe in the Church's representation of him. I no longer believe in his goodness or his protection. I can no longer understand how anyone else can maintain those beliefs, even if they insulate themselves as carefully as possibly from the vicissitudes of life, in a quiet monastery. Scholarship has made it impossible for me to accept the Church's lies, but the illiterate, who are spared that particular provocation, still live in society, where the tragedy of everyday life is painfully manifest. How can anyone believe for an instant that God—the Church's God, at least—is anything but a lie? At best, one might hope to convince oneself that he is a necessary lie, that, no matter how flawed faith is, it is better than the alternative, and that if its observance is merely habit, it is at least a virtuous habit. Not that I bothered to think such things, consciously and painfully, until I was provoked, first by circumstance and then by the figures of my dreams. Once the process begins, however, it proceeds apace."

"That I know," she murmured, thoughtfully. Then she said: "Thank you for telling me that. I am not sure whether I ought to welcome its implications or not, but enlightenment is good in itself, a species of freedom. Has Corentin told you what he plans to do in future with the power of the formula, if tonight's evocation is successful?"

"I doubt that his plans are firm. He intends to invoke Ollivier partly in order to seek his advice as to how to proceed thereafter—but he does intend to proceed, I think, if only by means of one tentative step at a time. He might take my advice too, but if I were to object to his continuation, and Ollivier did the same, the objection might only make his determination firmer. Genovela is afraid, because of what you have told her, that he might try to summon Gilles de Rais, and that Gilles might add his necromantic art to Corentin's, but I don't think that's what he has in mind at all. I suspect, given his youth and his temperament, that he might have larger ambitions—but he seems to be sufficiently prudent, for the present, to approach the prospect in a measured and unhurried fashion. Whether the entities that he hopes to enable have the same patience might be a different matter."

Corentin's mother had her own concerns. "He might attempt to summon Semiaza," she said. "If he does, it will be my fault…if it is a fault."

"I've read his instruction manuals, superficially at least," Primael said. "They provide formulae for reanimating the dead, not for summoning demons, although the distinction might not be as straightforward as it seems. Summoning the Devil is surely not the proposition that he intends to submit to Ollivier, if he succeeds in reanimating his voice. Perhaps the opposite; if he wants to try his uncertain power of command on a miracle-worker there are more obvious candidates. If he is content to be modest, he might settle for one of the legendary rivals of Jesus—Apollonius of Tyana, for instance—but if he consults Ollivier, he will certainly be advised that their reputations are inflated."

Beatriz de Tardivel had no interest in the possible inflation of the reputation of ancient sages. "You think that he might go in quest of a miracle—or two—in order to cure me, and Aidrena?"

""It would be an understandably egotistical beginning to a career in altruism. And it would be equally understandable that he has never breathed a word of that ambition to you or Aidrena—or to me, as yet. But this is guesswork."

"Surely it can't work," the chatelaine said.

"Probably not," said Primael. "Perhaps I am naïve, but I suspect that if the formula has been known for any length of time, and locations facilitating its operation have existed too, there must have been others who have tried to employ it for motives other than vulgar enrichment or the quest for sensual pleasure. If magic could make the world a better place, it would probably be a better place than it is. There must be problems standing in the way. The Church's faith, of course, says that magic is inherently evil, except for the magic practiced within its own rituals, but once we have accepted, or even suspected, that the difference between what the Church approves and what the Church rejects is not an accurate measure of good and evil, and might, in fact, have little to do with good and evil, that argument loses its force."

"Perhaps the formula only works within very narrow limits," Beatriz suggested. "perhaps it can enable a grief-stricken lover to recover a delusory compensation, but is impotent in the context of larger ambitions."

"That is possible," Primael agreed, "and has a certain dubious morality attached to it, although not one of which the Church would approve. Partly for that reason, however, I am suspicious of it. If magic works, I doubt that it does do within the restriction of moral judgment, only effective for approved motives. If the words of the formula have authority, at least in a defined location, that authority presumably has a raw power amenable to ignoble or ignoble ends, and subject to unintended consequences, like any other cause."

"You have obviously given the matter deep consideration," the lady who might be his daughter observed. "Have you really proceeded that far in a matter of a few rather eventful days?"

"A great deal of groundwork was laid at Paimpol, in debates that I have had with Ollivier and other scholars. Attempts to evaluate the possibilities of occult science have been an increasingly fashionable pastime, ever since the works of Albertus Magnus obtained a considerable circulation. They have been printed now, and will gradually make their way to every monastery in Europe, along with commentaries, replies and rival endeavors in philosophy. We have only begun the great debate, and the great enquiry, but we have begun it, and we have already made some progress in the sophistication of intellect. Petty wars between petty monarchs cannot interrupt it any longer, and nor can papal bulls. Only willful ignorance on the part of novices and lay readers can put a brake on it…although my own experience does suggest that as philosophy becomes more complex, willful ignorance and a refusal to engage with it become more frequent."

"But in sum," she said, returning to her own point, "you have no idea what Corentin intends to do after tonight's crucial experiment, and little or no idea what the consequences of his invoking Ollivier's spirit might be, assuming that he succeeds in doing that?"

"Indeed," said Primael. "But I feel, rightly or wrongly, that our conversation has put me in a better situation to play my part."

"Even though you do not believe in my revelation? Even though you think that I have only been talking nonsense?"

"That is not what I think," Primael affirmed. "You have told me things that I believe to be true, and which support ideas that have come to me as genuine revelations. None of what you have said is nonsense, and much of it is certainly the purest sanity, whatever doubts subsist regarding certain aspects of it—and given your assertion of the essential virtue of doubt, you can and should compliment yourself even on that. You are ill, my lady, but you are most certainly not mad. If you want such absolution as I can give, I am certainly willing to grant it, and if God disapproves of my doing so, then he must attribute the sin to my account, and not to yours."

"You're a generous man, Brother Primael."

"I am a sinner and a coward, my lady," Primael told her, "but perhaps I shall still have the opportunity to do penance for some of my sins."

XIV

"This is not the first time that you have attempted to summon Ollivier's spirit," Primael said, as they set forth into the forest. Corentin was carrying a satchel containing the manuscripts, carefully scrolled, while Primael and Genovela were carrying lanterns. Beatriz de Tardivel, who made up the party of four, was not carrying anything.

Corentin had not wanted Genovela to be part of the group, let alone his mother, but he had not had the authority to forbid them to come. Although Corentin was the Vicomte, the notional owner of the manse and the forest, his mother's word still carried a great deal of weight there; the conflict that would have ensued had he attempted to imprison her in order to prevent her accompanying him would have generated far more anguish than permitting her to observe. It was not as if there were any secrecy, any longer, about what he intended to do. Aidrena would doubtless have demanded to come too had she not been too weak to make the journey.

"No, of course not," Corentin replied to Primael's remark. "I have made the attempt before, at the Druid stone as well as in my apartment, albeit in daylight. I have felt his presence, but I have not been able to hear his voice. This time, I am sure the manifestation will be as full as possible."

"Because of my presence?" Primael asked, checking the deduction he had made in discussion with Madame de Tardivel.

"Yes. The link I had with Katarin was adequate to facilitate the invocation, but I'm not yet strong enough to bind other spirits. This will be an important step forward. With your help, Brother Primael, and Ollivier's, I truly believe that I am capable of mastering the art." He leaned closer to Primael and murmured, so that only the Benedictine could hear what he said: "I am already strong—far stronger, evidently, than Mother or Aidrena—but tonight's conjuration will make me

211

much stronger. I sense that…and so does Katarin. She is with us."

Primael knew better than to look around to see whether there a fifth member of the group might be moving through the shadows—but he believed what Corentin said. Delusion or not, Katarin was with them, and her presence, like his own, was crucial.

"Genovela's presence, and your mother's, will not be a hindrance, then, but a help," Primael suggested. "They knew Ollivier too."

"Very slightly," said Corentin, dismissively. "I was his pupil, and we worked together intensely while he was here. You knew him throughout his life. You were true brothers. The Abalains and the Quemerles were closely acquainted, were they not? All the old Breton families are interlinked—the Berthous too."

"Not as much as it might seem to an outsider," Primael said, although he had to admit that there had always been a certain sensation of kinship between himself, Ollivier and Herik Berthou, now Brother Michael, that was not shared with the younger monks. "Your own name is Breton," he pointed out to Corentin, "but your father would not have felt any brotherly bond with Ollivier in consequence."

"My father had a Norman soul," said Corentin, curtly.

"So had Gilles de Rais," Primael murmured.

"You've heard that rumor?" the young man said. "It isn't true. Mother's visions are deceptive. Ollivier tried hard to persuade her that, whatever she might think of God and the Devil, Gilles de Rais could not possibly be her father, but he could not do it."

Because it was not beyond the bounds of material possibility, as Aidrena pointed out, Primael thought.

And then, belatedly, the full import of that observation struck him. It was not, in fact, beyond the bounds of material possibility. He had had sinful intercourse with Corentin's grandmother, who had been pregnant before marrying in Montagu…but it was not beyond the bounds of material possibility

212

that he had not been the only person who had done so, and if he was not, then it was possible that another man might have fathered Beatriz: Gilles de Rais, or another nobleman of his licentious court…or even, in spite of the assurance he had given Beatriz when the idea was put to him, Ollivier Abalain. Ollivier had always insisted, after all, that Primael was a better man of God than he was, and if there was a kernel of truth in the visions visited on Beatriz by her epilepsy, it was that even God was a liar.

But how can I be innocent, since I am visited by visions myself? Primael thought. *I have been accorded prophetic visions, which had at least some truth in them, and I cannot believe that they came from God, or even Semiaza. They come from the forest, from the stone, but the forest and the stone are merely channels, which draw their power from the depths of the ages, and they remain quiet unless provoked. Their present provocation does not come from me, nor from Genovela, nor from Beatriz, nor from Aidrena…nor from long-dead Gilles de Rais. Where, then, if not from Ollivier?*

But surely that did not make sense? Ollivier was dead, and when he was alive he had only been a visitor here. On the other hand, he had supplied the formulae that Corentin had employed to stir the dead. And Ollivier had kept that secret from him, his friend and fellow scholar, as well as many other secrets.

I am not ready, Primael thought. *I need more time, to negotiate this labyrinth in my mind. I need time to think, time to put the pieces of the puzzle together, since it seems that I am the only person who can. But Corentin has already paused once, for my sake, and even though my feet are torn and bleeding, and I am limping badly, he shows no sign of pausing again. Ready or not, hurt or not, I must play my part…*

"Have you made all the preparations specified in the documents that Brother Michael gave you?" Primael asked Corentin.

"No," was the unsurprising reply. "I do not believe that they are necessary. "The power is in the formulae, the remainder is merely a hopeful program for cultivating the right frame of mind. Ollivier was insistent on that before our first experiment. Evidently, he compiled the documents he gave to Brother Michael because he feared that his illness might have been provoked by the failure of his preparation, and he was afraid for me, because he had no news from Tardivel; but I was the one who pronounced the formulae when Katarin came, and I am not ill. Indeed, I am stronger now than I have ever been. Have no fear, Brother Primael. I can invoke Ollivier's spirit, with your help. Katarin assures me that I will succeed, and that I need no other preparation."

"How can she possibly know?" Primael countered, warily.

"Oh, Brother Primael," the young man said. "You should have let me summon her last night. If you had heard her, and felt her, you would trust her."

But I have already heard and felt her, Primael suddenly thought, *and I did* not *trust her—rightly so, for she was evasive about her own identity, although, in truth, she might not have thought it a lie merely to cast doubt on the assertion that she was* Corentin's *Katarina, who really is delusory...*

But he could not follow the logical consequences of that revelation, for the moment. The train of thought was immediately obscured.

"Believe me," Corentin continued, "she knows. She knows what I am, what I can do. You will see…everyone will be able to see. When I have invoked Ollivier, you understand, it will be much easier to evoke other spirits. One link can remain specific, in the same way that the spontaneous visitations called hauntings can be limited to places as well as persons. Two established links open far wider opportunities. After three…the limitations dissolve and become feeble. Ollivier learned that long ago, in consultation with Cabalists who had some skill in the art."

"I remember mention of it in discussions we had, a long time ago," Primael admitted, dubiously, trying to dredge up the detail of the memory even though he thought that it was a distraction and even though his thoughts were strangely clouded. "We both considered it hypothetical then; if he tried the formulae at that time, they brought him no very tangible result. But if I recall correctly, what the cabalists of Granada told him was by way of a dire warning not to try the practice too far."

"It's habitual for magicians to issue such warnings, Brother Primael, as you know from your own reading," Corentin told him, airily. "Ollivier believed that they exaggerate the dangers in order to enhance their own prestige, and to provide a pretext for the evident limitation of their abilities."

"That certainly sounds like one of Ollivier's arguments," Primael had to concede. "To which I might have countered, although I cannot now remember for sure, that sometimes, warning of danger are simply that, and there is no need to search for more convoluted motives." *Upon which*, he thought, *Ollivier would have complimented me on being an honest man, ever reluctant to charge others with bad faith.*

"But you are determined, are you not, Corentin," Beatriz de Tardivel put in, anxiously, having had no difficulty in overhearing her son's last remarks, made in a loud voice, "not to attempt anything further tonight, or in the near future, than hearing Ollivier speak?"

"That has always been my intention, Mother," Corentin confirmed, a trifle impatiently. "I am proceeding in this matter with all due prudence, as Brother Primael can bear witness."

I am caught in a trap here, Primael thought. *If I tell him that I fear that his previous invocations might have had wider effects than he suspects, I will only make him more eager to test his art further. The dire example of Gilles de Rais will not deter him, as there is not an atom of real evidence that his downfall was due to any excess in the conduct of his occult research. Can I even be sure myself that the dreams I have had in Corentin's proximity, or the agitation of the trees in my presence, has any connection at all with his dabblings in necromancy, or the after-effects of a sin committed more than thirty years ago, when I was little more than a child? No, the best hope of putting a rein on this adventure, it seems to me, is that the invocation of Ollivier's spirit might work and that Ollivier might offer his own fate as a dire example of the awful effects of dabbling in necromancy...*

But he did not believe what he was saying to himself. Genovela, he thought, was right. Disaster was imminent...but the force that was impelling them all was too insistent, and their resistance too weak.

He knew, as well, that if Ollivier really did come in response to the power of the word, there was no reason to expect that he might oppose Corentin's further experiments. There was no way of knowing what Ollivier might say, or what his interests might be, now that he was no longer an embodied soul...

The prophet Samuel, Primael could not help remembering, had not told King Saul what he wanted to hear, or anything that could be of use to him. Quite the contrary. On the other hand, the legacy of legend and folklore was replete with helpful familiar spirits, although the Church had done its utmost to undermine them with propaganda in which all such familiars were diabolical. The early Church had struggled long and hard, Primael knew, against neoplatonist philosophers who regarded *daimons*—as opposed to demons—as benign. The Church fathers had condemned all such notions as heretical, and they were still prominent in the Dominicans' handbook of dangerous notions to be extirpated. On the other hand, Breton folklore, even today, still regarded the *dames blanches* as essentially benign and maternal, and even unfamiliar spirits, such as the Marie-Mortes, were not regarded as evil, except by the Church...

And yet, Primael could sense the danger that Genovela sensed. It did not come from the forest, or the stone, although it would surely come through them, but its origin, he felt sure, was far closer at hand...

For a moment, it almost seemed to be within his grasp, but then his thoughts were deflected again, as habit took over,

216

and his ideas veered in pursuit of another idea that had just crossed his mind, his relentlessly *scholarly* mind...

Was it possible, Primael thought, that the necromantic invocation of ancestral spirits had once been commonplace among many primitive peoples, and that its exclusion from the modern world was largely due to the hostility of modern religions? Had it once been thought ordinary for everyone to have a familiar spirit, a *daimon*, if not a loving Katarin, then at least an argumentative Ollivier...but *only one*. Intercourse, of whatever kind, with a wider host of the dead, seemed to have been regarded with suspicious dread long before the advent of Christ, if the testimony of the likes of Hesiod, Homer and Virgil could be trusted.

Ollivier and I were never brothers, he thought, *but we were daimons of a kind, to one another: daimons of a healthy kind, sources of wisdom, or means of stirring and provoking our own wisdom, rousing it from the torpor into which thought is ever ready to subside. Whereas Katarin, the succubus...*

But they had reached the stone, and Corentin was no longer by Primael's side. He was making his preparations—not those that Ollivier had sent to him, too late, but those with which he was already familiar. They did not take long, although Primael guessed that the seconds and minutes might be seeming overlong to the young man's impatience. Corentin was moving urgently, like a man possessed...as indeed, he was. But by what, exactly?

Corentin lit a fire, and carefully separated its brands into two, on either side of the signpost. He scattered incense on the burning twigs, and he inscribed symbols on the stone—not with the aid of woad dye, but with chalk, and there were only a few, not the bewildering confusion that Primael had seen on the signpost in his first prophetic dream. There were brief recitations. Corentin cut his left thumb with a knife, and allowed blood to leak on to the stone. Then, evidently, the stage was set for the essential incantation. It had all been done in haste.

Primael moved to stand beside Beatriz de Tardivel, who was watching her son with an expression verging on terror.

"You should not have come, my lady," he said. "There is danger here."

"I had to come," she replied, "I had to be here. I hardly know my son, but I love him. That is the way of things. You are the one who should not have come, Primael. Your feet are bloody, and you can hardly stand up, let alone walk."

Is it the way of things? Primael thought. *Is it even possible for parents to love their children if they do not know them?*

While wondering, he looked down at his feet. They were, indeed, bloody, but he had not felt any pain for some while. He had been aware that he was limping, but he had put the pain out of his mind…or had been insulated from it.

Genovela had also moved to stand very close to Beatriz, ready to catch and sustain her if she began to fall.

But who will catch me, if I begin to fall? Primael thought, and knew that no one would, not only because he had begun to fall a long, long time ago.

"Move away," said Genovela, speaking to him. "Go to Corentin."

Corentin was, in fact, already beckoning to him, inviting him—commanding him, rather—to come and take a position beside him, in front of the stone.

Primael obeyed. He had the freedom of choice, but he obeyed, coward that he was.

Primael did not reach out to touch the stone, but he had no need to do so. The link had already been forged, in the middle of the day and in the revelation of the previous night. He merely had to look at the signpost to be reunited with the soul of the stone, but he knew that the soul in question was merely a channel. The forest was more active than that, as it had proved when it had set the Dominicans to flight, but it had no agenda of its own. It had merely been reacting to the turbulent force from elsewhere.

Corentin did not take Primael's hand. He did not need physical contact with him, any more than either of them needed contact with the stone; they were bound by geometry, surprising in its elemental esthetic force.

218

Corentin began reciting the formulae. He had the parchment on which it was inscribed in his satchel, but he had not taken it out because he did not need to refer to it. Its presence doubtless helped, but the formula was within him now; he had already made sufficient progress to become a necromancer in his flesh and in his soul.

The stone was huge, and dark, a vast shadow in spite of the lanterns and the firelight. It seemed infinitely dark, in fact: a kind of void, in spite of its solidity, in which there was nothing to be seen. But in all probability, Primael thought, there would be little or nothing to see, whatever came of the invocation. At the most, he might feel the touch of ghostly fingers, and hear a voice other than Corentin's: Ollivier's voice, although it would presumably seem to emanate, at first, from the stone.

The first thing he heard, though, was not a voice; it was the agitation of the foliage of the mistletoe-clad oaks surrounding the circle. It was subtle, at first—so subtle that he was not certain that it was not caused by the movement of animals, or curious human beings—Genovela's wise women, for instance, coming to watch with her, or over her. The light of the two lanterns and the divided fire, however, cast the specters between the trees, beneath the crowns of the oaks, into shadows as deep as that of the menhir. It would have been very difficult for human, day-adapted eyes to see anything within, except perhaps for glinting eyes or the paleness of faces catching the lamplight; but the *dames blanches* were there, and visible, just the stars were up above, stubbornly defying the void, not benign in themselves, but nevertheless commanding a reaction, soothing, radiating peace in the house of peace.

But it was not enough. Primael could sense that, and knew that the pale spirits could sense it too. On multitudinous other occasions, it had been enough, and might be again, but for now the turbulence was too powerful.

It only seems to be individual, Primael thought. *It's focused in individuality, but the individual herself doesn't have that power, that authority. No individual does. She's merely a vehicle for the Babel of the dead, for the frustration of disharmony. It isn't the Devil, and it isn't evil, but it nevertheless possesses frustration and fury, which seethes and sometimes boils over. It's just a facet of the war, like the war of the Spider's heirs and the sick duke's surrogates. It's in me, and it's in Beatriz, and it's in Genovela, but most of all it's in Corentin, and it's Corentin whose necromancy has given it a form, an identity, a lie.*

And that, in the ultimate analysis, is the essence of it. It's a lie, because all Creation, and any creation, is a lie...

And in that moment of enlightenment, he regretted ignorance. The Marie-Morte, as she said, had shown him the way, but he hadn't taken it. Like the doubter he was, he had not been able to resign himself. He had pressed on, and on, and here he was, and what was about to happen was his fault as much as Corentin's, as much as Ollivier's, because he *knew*, and was free, and yet was impotent, because he was a coward...

Corentin paid no attention to the stirring in the forest, but continued intoning the formulae, in a measured fashion, but nevertheless in haste, possessed by an impatience that was not his own.

He is quite mad, Primael thought. *Like his mother, he is perfectly reasonable, outside the limits of his delusions, but within his delusion there is no room for anything but certainty, however absurd the certainty might be. He cannot doubt what he believes, no matter how ludicrous it might be. His delusion will not allow him to perceive its own falsity, its own absurdity, its own stark horror...*

Among the things that he now *knew*, among the tangled knots of his enlightenment, he knew that Aidrena was right, and that Corentin's father had not, in fact, killed Katarin...and Primael, unlike Aidrena, who had established protective mental obstacles of her own, immediately jumped to the additional conclusion that she had not been able to draw.

Too late.

220

Primael was suddenly gripped, internally, by an over-whelming sense of expectation, not yet of presence *per se*, but of imminent presence, as if something were trying to emerge, not within the space between the two fires, in front of Corentin de Tardivel, but inside his own body, inside his own soul, but only as a stepping-stone to moving outwards, into the world.

"I'm here," someone said—not Corentin, but Primael himself, although he was not aware of having made any deci-sion to speak, and the voice sounded hoarse, not quite his own—as, indeed, it seemed to Primael that it was not.

Corentin turned his head to look at him; Primael pre-sumed that Beatriz and Genovela were doing likewise.

"I'm here," Ollivier Abalain repeated—speaking this time, not from within Primael, but from without. And, as if to emphasize the separation, Primael felt fingers brushing his cheek. He was struck by the different between that touch and the caress of the Marie-Morte. The latter had been affection-ate, quasi-maternal. Ollivier's touch was demonstrative, brusque, a provision of evidence, not of tenderness.

"You're not alone," said another voice—Genovela's. Whether or not she was actually speaking for Ollivier's bene-fit, or to inform the entire company, Primael was not certain, but he saw immediately what she meant. A moment before, there had been near-darkness between the oaks. Now, there drifting patches of whiteness were more visible, moving in a circle around the clearing, as if in a slow, strange saraband.

But they're not enough, Primael repeated. *They can't soothe the fury.*

"The ladies are very kind," said Ollivier. "You too, Brother Primael. I could, and would, have returned anyway, given time, but your generosity in spending such long and tragic hours by my deathbed, absorbing the formula in your mind and in your soul, has made it so much easier. Not sim-pler, for the way is labyrinthine, but easier. I have been with you for a long time, but unclearly. Now that we have met, we shall be able to do it again, and it will become easier every time, until it becomes ingrained habit. Are you well, old friend?"

"Not entirely, I confess," Primael replied, although he knew that the dialogue was a distraction, and that Ollivier was not in command of the situation, "but well enough." That was a lie, but what did it matter?

"I'm glad to hear it," Ollivier said, "and I will pray that you stay that way."

Primael wanted to ask whether Ollivier knew of any reason why he might not, and a hundred other questions, but Corentin cut in.

"Can you see us, Brother Ollivier?" he asked. "Do you know how many we are, and who?"

"I have no eyes of my own with which to see you, Sire," said Ollivier, with a loquacity that Primael could not help but find absurd, in the circumstances, "but I know how many you are, and who. Forgive me, my lady, for not greeting you—and you too, Genovela. Death has made me forget my manners, it seems. You must forgive me, too, for not kissing your hands or offering you other tangible proof of my presence. If you interrogate Primael, he will be able to tell you that ventriloquy began as a religious rite and performance, still practiced in the era of the Pythia, and only became a matter of mimicry and fakery in relatively recent times, but even in its origins, I can assure you, its skill in prophecy was very limited. If you interrogate me, do not expect too much, I beg you."

That is unmistakably Ollivier, Primael thought. *The most pedantic spirit ever to have passed over from Bretagne, I dare say*. But he knew, as he said it, that it was a half-truth at best. It was the daimon Ollivier, the production of his own mind, the extension of his own soul, and the voice that was coming from the stone was, indeed, a matter of ventriloquy. His own presence here had, indeed, been essential to Ollivier's manifestation—but Ollivier was not the only spirit that had come in response to Corentin's summons.

Where is Katarin? Primael thought, even though he knew that *where* was a very slippery concept with regard to spirits. Corentin's conscious attention was elsewhere, for the moment, but that did not mean that Katarin was not present.

Ollivier and Katarin, Primael supposed, had only been the weakest of shades until this moment, incapable of any kind of existence without a host capable of maintaining them, but they were not entirely delusory, not entirely imaginary, and he assumed that, with appropriate assistance, they could and might become stronger and more powerful. There was a force behind them, a force permitting their impulsion and their metamorphosis, that was older than the world: the primal force, the animator of the Marie-Mortes and other entities far stranger than the Babel of the spirits of the dead.

Has that force an intelligence of its own? Primael wondered. *Has it a purpose of its own? Perhaps it has, even though it is vastly indifferent with regard to humans, their gods, demons and daimons. But it can be exploited, and it can be provoked. It can be provoked, and furiously.*

While the monk pondered, Corentin continued his dialogue with his former mentor. "If you cannot foretell the future," he said to Ollivier, "you can speak of the past and present. You can tell us where you have been since you died, and what the afterlife is like."

"I have not been anywhere," Ollivier replied. "Location is a worldly matter, an issue for bodies, not souls, although we are not incapable of it, as Katarin has demonstrated to you. As to what the afterlife is like, there are no analogies. Accuse me of speaking in riddles if you wish, but there are question to which it is direly difficult to frame answers, even for oneself."

That is certainly Ollivier's voice, Primael thought, *even though my vocal cords are aching.*

"I have come to seek your advice," Corentin said, still hastening to bring his prepared script into play.

"I know," said Ollivier. "We agreed that you would, if the occasion arose, although we did not know that it would arise so soon. My dying was inconvenient, I fear, in so many ways. It could not be helped. But you are not short of advisers, my son. You do not need me, while you have my Brother Primael."

"I might have been far more use to you and your proté-gé," Primael interjected, resentfully, "if you had taken me into your confidence regarding your experiments in necromancy. I might even have been able to perceive..."

"I'm sorry to have offended you," said Ollivier's disem-bodied voice, cutting him off rudely, "but I thought it prudent. I thought the dangers exaggerated, but I knew full well—in fact, I have a vague memory of your saying so once—that warnings are sometimes genuinely altruistic, sincere attempts to enable others to avoid danger. I would have told you every-thing, had I not fallen ill on the way back from Tardivel, but how could I know whether my affliction might not have been divine punishment? How can I know now? I never had your faith, Brother."

Neither did I, Primael remarked, inaudibly.

"It was not punishment," said Corentin, "any more than the sicknesses inflicted on my mother and my sister, neither of whom has ever done anything to merit divine wrath, while I...believe me, my friend, *there is no divine punishment*."

"You do not know that we have not warranted punish-ment, my son," said Beatriz de Tardivel. "Even Aidrena..."

But that is not the point, Primael objected, still silently. *That is not the basis of his conviction—but he does not know what the basis is, and cannot know, because he does not know himself, and cannot know the power that he has enabled...*

"I do know," said Corentin speaking with all the urgency of his false conviction. "Will you tell me, Ollivier, how to go about curing those sicknesses? Whom can I consult, and how?"

"How would I know?" Ollivier retorted, testily. "Do you think the dead hold symposia, exchanging their ideas? Do you think I am free to seek out the spirits of Galen and Hippocra-tes, Jesus and Albertus Magnus and speak to them in spite of the barriers of language and comprehension? Do you think the dead can read and write? Have you not asked Katarin these questions, and has she not told you that there are no answers here?"

Primael assumed that Corentin had done that, and had received exactly that reply, but that he had attributed Katarin's ignorance to her simplicity, or her ineptitude. He was trying hard to think of a question that Ollivier might be able to answer informatively, but he found himself trapped by his own certainty that Ollivier, in his present state of being, did not know and could not know, anything that he, Primael, had not already guessed.

"Ollivier," said Beatriz de Tardivel, "why are the Dames Blanches here, and why do they appear to be in distress while they are patrolling the environs of the clearing?"

"Out of kindness, I presume," said Ollivier. "They did not come with me, and are ever close at hand in Herbriant. They are patrolling for your protection, no doubt...but I do not know why they are in distress."

Primael felt a sinking feeling in his stomach. *Is that true?* he thought. *Am I, in fact more enlightened than Ollivier? But how could it be otherwise?* He had a horrible sense of inevitability, of his inability to do anything to prevent what was about to happen...and, in fact, of his inability to avoid being the agent of its outcome.

"Protection from what?" asked Beatriz de Tardivel, curiously. She did not know.

"From yourselves," Ollivier replied, confident even though he did not know either, no pedant ever being caught at a loss. "You took a risk in coming here, but the dangers are within, not without. The circle is a circumscription of your collective soul, for you are vulnerable here, and you are too many to be safe. Your curiosity is understandable, but your prudence should have enabled you to let Corentin and Primael to come alone to face the danger. No one is safe here, alas, in spite of such protection as the Dames Blanches can provide."

But that is guesswork, Primael thought. *Its truth is accidental. He does not sense the truth, as I do. He does not un-*

derstand that the flood of the dead's frustrations and resent-
ments is about to operate through Katarin...

Beatriz de Tardivel was still curious, or perhaps determined to create a distraction, sensing that one was necessary:
"What do you mean by a collective soul, Ollivier?" she asked.

"It is not the case, Madame," Ollivier replied, politely in
spite of the strained hoarseness of his artificial voice, "that the
soul—even such a reclusive soul as yours or Brother
Primael's—can really be contained and isolated within a kind
of hypothetical space. It cannot be surrounded by walls, like a
citadel, to withstand the siege of the world..."

That is good, Primael thought. *If we can only focus on
philosophy...*

But he had not even finished the thought when another
voice—a female voice, which he recognized as that of the
Marie Morte to whom he had talked in his dreams—screamed,
from the belly of the signpost, in literal panic: "Look out!"

And Primael ducked, as he had known that he would,
and because he had the choice. He dropped to the ground amid
the Asps of Jerusalem.

Later, he wondered whether he had really heard the voice
at all, and if so, whether it had really been the voice of the
Marie-Morte, and if so, how the Marie-Morte could possibly
have known that the warning was necessary, given that she
might simply have been a delusion. He decided, though, that
he must have heard it, and that it really must have saved his
life...although that might not have been its motive.

He certainly remembered hearing the twang of the metal-
lic string of the arbalest, and the whistle of the bolt, but he
knew that even old-style crossbow bolts traveled very rapidly,
perhaps not faster than sound, but fast enough to strike their
target before any such target could react. It was foolish to
think that a man who had only heard the twang of the bow-
string could possibly have had the opportunity to avoid the
bolt—but by the time it arrived at the place where Primael had
been standing, he had dropped to the ground, and he was not
hit.

Ollivier had been optimistic, he knew, to think that the only threats to the four necromancers came from within, and that the only protection they needed was the symbolic protection of spirits. He had been a fool himself to think that the Dominicans were men to take defeat gracefully, or even to heed supernatural warnings. He had been a fool to think that they were true men of God, who would play by the rules of the monastic Orders.

The Dominican, he knew, had also been a fool. He had been a fool to think that a man who had never fired such a weapon before, and had never practiced with one, could have the slightest chance of hitting his target as his first attempt. The bolt that he had undoubtedly aimed at Primael, the heretic magician who had appeared to raise the wrath of the trees against him, should not have passed within arm's length of him, and yet, it had passed straight through the space where he had been standing, and it had hit Corentin de Tardivel—who had not heard the twang of the weapon in time even to think of dropping to the ground—beneath his armpit, his arm having been raised in a dramatic gesture that he must have thought appropriate to the summoning of spirits...unless he had been reaching out in response to a caress.

At any rate, Corentin collapsed, without making a sound.

Beatriz de Tardivel screamed.

Genovela, drawing a dagger that had been concealed within her jerkin, bounded into the wood, with nothing on her furious mind but murder, not caring in the least that the Dominican who had fired the arbalest might not be alone.

Primael raised himself to a kneeling position by Corentin's side. The bolt had struck a rib, but arbalests were notorious for the force of their impulsion. The rib had not stopped the bolt. The iron tip had not struck the heart, Primael judged, but it had certainly shredded one of Corentin's lungs and had severed an artery. The shock of the impact had probably robbed the poor fellow of the capacity to feel pain, but the most that the mercy in question could achieve was to ease his demise.

Corentin coughed up blood, once, but after that, he could not cough again, and could hardly gasp. He gripped his mother's arms but he was not attempting to hug her. He was clinging to her for support, although he was already on the ground, with nowhere further to fall.

Beatriz de Tardivel collapsed on top of her son's body, sobbing hysterically, but her convulsions were those of ordinary sobs.

Primael had no doubt that Ollivier had gone, for the time being, along with Katarin, vanished into the nowhere from which they had both come, stealing away furtively like sly thieves of slight existence. He knew that it would not be his choice whether or when his lifelong friend came to him again, into his dreams or into his voice, He had no intention of invoking him by means of the power of formulae, but he knew that the link between them had been forged long ago, and could not be broken, whether formulae intervened or not.

Genovela came back. Her dagger was bloody

"Necessary self-defense?" Primael asked.

"Just vengeance," she replied, although she seemed slightly ashamed of what she had done. "The other won't get far," she growled, "even riding a mule as fast as he can. When I spread the word..."

Primael believed her. The Dominican did not know the country; in all probability, he would get lost in the forest. In any case, even if he managed to get out of Herbriant without being captured, it would not save him. Even in the midst of a war, he could be identified, pursued, caught and condemned. He was an accessory to the murder of an aristocrat. The secular authorities could not tolerate that, and his Order would surely disown him. A black friar who had been accomplice to the murder of the Vicomte de Tardivel on his own land, by means of a shot fired from ambush, could not be forgiven by men or by God, and if he were to be absolved after confession, it could only be immediately before his execution. In all likelihood, he would be excommunicated and denied even that mercy. The fact that his tall associate had only intended to kill

228

an obscure Benedictine monk—for whatever reason—could not be offered as an excuse; it would be too absurd even to voice, in the unlikely event that the opportunity to voice it were accorded to him.

Genovela ran to fetch help, in order to launch the pursuit of the assassin's companion, and also to send men to carry Corentin's dead body back to the manse.

In the meantime, Primael comforted Beatriz as best he could, although she had to hold him up as much as he was able to support her.

They held on to one another, clinging like father and daughter, although only one of them was apparently conscious that there might be more than mere mimicry in that semblance, and even though he could now consult Ollivier with regard to some of the possibilities, Primael knew that he would never know for sure.

Even if he summoned Gilles de Rais, or God himself, he would never know for sure.

XV

"It's all my fault," Primael said to Aidrena, the following day, when he fulfilled his promise, out of duty rather than rapidly-acquired habit. "All my fault" He did not elaborate, fishing hopefully for the denial.

"Everyone is at fault," Aidrena assured him, which was not quite the contradiction he had been hoping for. "We all had the opportunity to stop him, or make him pause. We didn't try hard enough. We let him ride to Paimpol in order to bring Ollivier back, because we had our own selfish reasons for wanting Ollivier to return. When he brought you instead, we were curious, and then glad, even though we knew that he would ask you to help him in his necromancy, and even though you admitted that you would. The responsibility is collective; you cannot monopolize the blame. But how is Mother? Can she survive, do you think?"

"I certain hope so," he said. "Thus far, she hasn't had an attack. The epilepsy, at least, seems to be showing a little mercy. Genovela is with her at present. I'll go back to sit with her later. We'll both do everything we can to soothe her woes."

"You won't go back to Paimpol, will you? You're needed here more than ever now?"

"No," said Primael. "I won't go back to Paimpol. If you'll let me stay, Lady Aidrena, this will be my home from now on. I'll be your almoner, if you wish. I'll keep my habit, if I may…if only out of habit."

"You'll have to ask Mother," she replied, "but I'm sure she'll agree."

"No," Primael told her. "Under the law, as the sister of the late Vicomte, you're the heir to the estate, not your mother. Until you marry, the manse and the forest are yours."

"Until I marry? That's not a possibility."

"You won't be short of suitors, given your dowry."

"That's not the reason. Corentin might have married, and had children, if the curse hadn't struck him down first, but now he's gone…well, perhaps it's a good thing that the family will die out, and the curse with it."

"There is no curse," said Primael, dutifully.

"Genovela says that the invocation worked," Aidrena said. "She said that Ollivier was really there, even though she couldn't see him."

Primael toyed with the lie, but decided that the burden on his conscience ought to be kept as light as possible if he were to bear it bravely.

"The invocation worked," he said. "Ollivier had to borrow my voice in order to make himself heard, but he was there. He had been there're all along, but the invocation made him stronger."

"So Corentin wasn't entirely deluded?" he said, stressing the word *entirely*, in order to give them both the recourse of denying the reality of Katarin's spirit, if they wished to make that choice.

All Primael said, though, was: "Not entirely."

Aidrena studied him carefully. "I haven't been entirely honest with you, Brother Primael," she said, tentatively.

"None of us is entirely honest, Lady Aidrena," Primael told her. "Not even with ourselves, let alone in our confessions."

"That's true," she admitted. "But we should at least try, should we not, to be honest with ourselves?"

"I believe that we should," Primael agreed, "no matter how painful it might be."

"Corentin wasn't," she said, "but that was because he was ill. Not mad, just ill. There is no curse, you say, but I'm not sure whether I can admit that. If he wasn't cursed, though, he was certainly ill. He wasn't evil. He wasn't honest with himself, but he wasn't really evil."

Primael made no reply to that. He could see that she was prepared to continue without prompting, and he was not at all sure that it would have been a good idea to prompt her if she had not.

"You remember," she said, "that I told you that my father didn't kill Katarin. I told Corentin too, but he wouldn't believe me, and I couldn't make him believe me. My father swore to me that he hadn't killed her, and he swore to Corentin too, but he said that he didn't know who had. I think that was true, in a strict sense, but I think he had a very strong suspicion. So had I. But neither of us wanted to admit it to ourselves. Father told me that he had explained to Corentin why he couldn't marry Katarin, and had explained it to Katarin too, because she didn't know any more than Corentin did."

This time, when she paused, she was seeking a prompt.

"Your father was Katarin's father," Primael supplied, "or thought he was. He thought that Corentin and Katarin were brother and half-sister."

"That's right," Aidrena confirmed. "Corentin wouldn't believe it. He was convinced that Father was lying. But Katarin did believe it, perhaps because her mother confirmed it. I don't know what happened between Corentin and Katarin after that. I can't know for sure who killed her, but if Corentin didn't know, it was because he refused to know. But he did love her, to the extent of obsession. That's why he was so desperate to bring her back."

"Ollivier believed him," Primael told her.

"I know," she said. "I didn't tell him what I've just told you. If I had..."

"It's not your fault, Aidrena," Primael said. "If anyone in this murky business is innocent, it's you."

He could see that she couldn't accept that. She wanted her share of the guilt.

She took a deep breath, and said. "Will you be honest with me now?"

Primael hoped that his anxiety was not manifest. "I'll try," he said.

232

"Good. Genovela says that immediately before the crossbow bolt was fired, a voice said: 'Look out!' The voice came from the stone, she said, but she says that voices can't come from the stone without being thrown. She says that it was a woman's voice, but that ventriloquy can produce voices of all kinds. Did you hear that voice?"

"Yes," Primael said, simply.

"And you dropped to the ground?"

"Yes."

"And it wasn't an echo of your voice?"

"No."

"Was it Katarin's?"

"I can't be sure, never having heard Katarin speak, but it seemed to me that it was the voice of a Marie-Morte, which I'd heard before in my dreams."

That could not possibly have been the answer that Aidrena expected, but she made no comment. Instead, she said: "Genovela says that you're a necromancer, and a powerful one, although you probably didn't know it yourself until yesterday."

"I can understand how she drew that conclusion," said Primael. "The Dominican thought the same. But I didn't *do* anything. If Ollivier's spirit returned from the dead as soon as he was buried, it wasn't me who summoned or invited it. If necromancers can prepare for their own deaths, it must have been his doing, although he made no mention of it in the papers he left with Brother Michael—not, at least, in the ones that Michael passed on to Corentin."

"But you have the formulae that Ollivier gave Corentin," Aidrena said. "If you *are* a powerful necromancer..."

"If I have any such power, Lady Aidrena," Primael said, "you have my word that I will never attempt to use it consciously—not in this house, nor in the forest."

"I believe that you could resist the temptation, consciously" she said, evidently aware of the import of his prevarication. "But what if mother were to ask you to summon Corentin's spirit...or the spirit of Gilles de Rais?"

"I would not do it willingly," Primael insisted. "Nothing on earth would persuade me to do either of those two things."

"Nothing on earth," she echoed, with sufficient emphasis to make it clear that she understood the limitation of that prevarication too. And she added: "But Ollivier is already here, is he not?"

"So far as I am concerned, he always has been," Primael said, "but in the final analysis, he is only a rhetorical device, a means of debating with myself. If I hear his voice, it is only in my imagination. And if I should happen to project it…it will still be my imagination."

She seemed satisfied with the promise he had given her, in spite of its limitations, evidently aware that it was as much as he could do. She trusted him. Even though she had only known him for two days, she trusted him. That was presumably Ollivier's work. He had planted the seeds of a reputation that Primael did not really deserve—but he would do his best to live up to it.

"Thank you for not treating me as a child," she said. "May I ask one more thing of you?"

"Of course," he said. "What is it?"

"Don't be as honest with Mother as you have just been with me. She's not a child either, obviously, but there are things she might be better off not knowing. She's stronger than me, physically…but far more troubled in her soul. Now that Corentin is gone, the curse will die with us, whether it's real or not, but it would be best, I think, if it dies quietly, without causing more pain than is inevitable. Don't you agree."

"I have not yet given up hope of discovering a treatment for your illness. Aidrena, nor for your mother's. I intend do everything I can to ameliorate them…except for experiments in necromancy. I will be as diplomatic as possible in conversing with your mother…but I think she might know more, or suspect more, than you think, and I am reluctant to practice outright deception."

Aidrena sighed. "Thank you again for your honesty," she said. "If you go to see Mother now, please send Genovela here. I'll talk to her, and do everything possible to reconcile her to your presence here. It will not be pleasant for you or the rest of us if she maintains her present hostility."

"Thank you," said Primael, and did as she had asked.

Beatriz de Tardivel made no attempt to subject him to a similar interrogation, or to make any further confessions in addition to the one she had already made.

"Genovela wants me to send you away," she said, when they were alone.

"I'm sorry to hear that," said Primael.

"I refused. I've told her that your presence here is necessary to me now, as well as to Aidrena. She'll accept that, I think. She has a good heart."

"I believe so," said Primael. "I shall do my best to make a friend of her."

There was a long silence, before Beatriz said: "He would not have got better would he? No matter what we did, he would only have got worse?"

"I don't know," said Primael, "but I'm sorry that I could not obtain the time to try harder."

"Ollivier should not have encouraged him—but he had no idea how dangerous it was. He thought of it purely as a scholarly problem. I could not—but I had no purchase on his obsession. There are matters in which a mother is the last person to whom a son will listen. Even so, I cannot help wishing that you had not fallen to the ground and that the bolt had struck you instead. Can you forgive me for that?"

"There is nothing to forgive," he said. "He was your beloved son. I am a futile old man. Had I realized exactly what was about to happen, I hope that I might not have ducked, but I cannot take refuge in ignorance. I knew that Katarin was present, and I knew that her intention was hostile. The danger was only too palpable. The only excuse I could offer is that I did not have time to think, and that my reaction was automatic—but I will not offer it. I ducked because I am a coward, because I did want to fall victim to whatever it was of which the Marie-Morte was giving me warning."

"But Corentin must have heard the warning too, and it wasn't courage that stifled his reaction."

"His mind was on other matters," Primael said, "and the warning was very vague—he had no way of knowing what the danger was, or from what direction it would come. After everything else is taken into consideration, though, the bolt was aimed at me; it should have killed me, if it had to kill someone."

"You do not believe, then, that God afforded you his protection?"

"No," said Primael, simply.

"Nor do I," she said, equally simply. "But he would approve, would he not? You are his man, after all."

"I doubt that, my lady. I forfeited God's protection a long time ago."

"Because you lost your faith? That is a very trivial sin, my fried—and if you still had your faith, you would be convinced that God never forsakes anyone." She smiled wryly as she said it, as befit a loyal acolyte of Semiaza, who believed that God was the great Liar.

After another pause, she said: "I hope that you are not going to neglect your own studies in necromancy, Brother Primael, because of last night's...accident. We might have need of it, you and I."

"It is a very dangerous study, my lady," said Primael, "and I think I have mentioned to you before as well as just now that I am a coward, as well as a futile old man. Furthermore, I have made a promise to your daughter, which I would be very reluctant to break."

"Indeed?" she said. "Children are sometimes more protective of their parents than their parents of them. She seems to have been very quick off the mark in extracting that promise. Do you have the papers on your person?"

Primael was taken by surprise by the question, but he knew that it was not really a question. She knew that he had

236

taken the formulae and the accompanying instructions from Corentin's satchel; she had watched him do it. Legally, they were Aidrena's property now, but he had neglected the opportunity to hand them to her, thinking—perhaps stupidly—that they would be safer in his own custody.

After a long hesitation, he said: "Yes."

"Give them to me, please," she said.

He could have refused. In a strict interpretation of the law, he would have had every right to do so. But matters of authority at Tardivel were not as clear as the specifications of the law. He gave her the papers.

"Thank you," she said. "I am right, am I not, in thinking that, since Ollivier has already been invoked, more than once, it will be easier to invoke him in future?"

"I don't know," Primael replied, honestly. "Perhaps his passage might have been eased...but I suspect that it is not sufficient to pronounce a formula of invocation. It might be necessary for the spirit to consent to answer it."

"Do you think so? Well, perhaps we shall see." Without any change in the tone of her voice, she said: "Is there a possibility, Brother Primael, that you might be my father?"

Taken aback, he said nothing.

"For two days," she said, as if by way of an explanation, "I have been searching for evidence of similarities between us. There are a few, but no more than I found when I searched Ollivier's features and studied his behavior. You will forgive my impertinence, I hope, in consideration of the fact that it has always been a matter that has troubled me deeply—understandably, I think you'll agree. I did not believe Ollivier when he denied the possibility that it might have been him, although I might have believed you if you had denied it. Since you did not, I shall assume that the possibility exists. Will you be kind enough to take it as a compliment if I say that I would far rather that you were my father than Gilles de Rais?"

Primael continued to say nothing.

""If it is any consolation to you." she said, "what I have learned about Gilles' court from various sources suggests that

237

you and Ollivier were not the only possible alternatives. My mother died before I could interrogate her as thoroughly as I would have liked, and I would not have trusted her word no matter how many saints she swore by. So, I believe the possibility that you are my father to be remote, perhaps less likely that I am the daughter of Gilles de Rais. Having said that, however, might I ask you not only to take the possibility seriously but to embrace it, and actually to think of me as your daughter? It's presumptuous of me, I know, but if you consider the matter seriously, as I have, I think you might find that we both have something to gain from the presumption, and nothing to lose. It will be our secret, of course—there are certain things that a mother ought not to tell her daughter."

Primael's tongue was still firmly tied. He could not speak.

Within his soul, though, Ollivier said: "The lady is correct. And for what it may be worth, I didn't lie to her when I told her that I could not be the guilty party. You were always a better man than I was, although more innocent. In my opinion, you would be failing in your moral duty if you refused her request, and if you require a further argument, the only hope you have of preventing her from using the formulae that you have just given her is to accept the proffered paternal authority, whether you are entitled to it or not."

It was definitely Ollivier's voice. Primael recognized it perfectly. He was a free agent, of course; he could have said no. But had he not been reminded, by no less an expert than a weary succubus, albeit a deceptive one, that the ultimate armament in the war within the soul is resignation?

"Yes, my daughter," Primael said to Beatriz de Tardivel. "I would be honored to be your father, and I shall be your father, if you wish, to the utmost of my ability."

"I do not ask you to love me," the chatelaine said, "but with your consent, I would like to try to love you."

"If I can convince myself of the truth of what we have just agreed to believe," Primael said, "I shall certainly be unable to prevent myself from loving you, and from regretting that it took so long to discover you."

"If," she repeated, colorlessly.

"Honesty forbids me to make a firm promise," he told her, "for I do not know myself well enough to say any more, as yet, than I have—but you can be certain that I shall try to believe it."

"Even though, in my conviction if not in yours, I am the Devil's mistress?"

"Even so," he confirmed.

He could see in her eyes—which, for a moment, were strangely reminiscent of those of a Marie-Morte—that she wanted to express her gratitude for that, but her curiosity proved too strong,

"Why?" she asked.

He was glad to find that he was not at a loss to offer her an answer, and that he did not have to ask himself, before doing so, what Ollivier would have done.

"Because it will increase my opportunity," he said, "during the few years that might remain to me, to be something other than a futile old man, something more than a scholar, and the least of the victims of the tyranny of the Word. And who can tell whether it might not enable either or both of us to find a way out of the labyrinthine toils of Hell?"

www.ingramcontent.com/pod-product-compliance
Lightning Source LLC
Chambersburg PA
CBHW060355030726
47497CB00003B/716

* 9 781612 278810 *